REPERCUSSIONS

By the Author

Dr. Kate Morrison Thrillers

Trigger

Pathogen

Troop 18

Repercussions

Visit us at www.boldstrokesbooks.com

REPERCUSSIONS

by

Jessica L. Webb

2017

REPERCUSSIONS

ISBN 13: 978-1-62639-925-9

This Trade Paperback Original Is Published By
Bold Strokes Books, Inc.
P.O. Box 249
Valley Falls, NY 12185

First Edition: July 2017

CREDITS
Editor: Jerry L. Wheeler
Production Design: Stacia Seaman
Cover Design by Melody Pond

Acknowledgments

I had a lot of help in researching various components of this book. Thanks to Kelly for sharing your experience with concussion, to Stewart for helping me frame Edie's history as a journalist, to Mikey for talking to me about guns, and to Connery for more than a few Sunday evening conversations about the Canadian Armed Forces.

A special thank you to Katie, my head of research and beta reader extraordinaire. Your input and support was invaluable. I'm so thankful you started it.

As always, thanks to my editor, Jerry. I am learning.

For my wife, Jen. Who has loved me every step of the way.

PROLOGUE

Edie eyed the concrete spiral staircase leading up to the bridge as she ran along the canal. It was still a block away and totally empty. If she'd had breath, she would have groaned. If the staircase had been full of tourists, she could have bypassed the thirty-six steps up to Rideau Street. But the tulips that drew the crowds were still rows of unfurling green buds. The crowds wouldn't arrive for another few weeks, when the tight-lipped and multi-coloured tulip petals blossomed.

Today the staircase was empty, so Edie took the corner hard without faltering. No excuse once her mind was made up. Counting each step, her footfalls light, feeling the burn in her quads and thighs. Pretending she didn't enjoy it. She smiled triumphantly at the lazy voice in her head that wished for an extra hour in bed. Slightly dizzy from the fast pace of the spiral staircase, Edie ran straight to the lights, the downtown core just now sluggish with early morning commuters. Timed just right, as always, Edie entered the intersection as the pedestrian light blinked permission.

Her thoughts were already three blocks ahead in her apartment, on the shower, then the coffee and maybe a leftover croissant from yesterday's department meeting. Even still, Edie registered each car, each cyclist, each bus, and each pedestrian. She'd been back in Ottawa for a year, after two years as a journalist and aid worker in Afghanistan, and she was still getting used to the change in pace, setting, and sounds. Today was calm, nothing pushed against the predictable fabric of this late April morning.

Two blocks now, and Edie slowed her pace, stores and offices giving way to houses and apartments. One block and she walked, tugging the thin toque from her head and running her fingers through her sweat-soaked dark hair, letting it fall against her neck as the air cooled her scalp.

Already breathing easier, already tasting her first cup of coffee, Edie checked the one-way street for cars. Empty. As she stepped onto the street, she registered the idle of an engine. Second step, and it revved oddly in this residential neighbourhood. Third step, and she heard the trip of tires not quite gripped to the road. She halted in the middle of her fourth step and saw the car as it careened around the corner, wrong way down this one-way street. Every muscle screamed at her to backpedal.

She did, sinews tight with spiked adrenaline, racing and tripping backward to the safety of the sidewalk, waiting for the car to screech to a halt. It didn't. Time for only one more step. Edie, desperate with fear-soaked certainty that the car was going to hit her, turned to launch herself out of harm's way. The car hit her hip mid-step, a shocking, dull ache, and sent her flying over the sidewalk. She only had time to duck her head and prepare for impact before she hit the brick wall.

CHAPTER ONE

One year later

"We can't have a meeting without coffee." Edie was adamant.

Her psychologist, Dr. Hera Wallace, agreed. They were setting up in the church-run community centre, preparing for the first concussion and acquired brain injury support group meeting. And that meeting required coffee, regardless of what the perfectly nice but unhelpful maintenance guy who stood before them was saying about the basement kitchen being under an inch of water from a leaking pipe.

"All I'm saying is the kitchen is out of bounds," the maintenance guy said.

"We've identified the problem, let's solve it," Dr. Wallace said. Edie smiled and continued to set up chairs. She could not count the number of times she'd heard that in the last eight months during therapy. "We are using the upstairs community room for another meeting, so we bring the coffee down here from that kitchen."

"Down two flights of stairs?" the maintenance guy said. "With a full 40-cup coffee perc?" He raised his bushy eyebrows in obvious skepticism. Edie did not appreciate the sexism she heard in his tone. She never did. And she felt a familiar surge of irritation liable to come spilling out of her mouth without filter at any moment. She couldn't blame that lifelong trait on her concussion.

"Actually, we'll be bringing down two full 40-cup coffee percs," Edie said, snapping open another folding chair. "Regular and decaf." Caffeine was on the post-concussion shit list. She'd started sneaking it back in about six months ago, happy to jump on the slippery slope.

The maintenance guy sighed. "You'll have to sort it out with the folks upstairs. I can get you a cart, but you're on your own for the stairs. My sciatica is too bad, and we're still fundraising to fix that lift."

Edie shrugged at Dr. Wallace as the maintenance guy left. "I can do it."

Dr. Wallace narrowed her deep brown eyes behind her glasses. *She has laser vision*, Edie thought. She drilled down past vibrato and bullshit and the lies that people told themselves, sifting and sorting them into unstable foundations of fact. She was sharply intelligent, direct, but also infinitely patient.

Dr. Wallace snorted indelicately. "That's a terrible idea."

"Hey, we need coffee. What if I promise to trip my ass down the stairs with that coffee and make sure to hit my head on every step?"

Dr. Wallace gave in and laughed. Irreverence was one of Edie's favourite character traits.

"You ready for tonight?" Dr. Wallace said.

She had asked a few months ago if Edie would be part of this group, both as a participant but also as a sort of mentor. She'd been through a lot in the year since getting hit by the car. The physical recovery from her pelvic fracture and a broken radius had been complicated by infection from the road rash. And of course, the concussion had knocked her off course more than anything else. For someone who prided herself on quick-thinking, gut-driven responses and her ability to pull together thoughts and words as a writer, the concussion had left her with a shaky sense of identity. Her core belief in herself had been shaken.

"Yes. I think I'm ready." Edie wanted to tell Dr. Wallace about her anxiety, about the surfacing of paranoia in her life, the odd sensation of thinking she was being followed. Perhaps this was a new and entirely unwelcome aspect of post-concussion syndrome.

The sound of feet on stairs and voices echoing down the hall interrupted Dr. Wallace's response. A few people had obviously come early, stepping tentatively into the room. Edie felt a moment of relief as Dr. Wallace went over to greet them warmly, welcoming them into the space. No time to get into Edie's newest neuroses.

Edie edged toward the stairs, allowing Dr. Wallace to welcome the participants to the group.

"I'll be up in a moment to help, Edie."

Edie waved away the offer, picked up the grocery bag of industrial coffee and filters, and headed up the stairs. She barely noticed the exercise until near the top of the second set of stairs. She'd been focused on physical and mental recovery, the appointments, exercises, and fitness filling the void left by her freelance writing, editing contracts, and teaching gig at Carleton University. All on hold for now, though Edie had high hopes of picking up a class in the fall. She had four months to put herself back together.

Edie wandered the top floor of the community centre, all beige hallways and patchwork floors with no helpful signs. She followed the sound of voices and passed a door where a meeting was already in progress. Not wanting to interrupt, she kept moving until she finally found the kitchen.

The small space was already occupied. The woman leaning against one of the counters immediately straightened when Edie walked in, and Edie couldn't tell if she was coming to attention or preparing for an attack. She was a few inches taller than Edie, and she had short, messy, sandy hair that disappeared into a floppy blue beanie that seemed to defy gravity as it slouched on the back of her head.

Edie quickly took in the loose green pants tucked into work boots and the fitted black, long-sleeved T-shirt barely hiding her impressively built arms. Edie tracked back to the woman's face to meet her guarded, but not unfriendly, yellow-green eyes. She was a glorious butch, and Edie felt a distant, almost forgotten moment of heat as instinct, intuition, and the whispers of attraction coloured her thoughts.

"Hi, I'm Edie," she said, walking over and holding out her hand. Start strong, start sure, one of her early mentors at the paper had always said.

The woman shook hands without hesitation. "Skye," she said. Her grip was strong, but she backed away again almost immediately.

"I'm here to make coffee," Edie continued, holding up the grocery bag as evidence.

Skye glanced across at the two percolators already plugged in and chugging away on the counter. Then she looked back to Edie.

"You with Dr. Wallace?"

"Yeah. We're just setting up for the first concussion and acquired brain injury meeting. You?"

"The PTSD group just started fifteen minutes ago. I told Dr. Wallace I'd babysit the coffee."

The woman grimaced slightly, like she'd just said more than she intended. A spark of curiosity made Edie want to dig deeper, but a whisper of caution told her not to.

"Well, what do you think? Can I squeeze in and start another batch?"

Skye shook her head. "We'll trip the breakers. The basement kitchen is on a different circuit if you want to—"

"Basement kitchen's flooded," Edie said. She walked into the kitchen, preparing to jump up on the counter. Skye stiffened and leaned farther back into the counter as Edie walked by in the small space. "I'll wait, if that's okay with you."

"It's fine," Skye said. Nothing about her body language said it was fine. Edie wondered how to put her at ease, what question to ask or comment to make that would ease whatever tension existed. She'd relied on that skill both as a freelance journalist and as an aid worker, but she no longer entirely trusted it.

Edie wedged herself between the sink and giant plastic tubs of sugar and flour. Skye watched her but not directly. *Wary*, Edie decided. Skye exuded wariness. The steamy burbling of the coffee percolators punctuated the silence in the kitchen. Edie watched the near-hypnotic, dancing tendrils of steam. Skye fidgeted in her peripheral vision, first with her sleeves, then she pulled a phone out of her pocket and almost immediately put it back. Then with a barely audible sigh, Skye jumped onto the counter, mimicking Edie's pose. Edie snuck a glance at the woman and Skye met her gaze squarely. Edie took heart from this small gesture.

"Dr. Wallace will be pissed if we don't talk," she said into the silence. Her statement was a tentative agreement to engage. Edie held her breath, suddenly wishing with a startling intensity that Skye would choose to engage. Silence stretched as Skye seemed to test the question, test Edie's motivation in asking, test the possible consequences of answering.

"'Pissed' is Dr. Wallace's natural state, I think," Skye said, and she smiled. Her smile was only a hint, Edie decided, as thoughts and emotions tumbled around inside her. It was a fraction of what she was capable of.

"You're not wrong."

Skye looked away, but her smile lingered. Shyness surrounded this tough woman, but Edie wanted to batter her cautious barrier. She tempered her emotions, unsure if she was going with her gut. Confused and angry at not being able to trust her instincts, she spoke without thinking.

"Is there any way to ask how you're involved in the PTSD group without asking about your whole life story?"

A terrible example of what her mentor would have called a demolition question. They were meant to dig fast and deep but they were guided, carefully placed, with a clear plan as to what was being carved away and exposed. No, this was simply a bomb dropped into a tiny room filled with two strangers and the smell of coffee.

Skye answered with silence, looking everywhere but at Edie. The percolators kicked into high gear, signaling the end of their cycle. Skye hopped off the counter and got everything ready quickly and efficiently. She left and returned with a wheeled cart for one of the 40-cup percolators. Edie stayed where she was, not blaming Skye for wanting to get away from her as quickly as possible. *I asked the wrong question.* She was surprised when Skye glanced up.

"I'll deliver this down the hall, then I'll come back and help you take this one downstairs," Skye said.

"You don't have to do that," Edie said.

Skye looked Edie up and down once. Clearly, she was found lacking.

"We always have more than we need," Skye said. "And, no offence, but there's no way you're getting that thing down the stairs by yourself." Skye loaded up the cart and wheeled it out of the room.

Edie blew out a breath and hopped off the counter. She opened and closed cupboards, looking for another percolator for the decaf. She was annoyed—with herself, with Dr. Wallace, with agreeing to be part of this group. She found a scratched silver percolator half the size of the other ones and pulled it out. Her thoughts began to spin as she shoved a huge filter into the top of the carafe and started measuring out the decaf coffee grounds. Self-loathing followed quickly on the anger as she spun and re-spun the brief interaction with Skye. Would she ever have a normal interaction with someone? Edie slammed cupboards as she looked for a water jug. Would she ever get it right again?

Edie plugged the percolator in and hit the power switch. Nothing.

"Fuck," she said, suddenly close to tears. Another new and exciting side effect of post-concussion syndrome. Edie never cried. Her brother, Shawn, had always been the crier. But not Edie.

"Bertha giving you a hard time?"

Edie wheeled around, not having heard Skye come back into the kitchen. She stood in the doorway with her hands in her pockets.

"What?"

Skye pointed at the percolator sitting silently on the counter. "Bertha. She's temperamental." If Skye noticed Edie's teary state, she gave no indication. "May I?"

Skye edged closer to the coffee perc, reaching around Edie with such extreme caution, taking such obvious pains not to touch her, that Edie wanted to laugh. The ricochet from sadness to laughter left her slightly hollow. She felt guilty she'd made Skye feel that ill at ease.

Skye carefully turned the coffeemaker and fiddled with the electrical cord at its base.

"See?" she said, pointing. "Bertha."

Edie looked. Someone had written BERTHA in block letters with now-faded black marker. She smiled. Skye's eyes were even more interesting this close up. More yellow than green with a ring of brown at the very outer edge. Skye returned Edie's smile but backed up quickly.

"Come on, I'll give you a hand."

Skye maneuvered the full coffee perc onto the floor, indicating Edie should pick up the handle on the other side. They awkwardly shuffle-stepped out of the kitchen to the top of the stairs. Edie silently acknowledged she couldn't have done this on her own. By the second flight of stairs, they'd developed an efficient, synchronized step. As they began the last descent, Edie's phone signaled a text. It was likely Faina, a friend she had met after her accident. They had become very close in a short period of time. The ringtone chimed then petered off into a strangled electronic whine, like a kid's toy running low on batteries.

"Sorry about that," Edie said. "My phone's been acting weird."

Skye looked at her sharply. "You mean you didn't choose that ringtone?"

"The dying Furby ringtone? Definitely not. Though my niece and nephew would have downloaded that if they could find it."

Skye said nothing, though she looked uncomfortable. Edie sighed. *No small talk, no big talk, no personal talk.* Apparently they could say hello and talk about coffee. Fine.

Just as they reached the bottom few steps, Dr. Wallace appeared in the doorway.

"I see," Dr. Wallace said gravely, then gestured for them to follow.

Edie looked at Skye, wondering about Dr. Wallace's reaction. Skye kept her eyes on the stairs but a light blush coloured her cheeks. Edie wanted to laugh, but that would have made her more uncomfortable. They deposited the coffee perc on the counter, Edie taking a moment to set it just right. When she turned to offer her thanks, Skye looked at her with an intensity that made her want to step away or step closer.

"My best friend," Skye said. She shoved her hands into her pockets and rocked back onto her heels. "My best friend has PTSD, and I started coming here to support her. We served together. But she re-upped a year ago. And I stayed with the group to help out."

It was the longest Skye had talked, and Edie wanted more. She wanted to ask about Skye's best friend, about her military past, about the slight strangle in her throat when she spoke. But before she could say anything, Skye turned and disappeared back up the stairs, taking her intensity, her interesting eyes, and her barriers of caution with her.

CHAPTER TWO

Carleton University wasn't really a beautiful campus. It could have been, given its proximity to the Rideau River. Most of the concrete and brick buildings faced each other instead of anything interesting except the River Building, which housed the pride and joy of Carleton University, the School of Journalism and Communication.

Edie wasn't heading to the River Building today. She walked to the generic concrete Dunton Tower at the far end of campus that held the Department of English Language and Literature. Maybe one day she'd get a chance to teach in the journalism department where she'd once been a master's student, but competition was fierce for those prestigious teaching positions. Edie had a long list of things she would fight for in her life. Prestige wasn't one of them.

Edie hadn't been here in over a year. She had just finished her first year teaching, all papers graded and marks submitted. She'd been taken off probation and offered a third course, Finding Voice in Creative Nonfiction, the following fall. All in all, she'd been elated. The two years in Afghanistan were shifting and settling into the past, her guilt at leaving with so much left undone was fading. Her gut had told her it was time to leave, but the guilt had ridden her hard for a long time.

The quick pace of teaching had helped her. Seeing the enthusiasm and raw talent of some of her students, as well as the apathy and terrible grammar of others, had begun to heal her. Regret had never sat well with Edie Black.

Determined to not let her past dictate the course of her thoughts, Edie opened the glass doors of the Dunton Tower. One lone student sat on a chair, ear buds in and staring at her phone. Classes were done for the spring semester, and the much quieter summer semester had not yet started. Edie took the elevator to the seventh floor.

Her office was an ugly, tiny space with a huge window just high enough to see the trees lining the path along the Rideau Canal. Four cubicles bisected the space, with a small round table shoved into a corner with a geometric imprecision that had always made Edie twitch. Edie could see the imprint from the Keurig coffeemaker on that round table. Someone had taken it home for the summer.

Edie stopped in the doorway as a ricochet of thoughts and memories, experiences and decisions went through her head. She remembered the last moments of happiness she'd had, confident she'd made the right decision to leave journalism, to leave Afghanistan, and to enter teaching. That happiness seemed distant now.

Tired already of introspection, Edie circled the cubicles until she reached her own in the back corner. The space was completely clean. Not a paper, not a sticky note, not a pen cap, not her *I* ♥ *Carleton* mug she'd bought on her first day. Confused, with a niggling thread of concern, Edie backed out of the office and headed to the far end of the hallway. A young woman looked up as Edie approached.

"Can I help you?"

"Hi, yes, I'm Edie Black. I was an instructor here last year—"

"Oh! Yes, you're the one who got hit by a car. The intoxicated driver. I saw it on the news."

The media coverage had been extensive after her accident, and this scene had occurred more than once during her recovery. Edie tried to play it like a journalist, shaping the conversation and leading it where she wanted to go. Trying to avoid people's sometimes intrusive curiosity.

"Yes," Edie said evenly. "I was wondering if you happened to know where my stuff is from my office? I'm guessing it got packed away."

"Well, sort of. Your brother came in about a couple of months after your accident last year and said you wanted everything collected. I figured they'd want the space anyway, you know?"

Edie didn't respond, thinking it was incredibly odd Shawn would show up to collect her things. For months after her accident, she'd been in so much pain, the last thing she would have been thinking about was files in her office.

The young woman chewed a cuticle as Edie's silence stretched on. "Maybe you don't remember?" she said. "Is that a memory thing from your coma?"

A coma. Was that what her story had turned into? Journalists and lobbying groups and concerned citizens had all converged on her once the details of her accident had been made public. The car that hit Edie had been driven by eighteen-year-old Yaz Khalid, member of a minor royal family and the son of an Arab diplomat stationed in Ottawa. He'd been drunk and high, and his diplomatic immunity had completely protected him. The lack of consequences for the young man's actions caused an uproar. The story had captured the city, the province, the nation. Edie didn't remember any of it, but for a few months, her life had been headline news.

Edie refocused on the very sweet, nearly vapid young woman. Where had they found her? Edie wished Faina was here with her to witness this odd exchange. They'd laugh about it, no doubt.

"No, not a coma. Did Martine give the okay for my office to be packed up?" Edie said, referring to the department head at the time.

More cuticle chewing. "Well, no one was here except me. I figured you'd want your stuff. He was a nice guy," she said defensively.

Anger surged in a wave of heat that went up Edie's collarbone and neck and into her face. She never used to blush. She'd always had absolute command over her expression and body language. Something else the concussion had stolen from her.

"Can you describe him to me? Please."

"He had dark brown hair and really nice eyes. He even brought his own boxes. He was wearing shorts and a T-shirt and flip-flops."

Concerned, disturbed, a yellow flag of caution. She needed to get away from this woman and call her brother. It could have been him. But with that description, it could have been anyone.

"Thanks for your help."

"You're welcome! Happy summer."

Edie opted for the stairwell over the elevator, needing some kind of movement to untangle her thoughts from her emotions. She'd call Shawn to confirm this story. She'd make a list of everything that should have been at her desk. She would...

What? She would *what*? Call campus security? Over some curriculum documents and badly written essays and a laptop so old the

IT department refused to service it again? They'd look at her the same way the woman at the desk had. They might even bring up her "coma." They would confirm her paranoia.

"Fuck," Edie muttered as she rounded the last set of stairs and pushed her way out into the sun.

Thankful she'd been too cheap to pay for parking on campus, Edie began the hike back to her car a few blocks away. This would get sorted out. It was just another example of a minor wrinkle she had mentally turned into an impossible mountain. She pulled out her phone and sent a text to her brother asking him to check in when he had a minute. Shawn was a pediatric surgeon specializing in oncology at the Children's Hospital of Eastern Ontario across town. He might check in three minutes from now or three days from now, depending on his schedule.

He and his wife Anna had two hilarious, bright kids, Elise and Colin, eleven and twelve, who Edie adored. The feeling was mutual. Shawn and his family were Edie's anchor in her nomadic, swiftly moving life, but they had never understood how Edie could switch locations and careers so easily. Edie had never been able to describe how she made decisions that just felt right. At least they had before her accident.

Edie took a set of stairs down into a courtyard lit up with the morning sun. During the regular school year, every stone bench and table would have been full of students. Today, she saw only two women sitting across from each other, talking. The woman wearing a purple print scarf around her head and shoulders suddenly laughed, a bright sound that echoed in the space, matching the brightness of the morning. Her laugh made Edie smile, even though she didn't know the joke. Both women looked over as Edie entered the courtyard and Edie nodded a quick, polite hello. Skye stared back at her in frank surprise.

Edie stopped abruptly. Skye had half turned on the bench and they stared at each other for a beat longer than was comfortable. Edie tried a smile, but Skye sat unmoving with no change in her expression. She was just about to break eye contact when Skye stood and walked toward her. Edie met her halfway, acknowledging the little of beat of happiness that ricocheted around her chest.

"Hi," Skye said, shoving her hands into the pockets of her navy blue pants. She wore a button up grey shirt, sleeves rolled up her forearms. No beanie today, and her sandy hair was styled with a messy, casual deliberateness. Jesus, she was gorgeous.

"Hi. It's nice to see you again. I never got to say thanks for your help the other night."

Skye shrugged and half turned away. "No problem."

Just pulling simple conversation from this woman required Herculean effort. Edie felt the challenge of it. She wondered how she could get Skye to talk without spooking her. To her surprise, Skye spoke first.

"You work on campus?"

"I did. In the English department. I'm hoping to pick up some courses again in the fall."

"You like teaching?"

"Most of the time. I haven't been in the gig long enough to be bitter about the amount of paperwork, but some days it's like teaching a seminar room full of hung-over toddlers, you know?"

Edie laughed to show she was joking, and Skye's eyes brightened. She even smiled a bit. Edie could get used to that.

"I led a platoon of infantry for five years," Skye said. "So now imagine armed hung-over toddlers."

Edie raised her eyes at Skye's unbidden offer of information. Even Skye seemed surprised at her admission. She blushed and took a step back, looking over her shoulder at her companion still seated at the table. The woman looked at Skye and Edie with curiosity.

"I should let you get back to…working?" Edie said, not quite ready to release Skye.

"Ah…yeah. Sort of." Skye hesitated, then spoke again. "Come on, I'll introduce you."

Edie followed Skye over to the stone table, and the other woman stood as they approached. She was stunning, with rich black hair, wide brown eyes, and honest-to-God dimples. Her skin was a light, warm brown, and she had a lovely smile.

"Edie, this is my partner, Adelah."

Edie shook the woman's proffered hand with disappointment. They made a beautiful couple.

"Edie Black. It's nice to meet you, Adelah."

"Lovely to meet you, Edie," Adelah responded in a lightly accented voice. "And just to clarify, I am Skye's business partner. She may be the handsomest butch in town, but my tastes run more to the femmes, I'm afraid."

Edie laughed at the unexpected response, then laughed even harder as Skye blushed and looked down at her boots, obviously trying to hide a grin. Adelah's brown eyes danced mischievously.

"You knew what you were getting when you signed me on as partner, Skye Kenny," Adelah said with obvious affection. "We're legally bound."

"What business are you two in?" Edie said. She was more than curious. She was driven to know Skye.

Adelah looked pointedly at her business partner, obviously waiting for her to answer the question. Edie thought she caught Skye give her a fleeting, pleading look, but Adelah simply raised a sculpted eyebrow. Skye sighed and answered.

"We run a small tech company. Basically, other companies contract us to write and repair lines of code, manage data systems, or develop site-specific software. We just picked up a long-term contract for audio scrubbing, taking out each individual byte of background noise for a production company in Vancouver."

Skye seemed to relax as she talked about her business.

"And the most unique aspect of our enterprise?" Adelah prompted.

"Our company is entirely virtual and all of our employees have some form of PTSD, anxiety disorder, or some reason why working in a traditional office environment would be difficult. We recently hired two individuals with autism. Between them, they completed a coding contract in three weeks that I told the client would take two months."

"That's incredible," Edie said. She remembered what Skye had said about her best friend.

"We're looking at partnering with the computer sciences department here at the university," Adelah said, picking up the thread. "Maybe take on an intern or two."

"*Maybe*," Skye said. "We're in talks right now."

Adelah rolled her eyes, a look she somehow managed to make look pointed instead of merely childish.

"We're expanding into training," Adelah said with a frustrated sigh.

"We're moving forward with caution," Skye retorted.

Adelah gave Edie a quick grin. Edie returned it, fascinated with their volley of conversation. Skye could talk. Interesting.

"So, Edie, you work on campus?" Adelah said.

"Not this past academic year. I was just telling Skye I'm hoping to teach a few courses in the fall."

"You took a sabbatical?"

"No, I was hit by a car last year, so I've been in recovery for the past eleven months."

"That must have been difficult," Adelah said.

"I'm sorry, Edie," Skye added softly.

Edie nodded her thanks to both women, but Skye's look of intensity truly captured her. She searched for a trace of pity and came up empty. She wanted Skye to see her as whole, not the broken and pieced-together person she sometimes resembled.

"I've been lucky," Edie said. "I keep making small goals for myself and meeting them. It's not overly dramatic, but it's working for me." She laughed self-consciously. Talking about her weaknesses wasn't easy. And self-doubt annoyed her. She was about to break eye contact when Skye spoke.

"The simple plans are the most effective if you stick to them. Good for you."

Edie took a breath. Rushing headlong into anything wasn't an option for her right now. Everything about her recovery was measured: exercise, relationships, reading, sensory stimuli, writing. Skye was an immeasurable quantity.

"I should get going," Edie said. She turned to Adelah. "It was nice to meet you."

"It was very nice to meet you, Edie." Adelah turned and sat back down on the bench, giving Skye and Edie a small amount of privacy.

"Will you have coffee with me after the meetings on Thursday?" Edie said.

Skye seemed completely taken aback. Her eyes widened and she pulled herself up, adopting an almost military stance. She searched Edie's face for a moment, then she relaxed slightly.

"You mean you won't have enough at the meeting?"

Edie grinned. "Nope."

"Okay. Sure," Skye said. "I usually stay with Dr. Wallace and help her clean up and make sure she gets to her car. After that?" Skye looked hopeful, and her nervousness was adorable.

"Perfect, yes," Edie said. "See you Thursday."

"See you Thursday."

Edie walked away, feeling Skye's eyes on her back. She was always curious about the minutes after an interview, always tried to imagine the mind-set of the people she had talked to, whether they felt satisfied or concerned or relieved with the conclusion. She had no way of guessing what Skye was thinking. And she really, really wanted to know.

Edie's cell phone whine-chimed in her pocket. She pulled it out, expecting to see Shawn's name. It was a text from Faina.

Baby D Dogs playing at the Ambassador at 8. Come with me.

Edie sighed. Faina had been pushing her to go out.

Not tonight, sorry, she texted back.

Faina's response was immediate.

You are ready. I'll pick you up at 10 before.

Edie shook her head and smiled. English was Faina's fourth language along with Arabic, Russian, and French. Describing time really messed her up.

Fine. A few songs. One drink.

Faina texted back a happy face and Edie shoved her phone into her pocket. She no longer felt the spring sun on her face as she crossed the final, ugly stretch of the campus to her car. She was nervous about going to a bar, with its combination of lights and sounds and music, movement and percussion, the effort to decode body language and decipher words amidst a chaos of noise. But her hesitancy wouldn't surprise Faina, who had met Edie at a really low point in her recovery.

Edie remembered that day very clearly. Six months post hospital discharge, and Edie had insisted to her family that she was ready to start going to appointments on her own. She wasn't. She sat in the physiotherapist's waiting room with a headache that threatened to physically knock her down. Light had streamed through the wall of windows to her left. She wanted to close her eyes, but the bloody pink of her eyelids made her nauseous. The TV behind the reception area blared news Edie had no hope of tuning out.

So she sat half-lidded and humiliated until Faina, the only other person in the waiting room, had rescued her by asking the receptionist to find an empty treatment area so Edie could lie down. Edie still remembered the feeling of relief at Faina's gentle and determined intervention. They had been friends ever since. Faina had chronic pain from an injury that had never been treated properly when she was a girl in Syria. She understood how pain could run your life. With Faina's friendship and support, Edie had learned to exist outside of pain. Faina had even insisted Edie try a massage/meditation clinic that specialized in treating pain patients, which had turned out to be a life saver. Faina had always understood.

That was why Faina's recent push to get her out to this bar made Edie uneasy. She had already seen a pattern in Faina's behavior. Some days she would be relaxed and being around her felt effortless, but sometimes she was tense, fearful, and even demanding. Edie chalked it up to the whiplash of pain. She could relate. Until recently, that had been her life.

Edie increased her pace as she took the last long, empty path toward her car. Evergreens crowded in from both sides, and Edie felt an unusual sense of claustrophobia. She'd been having that feeling of eyes on her back more and more recently. She thought she heard footsteps behind her but didn't want to turn and look to see an empty path, confirming her paranoia. Edie walked with hunched, tight shoulders, wishing Faina was walking with her, wishing they had made plans to sit in her apartment and talk and listen to music tonight. Wishing she could straighten her spine and walk with the confidence and ease she'd taken for granted before the accident had stolen it all.

CHAPTER THREE

Faina smiled when Edie opened her door, but Edie could tell something was wrong. Faina's slightly wavy black hair was tucked behind her ears, and she was dressed simply in jeans and a black T-shirt.

"Hey, what's wrong?"

Faina looked at her with dark, blank eyes, the half smile still lingering as if in afterthought. She shook her head slightly.

"Nothing, no. I mean, hello."

Faina stepped into Edie's apartment and kissed her lightly on both cheeks. Syrian born but raised in the UK since she was a teenager, Faina's accent and mannerisms were a mishmash of cultures Edie loved to explore when Faina was open to talking. Tonight did not seem like one of those nights.

"You ready?" Faina said, a smile too firmly in place.

"Sure. But tell me what's going on. You look a million miles away."

Faina just shook her head again as they walked out of Edie's apartment and down to the street level. It was a perfect, warm night and the bar was only a ten-minute walk.

"You look nice," Faina said. "Maybe you will meet a nice girl tonight."

Edie snorted. "Thanks. But it would be hard to meet someone and explain why I can only handle one drink and three songs from the set list before scuttling home again."

Faina let out a breath and looked away from Edie. "You will be fine, I think," she said. "Yes. You will be fine."

A band was already onstage and tuning their guitars, fiddling with amps and cords and mics when Edie and Faina walked in. The lead singer, a guy in head-to-toe black, greeted the audience, and Edie's stomach lurched at the answering cheer along with a piercing wolf-whistle and boots stomping. She was suddenly very unsure if she could handle this.

"There's an opening act?" Edie tried to yell in Faina's ear as they found their way to the bar.

Faina glanced at Edie over her shoulder. Her expression was a confusing mix of guilt, frustration, and concern. Then Faina just shrugged and kept pushing her way to the front of the bar like she was on a mission. Edie tried to think her way through Faina's odd behavior, but the band launched into their first song, a frenetic cacophony of electric guitar, bass, and drums. Edie, who loved all forms of music, unconsciously separated each component even as she heard them all together. As Faina ordered gin and tonics from the heavily tattooed and baby-faced dyke behind the bar, Edie felt her skin come alive. She'd forgotten how good live music could feel. She could do this.

Edie didn't think they'd find an empty table in this crowd, but she followed Faina's rigid back to a dark corner. Two men had just vacated a table, and Faina and Edie slipped into their chairs as they walked away, one of them nodding at Faina. Edie grinned at Faina, already forgiving her for pushing this. But Faina avoided eye contact, sipped her drink, and nodded halfheartedly along with the beat.

When the first song ended, Edie cheered along with the crowd. She also took stock. The muscles in her neck felt a little tight, absorbing the strain of this moment. She didn't know if the fuzziness in her head was the beginning of a migraine or the effects of having downed most of her drink. As good as this felt, she should probably quit while she was ahead.

"I'll probably only stay a few songs," she said to Faina as the band got ready to play their next number.

Faina only nodded, her lips pressed tight together, her eyes never leaving the stage.

"You okay?" Edie said, concerned and annoyed.

Faina finally looked at her. "Yes." She was very pale.

"You don't look—"

The band started again, their energy even higher than before, the lead singer flinging his head side to side at the opening guitar lick. The sight sank some of Edie's excitement. She would never again live with the ignorance of how brain-to-bone contact affected your thoughts, memories, problem solving, knowledge, and emotions.

Edie enjoyed the energy of the song at first, but it bordered on uncomfortable as the song continued. Edie closed her eyes, limiting one stimulus to help her deal with another. The drumbeat bothered her most. The sharp rhythm was out of place. It echoed oddly, like it was bouncing off the wall behind her and hitting her head with almost concussive force.

Edie shifted in her seat, turning her head from side to side in an effort to relieve the pressure. Nothing worked, and the sensation escalated. Edie opened her eyes. She began to panic as the feeling intensified, locking down each vertebra as it ascended her spine. Edie wanted out, needed to get away from whatever this drumbeat was doing to her body. She blinked and willed herself to move.

It wasn't working. Why wasn't she moving? She felt Faina's hand on her wrist. Her mouth was moving, as if she was talking. Edie couldn't even hear the music anymore, just the drumbeat assaulting her from all sides. It ratcheted up another impossible notch and Edie felt the need to scream but the sensation had reached her neck, immobilizing her voice and muscles. As she succumbed to the numbing beat, a hand slipped around her neck and the last thing she remembered was a low, commanding voice in her ear.

❖

The sound followed Edie into her dreams but it was subdued now, like a door had been closed. The beat felt comfortable now. It enveloped her, it surrounded and held her like a weighted blanket covering her from head to toe. The beat asked questions and she answered.

"The savageness of man lies not in the actions but in the echoes of silent history."

"Can you repeat it?"

"Fortune has no will where flowers refuse the fertile soil of deliberate thought."

"No, repeat it."

"Waves can tell lies as oceans—"

"NO!"

❖

Edie woke in her own bed. It was morning, the curtains of her windows letting a slant of sunlight onto her comforter. Edie moved her body cautiously. It was going to be one of those days. Her headache was heavy through her body, a deep, low thrum of constant pain. She kept her eyes closed, but the simple act of waking had ratcheted the pain.

Eight out of ten, eight out of ten, eight out of ten, Edie chanted to herself, as if repeating the pain scale could hold the number steady. Nausea crept in on her next breath, and Edie wanted to cry. *Crying will make it worse, nine out of ten, don't cry.*

Edie didn't feel like she was in command of her body for a long time. She raised herself slowly, intent only on reaching the bathroom, taking her meds, and coming back to bed.

"Edie," a voice called tentatively from the living room.

Faina. Edie remembered the explosion of images and sounds from the night before. Her heart hammered like the beat of the drum, and panic wrapped itself around her chest and made it hard to breathe. God, her head hurt.

"Edie? You okay?"

No, not okay. How did she get back here? Edie ran a hand over her stomach, felt the soft cotton of her favourite T-shirt to sleep in. No memory, and it hurt to think. It hurt to be angry, but she couldn't help it.

Edie leaned against the wall and cracked an eyelid. Faina was wearing the same clothes she'd worn to the bar last night. Her eyes were red and tired and guilty.

"Get out."

Edie's voice had no force. It was too thin and could not convey her anger.

"Edie, I'm—"

"Out. Now."

Edie was going to throw up. She needed Faina gone.

"I'm so sorry. I didn't know they would…I didn't know."

Edie closed her eyes. She heard sorrow in Faina's voice, deeper than this mistake. She could not, she would not think about it now. Faina hadn't moved. Edie needed her to move.

"I'll go," Faina said. "I won't be at the clinic tomorrow. I think you should make an appointment."

Her words sounded forced, but the thought was just another assault on her head. The front door closed, and Edie shuffled the last few steps into the bathroom. Her hands shook as she opened a blister packet and put the small pill on her tongue before pressing it to the roof of her mouth. It would kick in quicker, and she didn't have to worry about throwing up what might be her only relief.

The nausea intensified and Edie rode it out before shuffling back to her bedroom, one hand on the wall to hold the world steady. The sheets felt itchy on her overly sensitive skin and the need to cry rose up, a pressure against her eyelids. With no willpower to keep them at bay, Edie let the tears leak from her eyes into her pillow. Then she finally slept.

❖

The migraine took three days, and Edie felt hollowed out and weak even after the pain was gone. The anger didn't help, but Edie couldn't let it go. Faina kept texting to make sure she was okay. Edie ignored them all. So much for a new friendship she thought she could count on. Faina's insistence on going to the bar that night nagged at Edie. The fact that her memory of the night was blurred and blanked by the subsequent migraine didn't help.

By Wednesday morning Edie knew she needed to get out of her apartment. She had group tomorrow night, plus that date with Skye. A coffee date, but a date nonetheless. She clung to the thought as the migraine ravaged her body, stripping her of thought and will.

She had to be better for Thursday.

She forced herself out of her apartment for a meditation/massage appointment, ignoring the fact that Faina had introduced her to her massage therapist, Pino. As usual, he said very little. He chose a meditation track, gently working the muscles in her shoulders, back, and neck.

She always left with the scent of lavender in her hair from the essential oils they used. Edie always woke alone, her muscles relaxed, the voice replaced with gentle strings. Surfacing from the lethargy of her massage seemed to take so long, but Edie was used to it by now.

Even though she was often disoriented, the pain was invariably lessened and Edie would do almost anything to keep the pain away.

After her massage appointment, Dr. Wallace's office was another calming space after several tumultuous days.

"Would you like to start with the reason you're shaking?" her psychologist said.

Edie grimaced. "Bad decision followed by a bad few days."

Dr. Wallace cocked her head to the side, her nonverbal prompt for more.

"I let Faina convince me to go see a band the other night. It was fine until it really, really wasn't. I'm not sure if I passed out, blacked out, or if my fucked-up brain has just decided to redact the part where I got out of the bar and got home."

Edie's temper rose with every word, the anger finally her only focus without pain.

"Who are you upset with?"

"Faina, for starters. There was really no reason for her to push me. I mean yes, we've gotten pretty close in the last few months, but I can't possibly be her only friend in the city."

"Are you also upset because she is your only friend?"

Edie opened her mouth to retort, then shut it again. The question made her uncomfortable. Edie had Shawn and his family, and she had friends and acquaintances and connections all over the world. But Faina was her only friend in Ottawa. The only one who would ask her to go out and see a band on a random Monday night.

"Are we making lists of my BFFs now?" Edie grumbled.

Dr. Wallace grinned. "That was a terrible attempt at deflection, Edie. You're slipping." Her smile disappeared. "You feel betrayed by Faina."

"Of course I do. She always seemed to understand my recovery. I could talk to her about not trusting myself anymore, about being afraid that I didn't know my own limits. When I didn't feel safe with myself, I felt safe with her."

Dr. Wallace sat very still. She was either waiting for Edie to expand on what she said, or she was developing a question that Edie wasn't going to like.

"Do you consider her a partner?" Dr. Wallace said.

Anger always made Edie's tongue looser.

"I'm pretty sure she's straight, and I've never felt attracted to her. So, no," Edie said shortly.

"That's not what I asked. A partner is someone who is committed to your happiness and can put your needs above theirs when the situation is warranted. Someone who will share in all aspects of your life, the good and the bad."

"Shouldn't a friend be that for me, also?" The question made her feel vulnerable, like she was exposing an embarrassing lack of knowledge about what being close to someone meant.

Dr. Wallace took a moment to choose her answer, never a good sign. When she spoke again, her voice was gentle.

"I think you need to learn to trust yourself. Yours should be the most influential opinion in your recovery. Right now it's not. A friend should respect that. And a partner, when you're ready for one, should make you feel safe enough to try and fail. And to succeed."

Dr. Wallace's words followed Edie the rest of the day. By Wednesday night, she still felt low. The headache was long gone, but she still felt drugged. She found her thoughts slipping for no reason, words and phrases drifting like barely heard conversation through her head. Her days had become lethargic, ponderous, and slow. She also felt like she was being followed, the weight of someone's constant gaze making her edgy. She hadn't wanted to admit to Dr. Wallace she was feeling paranoid. What if it was the final checkmark on some diagnostic list that meant Edie wouldn't ever recover?

Edie knew the thought was irrational. The combination of sluggishness and edginess was nearly more than she could handle. Climbing into bed, Edie vowed to go for a run in the morning, paranoia or not, and get herself back on track.

CHAPTER FOUR

Dr. Wallace was talking quietly with a couple in the corner when Edie walked in to help set up at the community church. The conversation looked private, so she nodded briefly to her before taking the two flights of stairs to the top floor. Edie's morning run had helped but she still felt edgy, hearing and seeing things that weren't really there. Whispers and footsteps and car engines. She had gone for a run, bought groceries, journaled. She had practiced meditative breathing and thought about her coffee date with Skye. It was the only time she'd smiled all day.

Edie found Skye in the exact same spot as the week before, leaning against the kitchen counter. Tonight she had on jeans and a dark blue thermal shirt. And this time she smiled as soon as Edie walked in. Edie's heart stuttered in her chest and she took a moment to breathe. She had no idea how much she'd wanted someone just to be happy she walked into a room.

"You made it," Skye said.

"Of course, why wouldn't I?"

"I thought maybe you'd change your mind."

"About sharing stories of fucked-up brains with strangers while drinking shit coffee? How could I miss it?" Edie heard the bitterness in her voice. She hadn't meant to unleash it. Couldn't figure out how to draw it back in.

Edie searched Skye's face, trying to figure out how to talk her way out of this.

"I meant our date," Skye said evenly. "Is something wrong?"

"You were worried I'd change my mind about having coffee with you?"

Silence permeated the kitchen, punctuated by the energetic burbling of the coffee percs. Skye and Edie looked at each other across the small space, each obviously trying to figure out how the conversation had veered so off course so quickly. Edie knew it was her fault. She needed to make it right, but Skye spoke before she could.

"Let's start again, okay?" Skye waited for Edie's nod. "It's good to see you, Edie. I'm looking forward to having coffee with you after the meetings tonight." Her cheeks coloured light pink.

Edie took a breath. She could do normal conversation. She even used to be good at it.

"Me, too. I've been looking forward to it all week."

"Yeah," Skye said and smiled.

Edie returned the smile, feeling her thoughts settle for the first time in a long time. She'd climb her way back to normal again. So she'd made a stupid decision and been knocked back a few steps. Edie heard the echo of the drumbeat from the bar, and her heart rate accelerated to match it. She had a flash memory, with Faina's hands on her wrists and someone else's voice in her ear. Words drifted by with the beat. Was it lyrics she'd been hearing?

"Edie?"

The church kitchen. The smell of coffee. Skye looking worried. Edie shook her head lightly.

"Sorry. I'm here." *Am I?*

"Is something wrong?"

"It's been a rough week."

Skye nodded like she understood. Maybe she did.

"Will you tell me about it?" Skye said.

Edie checked her watch. The meeting would be starting soon. "Sure, I can admit my recent failures. But I expect some in return. Deal?"

"Deal," Skye said, and she pushed herself away from the counter. "Let's make a coffee delivery."

Once the coffee was delivered and chairs set up, Skye disappeared upstairs and Edie settled into her meeting. Dr. Wallace was working upstairs with the PTSD group tonight. Her colleague, a gentle giant of a man, facilitated Edie's group, asking guiding questions and encouraging the participants to reflect and articulate their journeys through a brain injury.

Edie spent most of the hour and a half trying to regulate her emotions. She worked at riding out the rough waves, building evidence of her amazingly fast recovery, listing all the things she could do now that she couldn't just a few weeks ago, focusing on the flame of heat in her chest that was her coffee date with Skye. By the end of the meeting, she was drained but balanced. She could recognize the victory in that.

After helping put away chairs, Edie said good night to the facilitator and took the nearly empty coffee perc back up the stairs. The kitchen was empty, though Edie knew Skye's group finished first. Edie washed out the coffeepot and arranged the kitchen, wondering about Skye's absence. As she considered going to look for her, Edie's phone rang. She checked the screen and saw it was her brother, Shawn. They'd texted only briefly in the last few days. She picked up the call.

"Hey, little brother."

"Hey, E." Her brother sounded tired.

"What's going on? You at work?"

"Yeah. Just finished eight hours of surgery that should have been one."

"So a long fucking day."

Shawn barked out a short laugh. "A long fucking day," he agreed.

Edie listened to the silence on the other end. She could picture her younger brother pulling himself together.

"You need to go home, Shawny," Edie said gently. "Let Anna remind you that you're a gifted surgeon with a big heart, and those kids and families are lucky to have you."

"Yeah. Thanks, E."

"Anytime. That's what big sisters are for."

"I've always wondered," Shawn snorted. "So why did you want me to call you? Everything okay?"

"Yeah, fine," Edie said, deciding not to tell Shawn about her temporary setback. He and Anna had spent enough time worrying about her recovery. "I just had a question for you. After my accident last year, did you go to my office on campus and pick up some boxes of my stuff?"

"Yes," Shawn said, sounding surprised. "You were adamant. It was just easier to do it than argue with you."

Edie felt a shiver of despair at having no memory of these conversations.

"Do you need it? I can find where—"

"No, Shawny. It's fine. It's just…"

What could she say? *It's just that my brain has been hijacked by paranoia. I think I'm being followed. That someone is stealing my belongings. That maybe I'm losing the battle with my sanity.*

"E?"

"I'm good. Really. Thanks for calling me back."

Just then Skye rounded the corner with the coffee perc. She saw Edie was on the phone and started to back up. Edie waved her in.

"Listen," he said. "I've got to check on a patient before I head home. You want to come over this weekend? It might be warm enough to barbecue, and Elly and Colin would love to see you."

"Yeah, that might work. I'll text you. Love you, little brother."

"Love you, E."

Skye was quietly unpacking the cart when Edie finished the call.

"My brother," Edie said, indicating her phone.

"Everything okay?" Skye said as she hopped up on the counter.

"Yeah. Shawn's a surgeon specializing in pediatric oncology. He has some rough days."

"I'll bet."

Edie shook her head free of her unsettling thoughts. "Ready to head out?"

Skye grimaced. "Dr. Wallace is still in with one of the guys from the group. He's on edge, and I'm not really comfortable leaving her alone. I'd like to help pack up and walk Dr. Wallace to her car. I'm really sorry."

"No problem," Edie said, trying not to show her disappointment. Neither of them moved from their spot on the counter, and the silence stretched until they both grinned at each other across the small space.

"This is really no different than a coffee shop," Skye said into the silence. "Can I take your order?"

Edie laughed. "A grande mocha with whipped soy and cinnamon sprinkles, please."

"Roger that," Skye said. She grabbed a paper cup and pulled the spigot on the coffee perc, added a packet of sugar and a splash of milk and handed it to Edie. "Your grande mocha, ma'am."

Edie laughed again. She loved the way being around Skye made her feel so much lighter. Anticipatory. The thought of spending even ten minutes in this community church kitchen just talking with Skye suddenly seemed like a huge gift. Edie took a sip of coffee.

"It's a shit grande mocha, but I'll take it," Edie said, her eyes dancing mischievously.

Skye muttered something that sounded like "coffee snob," but Edie could see the laughter in her eyes as she prepared her own coffee and settled back on the counter.

Then suddenly there was silence, as if they'd just transitioned from casual acquaintances to two women on a date. It had been a long time since Edie had gone on a date. She remembered that she usually felt confident. Hopeful it would work out but not too invested if it didn't. This not quite date in a run-down kitchen with shit coffee at nine thirty on a Thursday night with Skye felt important. Edie wanted this to go well, and she didn't know where to start. She shifted into journalist mode, a place of comfort.

"So, I know you own a tech company and you used to serve in some capacity in the armed forces. Is there a connection between the two?"

Skye tilted her head back and forth. "Yes and no."

Edie waited for more.

Skye seemed to take the silence as a cue to continue. She took a breath and straightened her spine, as if she was about to give a report. "I've always been interested in the technology, ever since I was a kid. I started at the Royal Military College when I was seventeen and got my Bachelor of Science in computer science. I also trained as an infantry officer and led a light infantry battalion with the Royal Canadian Regiment. My plan was to stay for the three years I owed the CAF, then work private security to raise the capital to open my own business."

"And is that what you did?"

"No, I re-upped. So another five years with the Royals before taking my leave. Then I worked private security in the UAE for two years. Long hours, good pay. I've been back in Ottawa about that long."

Edie wanted to ask so many questions. *Why the re-up? Why the Royal Military College? Why infantry?*

"Why didn't you become an intelligence officer?" Edie said. "Wouldn't that have fit better with your education?"

Skye's expression darkened, but she covered it quickly with a shrug. "I could have. But I joined the armed forces to serve. Boots on the ground, that kind of thing," she said vaguely.

Skye's story interested Edie, and she got the sense they were barely scratching the surface. She took a sip of her coffee, silently counseling herself to be patient.

"Five years," Edie mused. "You must have gained rank in that time. Captain?"

Skye looked surprised. "Major," she responded. "You know a lot about the armed forces."

Edie reminded herself this was a date, not an interview. She liked Skye and, more importantly, her gut was saying she could trust Skye.

"I spent two years in Afghanistan," Edie said. "I wasn't embedded with Canadian troops, but I spent a lot of time around them."

"As a journalist," Skye said. Edie noted how often Skye made questions as statements.

"Right. I started there on assignment with *Sun News*. I wasn't a war correspondent, not by training and not by interest. Mostly I focused on humanitarian, cultural, and historical angles. I did that for about six months and then ended up working with a humanitarian aid organization and took freelance writing gigs wherever I could."

Edie could feel the heat of Afghanistan against her skin. Her time there had been tumultuous, satisfying, and scary. She'd made lasting friendships and had a brief, intense relationship with a fellow aid worker from Germany.

Edie opened her eyes to find Skye watching her.

"You liked it there," Skye said softly.

"I did. The Afghani families I met were good, solid people. Their sense of independence and community is so different from the more isolated North American way we grew up. Most of my job as an aid worker was to organize resources and supports more efficiently. Basically I was trying to help them help themselves. But government aid agencies aren't known for efficiency."

Skye laughed. "Try working with the army," she said wryly.

Edie grinned.

Just then Dr. Wallace came into the kitchen. She looked tired. Edie checked her watch and noticed it was almost eleven.

"Ah, you two didn't need to stay," she said.

"It's no problem," Skye said. "All done for the night?"

"Yes. And ready for a bubble bath and a glass of wine," she groaned.

"I'll clean up in here and then walk you out," Skye said.

"And I'll help with the chairs," Edie added.

"I'm going to model good self-care and accept your offers of assistance," Dr. Wallace said. "Bless you both."

Less than ten minutes later, the three women were on the street in front of the community church. They could hear street sounds a few blocks up, the bars and restaurants of the Byward Market just now in full swing. Edie and Skye walked Dr. Wallace to her car, said their good nights, and waved as she drove off.

Edie felt tired, but she didn't want this night to end.

"Want to grab a drink or something to eat?" she said to Skye.

Skye checked her watch. "Rain check? I've got a meeting that starts in about half an hour."

Edie considered this. What kind of meeting started at midnight?

"A work meeting," Skye clarified, obviously reading Edie's confusion.

"At midnight."

"Uh, yeah," Skye said. She shifted her balance, clearly uncomfortable.

"Time difference?" Edie pushed.

"No."

Edie waited, but Skye didn't offer anything more. The light from the front of the church cast Skye mostly in shadow. Edie couldn't read her expression, but she understood from the set of her shoulders that Skye was feeling defensive. Edie got the sense she was being brushed off. She didn't want to end the evening that way, but she couldn't find another way out.

"I can show you," Skye blurted into the silence. She pulled her hands out of her pockets and held them stiffly down at her sides. Her words and her body language conflicted.

"Show me what?" Edie said, confused.

"The meeting. It's virtual. My loft is just around the corner. If you want to."

Edie weighed Skye's offer with her clear reluctance. She went with her gut. "Okay, I'd like that."

Skye relaxed her shoulders. "Let me just text the guys so they know to expect someone new."

Skye indicated with a tilt of her head which way they should walk, then pulled out her phone and tapped away quietly. Edie waited until Skye had shoved her phone back into her pocket before she asked her questions.

"Why do you have a meeting set for midnight? Who needs a warning that I'll be showing up? Is it weird I'll be at the meeting?"

Skye looked at Edie and grinned.

"Definitely a journalist," she muttered, then answered the questions. "We call it the Twelve and Twelve, or mostly just the Twelve. Because we never meet in person, all my employees know they can check in at noon and midnight every day if they have questions or if they just want to connect or to collaborate on a project. The virtual office is available twenty-four seven, and there's a bulletin board where anyone can leave a message. Some of my employees rarely log in to the daily meetings, some show up for every one, and I have one employee who hangs out in the Twelve all day."

"Why?"

Skye shrugged. "He says he likes it. Says he feels connected even when no one is there. It's a social environment without most of the stressors of a social environment."

Edie ran through what little she knew of autism spectrum disorders and post traumatic stress disorder. She knew social interaction could be a barrier for both.

"And he's the kind of guy who would want a heads-up that you were bringing someone new to the meeting."

"Right."

Skye indicated they should turn down a side street. Edie noted they were moving parallel to her own apartment, but about four blocks away. She also felt a tightening across her shoulder blades. The sensation was familiar. Edie didn't want it to be. She ignored it.

"You didn't tell me about your bad week," Skye said.

Edie laughed shortly. "It was pretty shitty. Worse than your grande mocha."

"Hey now," Skye protested, laughing. Edie didn't say anything more. She didn't want to talk about it. She didn't want to listen for echoing footsteps behind them. "Will you tell me more?" Skye said.

Edie sighed then told Skye about Monday night's incident at the bar. She found herself caught up in the story, more so even than with Dr. Wallace. She tried to remember and describe those last few seconds before her memory got swallowed up by the misfired neurons.

Edie came back into herself suddenly. She was aware again of her surroundings, aware that Skye at some point had put her hand lightly against her back. Aware that Skye's whole body was tight and she was walking slightly behind Edie.

"What—?"

"Keep walking," Skye said. Her voice was low, her words clipped. She guided Edie with a hand to her lower back. Edie had been hoping for gentle and connected, but it felt commanding and protective instead. "Creepy guy behind us. Been there at least a block. Take the next left, three doors down is a steel blue door. It will be open."

"But—"

"Do it."

Edie bristled at the command. She'd navigated Kandahar on her own for two years. She didn't want to end this date feeling vulnerable and bossed around.

"Please," Skye said quietly, just as they reached the end of the block. "I know it's probably nothing. But please."

Edie just nodded. *Maybe something.* The words stayed in her head as she rounded the corner, found the steel blue door, and pushed it open. A hall light came on and illuminated the bare space dominated by a set of stairs. Edie waited, muscles tight with strain, with anger at her paranoia made real. Frustration that she couldn't think through this. Embarrassment that Skye would see her this way.

A light at the top of the stairs came on, and a door opened. Skye came out onto the top-floor landing.

"Hey. Come on up." Skye tapped at the screen of her phone. Edie heard the locks engage on the door behind her.

"Slick," Edie said as she climbed the stairs to Skye. "You really know how to impress a girl."

Skye smiled distractedly as she held the door for Edie and gestured for her to enter. The landing was a small space, and they stood very close together. Edie took a moment to look into Skye's eyes.

"What happened?"

Skye shrugged. "Nothing."

"Try again. This time with more words."

Edie had the satisfaction of seeing Skye's eyes widen.

"Fine. White male in dark jeans and a light T-shirt, five-ten, short brown hair, slight accent, maybe Eastern European. I asked him for the time and where I might get a taxi. He knew the name of the cross street. Then he kept walking, and I took the back entrance to my loft."

Silence permeated the small space between them.

"Better," Edie whispered. Then she smiled. "And thanks."

Skye let out a breath as Edie moved through the door. Edie felt a warmth in the pit of her stomach, knowing she had that effect on Skye.

Skye's loft was massive—not necessarily in floor space but definitely in height. At least a floor and a half if not a full two floors of space vaulted above her. Two sides were exposed brick, a dull reddish brown patched together in swaths of concrete. The other two walls were plain whitewash, interrupted on the lower level by intermittent four-pane windows that overlooked the street.

Edie walked a little farther into the room, aware of Skye shadowing her nervously, as if she was waiting for Edie's approval or derision. Edie kept looking around. A thick rug with a couch, coffee table, and television sat in one corner. A kitchen with wooden cupboards and a gleaming, brushed steel island with bar stools dominated another. The whole back section of the loft was overrun with electronics.

Open shelves of metal boxes, wires, blinking lights, and fans formed a three-walled barrier around a standing desk and an old, dilapidated maroon leather chair. Edie squinted past the lights into the far corner. She thought she could make out a bed tucked into an alcove.

"You live here?"

Skye moved into the space and tapped again at her phone. More overhead lights came on, and Edie could see two industrial fans with massive black blades circulating slowly in the upper levels. Another set of metal stairs ended at a door on the second level.

"Yeah. It's home and office," Skye said. "It's a work in progress."

"It's incredible," Edie said honestly, still trying to take it all in. "I've never seen anything like it."

Skye ducked her head, but Edie thought she looked pleased.

Edie pointed to the stairs. "There's more?"

"A small, unfinished apartment. Mostly storage. Feel free to look around or have a seat. I'm just going to grab a few things," Skye said as she entered her office space. Edie walked to the windows, realizing how tall they were as she approached. They seemed dwarfed by the enormity of the space around them. Then she dropped onto the comfortable couch and a moment later Skye sat beside her, arms full of laptops and headphones and other gear Edie couldn't immediately identify.

"So there are several ways to join the meeting. Audio only is an option, passive 2-D video where you just watch on the screen, active 2-D where we can make you an avatar and you can interact, or VR, which is really the whole package." Skye held up a pair of sleek goggles. "Have you ever interacted in a virtual reality environment before?"

"Once, for an article. But that was a few years ago. I bet technology has changed a lot since then."

"No doubt." Skye paused. "I'll leave it up to you how you want to enter the meeting. If you've had any experience with VR, you know it can be disorienting until you get used to it. And the effects can last after the VR session is over."

Edie searched for condescension, overprotection, or command in Skye's tone. She didn't find it.

"I'll give my brain a break and pass on the VR today. Can I make an avatar, though? I'll make it better than the Mii my niece and nephew made. They gave me way too many wrinkles."

Skye laughed as she flipped open the MacBook Air in her lap. She deftly maneuvered through screens and typed in commands. Edie recognized none of the platforms or servers Skye was navigating. She passed the laptop over to Edie.

"Here, you've got a few minutes to make a basic avatar. I'll log us into the session."

Edie chose the basics for her avatar: medium-length dark hair, brown eyes, slight build, jeans, and a T-shirt. Skye seemed fully absorbed in whatever she was doing on her own laptop, and Edie studied Skye in her element. In her own space, she navigated the cyber world, relaxed. But Edie could also picture her leading a team of troops, her body and mind in tight synch. Command in her tone. Edie thought about Skye's touch on her back while they were on the street. She shivered.

"You're staring at me," Skye said without looking up from her laptop.

"This has been a strange date," Edie replied without thinking.

Skye went still, and when she looked up, her expression had become guarded. "I can take you home, if you'd like."

"No, sorry, that's not what I meant. I like this date. I like being around you."

God, had she ever fumbled this badly on a date?

Skye saved her. "Me, too." They smiled at each other and the sweetness of Skye's expression settled Edie. "Okay, we're about to get started. I'll be in the VR world as well, so you'll see me and hear me in both environments. Your mic toggle is here, volume here, chat feature here, if you don't want to speak. The meeting shouldn't last longer than fifteen minutes, and you can exit by clicking here. Any questions?"

"Nope, I'm good."

Skye lifted the sleek goggles but paused before she put them on. She fixed her yellow-green eyes on Edie's with an intensity that made Edie's stomach clench.

"Is there any reason why someone would be following you?"

"Not that I know of."

"But you didn't seem surprised." Question as statement. A Skye Kenny specialty.

"I…" Edie had no idea how to finish the sentence. She shrugged helplessly. Skye said nothing.

Skye's alarm sounded on her phone. She silenced it, brushed her fingers lightly across the top of Edie's hand, then put on her goggles and settled back into the couch with her phone in her hand.

Lines of code tore across the laptop's screen in rapid sequence, then Edie saw the clean, sharp logo of a striped blade and the word "Strictus" across the top. The logo disappeared and Edie found herself dropped into the virtual office. At first it was a bird's-eye view of the office space, complete with a meeting table and chairs, a wall of whiteboards, a kitchenette with coffee and a water cooler, posters on the wall, a digital clock that displayed military time, and a potted plant that seemed to be growing a pineapple. The view slowly lowered until Edie was looking out at the room from the perspective of the table. Edie could see four or five avatars moving around the space. Each had a name hovering over its head.

Beside her on the couch, Skye tapped at her phone, then reached over and touched the keyboard in Edie's lap.

"You can toggle between first and third person by—"

Edie brushed her fingers away. "I'll figure it out. Go run your meeting."

Skye grinned, tapped her phone again, then spoke. "Hey, everyone, we'll get started in about thirty seconds. I want to introduce you to Edie, she'll be hanging out at our meeting today." Skye's avatar sat at the table, opposite Edie. She looked the same except she wore a camo baseball hat.

Through the speakers of the laptop, Edie heard a chorus of hellos and then one voice boomed, "Friend or foe?"

Edie checked her mic was on before answering, "Definitely friend."

She isolated the voice to a corner of the room under the clock. The avatar was a young man in a hoodie, the name hovering over his head said Gordon, and he bounced on a trampoline. As Skye threw out questions, a woman with long red hair stood by the whiteboard and the words appeared there in virtual marker. Edie didn't entirely follow the thread of the conversation, the tricky line of code a problem that completely eluded her limited understanding. Instead she watched the avatars. Some stood very still, another drank from a coffee cup at one minute intervals, and Gordon bounced on the trampoline, even as he asked and answered questions. Another avatar suddenly appeared at the table next to Skye and Edie recognized her even before she read the name Adelah hovering above her head. The private chat window in the lower right corner of Edie's screen opened up, a message from Adelah.

Hello, Edie. Nice to see you again. I heard Skye was bringing you to the meeting tonight.

Hi, Adelah. I hope it's not a problem I'm here, Edie typed.

Not at all. Skye would not have brought you if it was.

This space is amazing. Feels so real.

Thank you. It's Skye's code and platform and my design.

Impressive. I bet she brings all the girls here.

You're digging, Adelah typed, accompanied by a smiley face. *I think you can guess Skye has never brought a date here. You must be special.*

Edie blushed in real life. Adelah's avatar, obviously more complexly coded than Edie's, winked at Edie across the table. Skye, clearly catching the interaction, paused in the middle of what she was saying. On the couch beside her, Edie saw Skye start to reach over to the keyboard, then snatched her hand back and kept talking. Adelah laughed at the table and sent a winking smiley face to Edie before the private chat window closed.

Edie half listened to the meeting as she explored the virtual meeting space, getting bolder as she realized she could explore without interrupting the meeting by toggling to third-person view. She saw herself sitting at the table, relatively static except for the occasional blink. She found a row of old-school file cabinets in various colours next to the small kitchenette, each labeled with names. About fifteen minutes into the meeting, she heard Skye ask if anyone had any more questions, and when there were none, she wrapped up the meeting. Edie toggled her mic to say good night and thank you, then the avatars rapidly disappeared as the office lights dimmed, leaving Gordon alone jumping in the corner as Edie's screen showed the Strictus logo, then went blank.

Skye pulled off her goggles but kept her eyes closed as she ran her hands through her short hair.

"All good?" Edie said.

"All good," Skye confirmed. "I just need a moment to ground myself. I find it limits the vertigo."

"Take your time, I'm familiar with vertigo," Edie said.

Without opening her eyes, Skye found Edie's hand and held it. Edie could not remember a time in recent memory when she felt this happy or this comfortable in her own skin. Even the episode with the man on the street seemed far away. Edie leaned back into the couch cushions and closed her eyes, feeling the pulse in Skye's wrist, loving the intimacy of the moment.

She opened her eyes moments later to find Skye looking at her, their hands still joined.

"I should get you home," Skye said quietly.

Edie blinked. She could no longer deny how tired she was. She wanted to stay, she wanted to lean in and kiss Skye, to have a glass of wine, to learn more about this sweet, somewhat secretive woman. She wanted to tell her everything: Faina's betrayal, how scared she was that she was losing her mind, how she missed her old self and worried she would never be the same. Her tears began to surface, but she pushed them back, horrified that Skye might see.

"Yeah, okay," Edie said, sitting up abruptly and dropping Skye's hand.

"Walk or drive?"

Edie rubbed at her eyes. "Drive would be good, thanks."

They remained silent as Skye walked them through the loft to the back entrance with an identical set of stairs that led to a garage and workshop. Edie couldn't tell if Skye's Jeep was navy blue or black. Either way, it fit her perfectly. Edie climbed in and Skye tapped her phone and the garage door opened. Edie didn't notice she hadn't given her address to Skye until they were turning onto her street.

"You know where I live," Edie said.

"Google told me," Skye said, somewhat apologetically.

Edie said nothing as Skye pulled up in front of her apartment and turned off the ignition. Silence reigned as Edie tried to find the energy to get to her door, to say thanks for the date, to find a way to ask to see Skye again.

"Tonight was too much?" Skye said. Edie didn't know how she felt about Skye's ability to read her so well.

"I'm tired, but okay," Edie said. She faced Skye, searching for her eyes in the streetlight. "Thank you for tonight."

"You're welcome," Skye said. "Come on, I'll walk you to your door."

Before Edie could protest, Skye was out of the car and around to the passenger door, opening it and holding out her hand. Edie took it, feeling charmed and ridiculous all at once.

"You don't have to do this," Edie said.

Skye started walking her to the front door of the apartment building.

"First of all, there was a creepy guy," Skye said. "Second, an as yet unverified history of thinking you're being followed. And third—"

"You're a gentleman," Edie finished and laughed as Skye shook her head.

"Well, I was going to say that it's the proper way to end a date."

They stood on the top step at the entrance to Edie's apartment. Edie took a breath.

"I'd like another one. A date," Edie said.

"Me, too."

Somehow knowing Skye wouldn't make the first move, Edie leaned in and kissed Skye. She could feel the tension in Skye's body through her incredibly soft lips. Skye held her breath as she kissed her back and Edie kept kissing her, tugging gently at her lips until Skye let her breath out in one long, jagged expulsion of air against Edie's sensitized skin. Edie pulled back. Skye's eyes had lost just a little of their laser focus. Edie liked that.

"I bet you have my cell number, don't you?"

Skye simply nodded.

"Good. So you'll call me."

Another nod.

Edie leaned in and kissed Skye's cheek. "Tonight was perfect. Thank you."

Skye didn't move as Edie unlocked the front door and made her way up to her apartment. She let herself in, turning on only one table lamp as she went to the front window that overlooked the street. She saw Skye disappear into her car but not start it. Edie wondered what she was doing, and then her phone chimed in her pocket. She didn't recognize the number.

It's Skye. All good?

Edie smiled at the screen. *All good*, she texted.

Can I take you to dinner on Saturday night? Or I can cook for you at my place if going out is too much. Game day decision.

Yes, sounds perfect.

One request.

Okay...

Will you tell me about thinking you're being followed?

Edie sighed. Of course she would. Right now, she even wanted to.

Yes. Promise.

Okay. Thanks. Be safe.

Good night, Skye.

Good night, Edie.

CHAPTER FIVE

Edie's favourite coffee shop was busy. Too busy. Chatter competed with coffee machines which competed with music. The din created by so many people had always been a draw for Edie. She felt inspired being around that many people, the free flow of unconscious words like poetry that made her want to listen closer.

Not today. Today her favourite coffee shop was a confusion she couldn't afford. She paused at the window and checked out the posters for the band they were featuring two weeks from today. She considered asking Skye if she'd like to go. A bubble of happiness caught in chest.

And burst there.

Her last disastrous experience at a bar was still too fresh in her mind. Thinking of that night was disorienting and disturbing. Instead she thought about her night with Skye, the sweet first date and the anticipation of another tomorrow. Edie had slept in this morning but had woken groggy and happy. She'd woken thinking of Skye.

Edie carried on, leaving the darkness of the night at the bar on the sidewalk outside the coffee shop. Three blocks down, her favourite small bakery was nearly deserted, the only sound the melodic tone of the afternoon host on CBC Radio drifting out from the kitchen. Edie ordered a coffee and mulberry Danish, mostly because she liked the sound of the two words together. Her cell phone vibrated insistently in her pocket as she paid, gathered her snack, and found a spot in the sun. She pulled out her laptop and notebooks and set herself up to start working on the fall's syllabus before pulling up the text on her phone. It was Skye.

Hey. Just wanted to chat. Use this link on your laptop. Password is best adjective to describe Hera.

Why the weird instructions? Why didn't Skye just text?

What's going on? Edie texted back. She was curious about the link and surprised by Skye's odd behavior.

Please.

Definitely odd. Edie typed the link into her browser and a white box appeared on a blue background with the Strictus logo Edie recognized from the night before. Skye was contacting her from work? She typed "pissed" into the text box and immediately another screen opened up. She saw her name and Skye's, like an old-school chat room. The prompt told her Skye was typing.

Two minutes then I'm shutting this down. You are being followed. I'm close. You are okay.

Edie read the words twice, her body reacting with dread and nausea even as her brain struggled to catch up. But there it was on the screen. Her paranoia made real in black Arial font. Edie tried to keep her eyes on the screen, but she had to look around the small bakery. The only other customer was a mom who texted with one hand and rocked the stroller beside her with the other. The man who had served her shuffled baked goods in the display. The bakery was quiet and light.

"You are being followed...You are okay."

Edie? The cursor blinked.

Edie put her fingers on her keyboard. They shook as she typed.

What should I do?

The prompt told her Skye was typing. The wait was endless. She felt exposed, her spot in the sunlight made her a target on display.

Stay for ten minutes. Act normal. Stay calm. Then pack up and walk down to Murray Street. Get a cab at the corner. Go directly home. I'll meet you there.

Where are you?

Close. You are safe. One minute then this window shuts down. Don't use your phone to contact anyone.

The shaking in her hands was bad. How was she supposed to act normal if she couldn't even pick up her coffee? She typed.

I'm scared.

Find anger. Scared later. If you see me pretend you don't know me. Thirty seconds.

Edie fought the swell of panic. Skye was a lifeline about to be severed. She looked around again. The smell of yeast and coffee, the near heat of the sun through the window. A perfect afternoon completely shattered. Edie felt the invasion. And she felt her anger. She anchored to it and typed her last message.

I'm okay. I've got this.

I know. See you soon.

The window shut down, and Edie counted ten breaths in and out. It took forever.

Eight minutes. Act normal. Take a sip of coffee. Pretend eyes were not on her. Everywhere. The back kitchen, the man in the business suit on his phone across the street, the glare of the sun off a car windshield that hid a potential occupant. Eyes everywhere. She'd felt them for weeks. They'd begun invading her dreams, along with the voice that asked so many questions. She didn't know what they all wanted.

"Enough." Edie whispered the word into her mug as she picked it up. Her hand was steadier.

Four minutes, and Edie shut her laptop. She scrolled through pictures on her phone. She drank her coffee, but she couldn't eat the pastry. Too sweet right now. She wrapped it in napkins and tucked it away. That was normal, wasn't it? She'd lost sight. She was evaluating her every movement. Breathe.

One minute, and her heart hammered in her chest at the thought of leaving this quiet, safe space. Slightly dizzy, she stood, her heart rate way too high. Full breath, down to her toes. Not a good time to pass out. Edie gathered her things and walked the seven steps to the door. She felt the warmth of the wood and metal under her palm. The sun was so bright she felt pierced by it. Edie tried to convince herself she had walked into a normal afternoon. A regular day.

She heard it. An engine idling, then gunning. It was approaching too quickly. It wasn't stopping, there was no time, she had to run. If she jumped now, the car wouldn't hit her, she could escape the pain of it all.

Breathe.

The scene resettled. A car drove slowly up the street, braking sluggishly at the stop sign. It wasn't going to hit her. That was then, not now.

You're being followed.

Danger shadowed Edie on the brightly lit street. She tried not to look for Skye in the street, instead tried to feel the pull of her in the air. Was that possible, after knowing someone for such a short period of time? After one kiss?

She was almost at Dalhousie Street. She could catch a cab there, no problem.

Someone was behind her. Steps in step with hers. Edie wanted to turn and look. Was this real? Was this her scrambled wiring, a fuse shorting in her brain, a connection gone awry? Every muscle in her back and neck tensed, but she kept walking. Eyes ahead on the street, half a block until the main intersection.

A man stepped out of an alley directly into her path. She stopped immediately, an awkward stutter-step. The steps behind her became a presence, a softly muttered curse, breath against the back of her head. The man walking toward her stepped to the side, then he held his arm up, as if showing her a picture on his phone. The screen pulsed a rapid explosion of white light, a hundred strobe lights in the millisecond before she could blink or turn away. Hijacked. *Is this real?* Edie was paralyzed. *Did I close my eyes?* Someone brushed by her right shoulder, and she shrank away from the touch, which pushed her toward the flashing light. *I should blink.* The thought was far away. *Skye.* That thought was even farther.

"What the fuck, man?"

Shouting, a flurry of activity and the light gone. Edie blinked. Someone on a bike came screaming up the sidewalk. Looked like a bike courier, spiked helmet, army pants tucked into socks. Beat-up saddlebags matching the beat-up bike.

"You're a fucking hazard, get out of the way."

Did she recognize that voice? Edie edged away from them all, even as she registered something familiar about the bike courier.

"You should not be on the sidewalk."

Russian accent. Jesus. Like the other night. Last night? What was this? Edie stepped around the bike courier and the two men and kept walking. Almost at Dalhousie Street. Had there been lights? Real or imagined?

"You want your shit delivered? I get it delivered. Now move."

Skye's voice. This Skye was all angles and spikes and edges, no hint of reserve or shyness. Edie breathed. Skye was at her back. Skye was watching her. A cab idled at the intersection a few steps away.

Edie flagged it down, such a casual, normal gesture. She got in, gave her address, and closed her eyes. Lights danced and she felt nauseous. Tears threatened but anger burned them away. Then, a deep relief. It wasn't her imagination or her messed-up brain. Something was going on. And Skye believed her.

The cab took only minutes to get to Edie's apartment. Edie paid the driver and hurried up the front steps, remembering how she'd stood here last night with Skye. Her hands shook as she unlocked the door, entered the quiet front hall, and relocked the door behind her. Edie took a breath. And another. The trembling wouldn't stop. She took the stairs to her apartment, unlocked and relocked the door, dropped her bag on the coffee table, and sat on the couch. She didn't move. Edie stared straight ahead, letting thoughts and images cycle in and out of her head. She began to line up events like she was investigating a story. No luck. She had to consider the source. She needed help.

Edie's cell phone chimed. Skye.

I'm here. Buzz me in.

Edie stood and crossed the floor, pressing the old-fashioned buzzer next to her door. She leaned against the painted wood and waited until she heard Skye's quick tread on the stairs. They stopped outside her door. She heard a knock.

"Edie, it's Skye."

Edie put her hand on the doorknob. Last chance for this to be all a misunderstanding. Last chance for Skye to see her as a whole, together being.

"Edie?"

Edie opened the door. Skye walked in, closed and locked the door, and stood at near attention. She was still sharp edges, controlled movement, evaluative stare. Her voice was a harsh whisper, her words demanding. Edie saw her Skye in her slightly wild and fiercely protective eyes.

"Are you okay?"

Edie nodded.

"I think you should come over to my place. Pack a bag."

"No. I'm fine here."

Skye's eyes flashed and Edie caught a glimpse of the commanding officer. But she was not a subordinate.

"Edie…"

"Were you following me today?"

"Yes."

"Why?"

"I was worried."

"You didn't tell me."

"No."

Skye was unapologetic. Edie was resistant. This wasn't going anywhere.

"I don't want to do this here," Skye said finally, softening her stance just slightly.

"We're not doing anything," Edie said. Her voice sounded robotic. That should have been a red flag, but Edie felt grounded in her stubbornness. It was familiar and safe in a world that suddenly wasn't.

Skye looked around the front entrance and found an envelope and a pen and began to write. Edie watched curiously as Skye wrote quickly and passed the envelope over to Edie.

Your apartment might be bugged.

How can you tell? Edie wrote back.

Can't. Need proper equipment. Have it at my place. Come over. We'll talk.

Edie sighed. Skye was being so reasonable. And helpful. Right now she needed someone to share the load. She took the notepad back and scratched out a message.

I have an appointment in an hour with Dr. Wallace.

Skye nodded, and her eyes brightened.

I'll take you.

Resistance rose up and disappeared just as quickly. Another sigh. "Okay," she said out loud.

Edie turned and walked to her bedroom, thankful her legs were steady. She packed a bag without really thinking and walked back to the living room. Skye was busy tapping on her phone which vibrated every few seconds. Skye's eyes would flick up to the screen then she'd keep typing. It looked like an intense text conversation.

"That about me?" Edie said.

Skye looked at the bag in Edie's hand and kept typing before she pushed away from the wall and shoved her phone in her pocket. She crossed to the window and glanced out.

"Cab's here."

Outside, Skye was alert, maneuvering Edie with subtle gestures and a brisk pace. Edie allowed herself to be directed, though she was tired and irritated. As the cab made its way to Dr. Wallace's office at the edge of downtown, where buildings met residential neighbourhoods and local grocers and public schools, Skye scanned the streets and occasionally tapped on her phone. Edie stared blankly out the window and tried halfheartedly to stop the anger mounting in her stomach.

They reversed the routine, getting out of the cab and into the building. Edie felt like a politician with her bodyguard hovering beside her. Skye had the sunglasses, the vaguely threatening presence, the intensity. This would be funny any other moment. Any other moment that didn't mean an unnamed threat was lurking.

Edie wanted her life back. She wanted anonymity and she wanted the gentle, sweetly awkward Skye back. But that Skye seemed farther and farther away. They sat in Dr. Wallace's small waiting room. Skye continued to tap at her phone. Edie closed her eyes and tried not to surrender to the fear hiding in her anger and irritation.

Edie heard voices approaching the treatment room door but kept her eyes closed as the previous patient left. She felt Skye stiffen and shift closer as the person brushed by in the small space.

Edie opened her eyes to see Dr. Wallace evaluating Edie and Skye sitting together. This would require some extensive explaining.

"Edie?" Dr. Wallace's tone and expression asked a hundred questions.

"Yes, I'm ready," Edie said as she stood without acknowledging Skye's presence. She began to follow Dr. Wallace back into the therapy room when she heard Skye call her name. Edie paused without turning around.

"I'll be out here," Skye said. "I have some calls I need to make. I think you should tell Dr. Wallace everything."

Edie did not want to admit Skye's request made sense or that she was relieved to know Skye was waiting for her.

Dr. Wallace sat comfortably in her chair across from Edie with her eyebrows raised.

"I have some things to tell you. I'm not sure where to start," Edie said.

"Start wherever you'd like. We can always fill in the blanks later."

"I think the incident at the bar earlier this week is part of a bigger…

issue." Edie could not bring herself to say the word "plot." It felt too dramatic. It felt too scary. "I've had the sense I was being followed for a few months now. And then it happened again the other night with Skye, and then she followed me, and another incident happened out on the street just now…"

Dr. Wallace held up her hand. Edie felt her heart beating inside her chest. It was too high, her blood pressure increasing with every confession.

"Take a breath, Edie. Let's unpack this. When you're ready, start with what happened most recently."

Edie took a breath. And another. And then she started to speak. It took almost forty minutes for Edie to dump out all her fears and suspicions. Dr. Wallace asked a few clarifying questions but mostly she sat and listened, though Edie could sense her agitation with this strange therapy session. When she was done, Edie sat quietly.

"Have you taken this to the police?" Dr. Wallace said.

"No." Edie shifted in her seat. "I'm not even sure what I'd say. I'm not sure it's significant." She knew in her heart that it was.

"If Skye thinks you need protecting, I'd say that's significant."

Edie didn't respond.

"I'm not sure what you know of her history, she was in the—"

"Canadian Armed Forces. I know." Edie could not explain why she was acting like a sullen teenager. Why she was still so resistant to seeing this as a real issue. A dangerous problem. A threat.

"She also works for a private security company. Surveillance and protection."

"Still?" Edie said.

Dr. Wallace nodded. "I think we should suspend the therapy portion of our session and bring Skye in to talk about what happens next. What do you think?"

Edie's shoulders slumped. She had no energy for this, but she went to the door to ask Skye to come in, stopping abruptly when she saw Skye was not alone. She sat next to a tall woman with short, straight brown hair. The woman was leaning in close to Skye, their heads bent together, talking rapidly in a low tone. When Edie stepped into the small waiting room, both women looked at her and immediately stood. Edie kept her eyes on Skye though she noted the other woman's height, the broadness of her shoulders, and the blazer over her T-shirt and jeans. She smiled warmly at Edie.

"Edie," Skye said, "this is Constable Jane Caldwell with the OPP."

The constable stepped forward to shake Edie's hand. "I'm off duty, so it's JC." Her grip was strong, her hand warm like her smile.

"Nice to meet you," Edie said robotically. She looked back and forth between the two tall, muscled women who dominated the small waiting room with their energy. "I'm guessing Skye called you about what happened this morning."

Behind the cop, Skye lifted her chin and set her shoulders, like she knew she might be in shit for this decision but refused to back down.

To her credit, JC didn't once check in with Skye, she kept eye contact with Edie as she spoke.

"Yes, and some of the other incidents as well. I'd like to—"

"Why don't you both come in," Edie interrupted. "We can use Dr. Wallace's office as a war room." She turned abruptly and reentered the office, the two women following her. She sat woodenly and stared at the desk as Skye made the introductions. JC then sat beside her and Skye leaned up against the wall, arms crossed over her chest, her eyes on Edie, as if preparing to knock down her defenses. Edie stared at the lines and whorls in Dr. Wallace's desk. The irritation and anger were back.

"Ms. Black?"

Edie tuned back in, unaware that she'd drifted until JC's gentle voice called her back.

"Yes?"

"I'd like to verify what I've learned from Skye so far, and then I'd like you to think about anything else that could possibly be related to these incidents. Is that okay?"

Edie recognized the interrogation technique: the invitation to participate, the building of trust, and the reiteration of the value of her opinion. Edie nodded, and JC read from her phone point-by-point details of everything Edie had told Skye and what Skye had witnessed. Edie kept her eyes on JC's hands as she listened, aware of Dr. Wallace on one side and Skye on the other. JC completed her list and looked up at Edie.

"Ms. Black, is there anything else you can think of to add to this list?"

"Edie," Edie corrected absently.

"Edie. Anything at all?"

Edie thought about all the times in the last few weeks and months that she thought she was being paranoid. All the times she'd kicked herself for being unable to properly evaluate and react to her environment in a normal manner.

"No, that's everything."

"Okay. Can you think of any reason why someone might be after you? Why someone might want to scare you or threaten you?"

That gentle voice again, the gentle cop voice. Even knowing what she did about interrogation, Edie still wanted to trust that voice. But she looked past her to Skye. Her intense, yellow-green eyes gave her the courage to speak.

"I don't know."

JC waited, the silence oppressing the room. Edie felt stupid and vulnerable and so fucking tired. She clamped down hard on her threatening tears, tightening the muscles in her stomach as she gripped the upholstered arm of the chair and closed her eyes. No way was she going to cry in this room full of powerful women. She opened her eyes but would only look at JC.

"I'd like to take this to my superiors," JC said. "I'll be honest with you, I'm not sure this is enough for us to launch a full-scale investigation. Right now we don't have enough evidence to tie this all together. More significantly, there are no leads at all as to who might be behind any kind of systematic threat or attack." JC paused as if reluctant to say what she needed to say next. Edie decided to rescue her. And to take some control back from this interrogation.

"And because of my highly publicized history with a head injury, it's possible that whatever evidence you've gathered from me so far will be called into question."

Edie did not want the sympathetic look from JC, but got it anyway.

"Come on, JC, that's ridiculous." Skye pushed off the wall and advanced on JC. Her shoulders were rigid with strain, and her expression was dark and dangerous.

"Skye," Dr. Wallace said evenly, holding up a forestalling hand. "Let me see if I can handle this." Skye leaned back against the wall, clearly still pissed. "Constable Caldwell, if you need verification of Ms. Black's current, exceptional level of cognitive functioning, I can obtain that for you."

Edie relaxed just a little at her words as well as her tone.

JC shook her head, obviously frustrated at the multi-side attack. She took a breath before she spoke.

"I'm not saying I don't believe her…" JC stopped and turned to Edie. "I'm not saying I don't believe you. I do. I will take this to my superiors, and we will begin an investigation. I can guarantee that. What I can't guarantee at this moment is any kind of security from the OPP. We don't have enough evidence to warrant that kind of manpower at this point. Honestly, I think your best bet is to lay low and have Skye here be your protective detail."

Constable Caldwell clearly did not expect the immediate and adamant reaction from both Skye and Edie. As Edie started protesting from one side and Skye launched herself away from the wall for a second time, JC sat back in surprise.

Dr. Wallace once again interrupted. "Maybe let's all just take a moment with this suggestion, shall we?"

Edie bit back an angry retort and deliberately tried to calm her breathing. She did not need protection. The police could figure out what was happening and deal with it. If it even *was* anything. She didn't need her movements monitored, didn't need yet another major disruption just as she was getting her life back together.

"Edie? I'd like to check in."

Great, a therapy session in front of Skye and JC. Fucking perfect. Edie took a breath and released it. Dr. Wallace used that phrase to bring Edie back when she was cycling through a non-productive spiral. Another breath. She looked at her psychologist.

"I don't want a security detail."

Dr. Wallace nodded. Edie felt Skye and JC stiffen from across the room. Dr. Wallace ignored them.

"I understand. But I'd like you to take a minute and consider the list of unexplainable events in the last few months. And then I'd like you to tell me if you think you *need* some form of protection while the case is being investigated."

Wants and needs. Edie wanted her life back. She wanted to be looking forward to her second date with Skye. Then Edie remembered how it felt to be followed, the fear of someone behind her, the disorienting tricks someone was playing on her mind. And she remembered her absolute confidence that Skye had her back.

Edie sighed and leaned back in her chair. "Yes," she said in a small voice.

Dr. Wallace turned next to Skye. "I understand you have objections?"

Skye squared off at near attention. "No objections to Edie requiring some form of security. I can tap my contacts and find a suitable—"

"I'm not sure anyone else should be brought into this," JC said. "Why can't it be you?"

The silence was awkward. JC looked confused.

Dr. Wallace looked between Skye and Edie as if evaluating the temperature of the silence. "Ah, I see."

JC snapped her head around to the psychologist. "What am I missing?"

Dr. Wallace said nothing.

"I kissed her," Skye blurted into the silence. She put her arms behind her back, shoulders rigid, her gaze fixed somewhere over Dr. Wallace's head.

"Jesus." Edie rubbed her hands across her eyes. Dr. Wallace looked impassive, though Edie could detect a hint of a smile.

JC seemed to need a moment for the information to sink in, then she grinned at Skye. "Kenny, that's pretty fast work for you."

"Fuck off, Caldwell."

"Okay," Dr. Wallace said. "We've identified the problem, now let's solve the problem. Skye, could you please elaborate on your concerns about looking after Edie while the police are investigating her case."

Edie's heart sank. Dr. Wallace had chosen her words very carefully, posing the question so Skye couldn't easily maneuver out of this. Dr. Wallace wanted Skye as Edie's security.

"It's inadvisable for the security detail to have any kind of personal relationship with the protectee," Skye said without inflection. She was still standing at attention.

"I see," said Dr. Wallace. "And how long have you known Edie?"

"Eight days."

"And you believe that knowing Edie for these eight days somehow impairs your ability to make sure she is safe?"

"It might. I won't take that risk."

"Skye, is there any other reason you think precludes you from being the best protection for Edie, other than your admittedly very new relationship?"

Edie suddenly very much did not want Skye to comment on their relationship. She did not want to hear they didn't have a chance. She did not want to hear that one date, one kiss, had ruined the chance for anything more. She did not want to hear that Skye was using this as an excuse to back away. Edie felt the need to protect herself.

"Hardly a relationship," Edie said, looking only at Dr. Wallace. Still, she thought she could see Skye flinch.

"She kissed you," JC said, seemingly half in amusement and half in clarification.

"Technically, I kissed her."

"Not surprising," JC said with smug satisfaction.

Edie wanted to ask what she meant but kept her mouth shut. Once again, Dr. Wallace mediated the situation.

"Constable Caldwell, why don't you and I step outside? I think at this point, Edie and Skye need a moment to work this out for themselves."

JC looked as if she was going to protest, but she stood up instead. Dr. Wallace followed her out of the room. As JC passed Skye, Edie saw her punch Skye on the bicep.

"Don't fuck this up, fire buddy," JC said.

Once they had left, the room became very, very quiet. Edie turned in her chair to look at Skye, who stood completely still, staring at a blank spot on the wall above Dr. Wallace's desk.

"What's a fire buddy?"

Skye flicked her gaze to Edie then back to the wall.

"The person you're assigned to in Basic Training. Your Fire Team Partner, FTP. You have to stay within three feet of each other for the entire twelve weeks."

"JC was your FTP? Your fire buddy."

"That's right."

More silence. Edie sighed. "Will you come sit down? Please."

Skye sat in the chair next to Edie. She leaned forward with her elbows on her knees. When she looked up, Edie saw her Skye there. But she also saw the hardness. Soldier Skye. Edie's stomach flipped.

She remembered holding Skye's hand. She did not want her to go anywhere.

"You've worked security before. Protective detail."

"Yes."

"But you don't want to provide security for me."

"I don't think it's a good idea. I know several really good security agents. I can call them right now. They're good people. I promise."

Skye pulled out her phone. She seemed almost frantic to get away. Edie didn't want to deal with the sadness of that thought.

"Tell me what you think is going on."

Skye stopped tapping at her phone. "What do you mean?"

"I've given my version of events, and everyone has agreed that something is going on, but no one seems to want to speculate. What do you think is happening to me? Why do you think I need protection and a police investigation?"

"I know someone is after you. I suspect whoever it is wants to evaluate your reaction to a variety of sensory tests, but I don't know why. I know with absolute certainty you should have twenty-four-hour protection until the police get some answers and can step in to ensure that you are protected and secure."

Edie was numb to the fear. It just didn't exist. But she suddenly knew exactly what she wanted.

"I want it to be you."

"Edie..."

"I want it to be you," Edie said again, this time with more force.

Skye dropped her head into her hands. Edie let the silence stretch. Minutes passed. Edie could hear the low murmurings of Dr. Wallace and JC in the waiting room. When she spoke, Skye spoke to the floor.

"I'll do it on two conditions."

"Okay," Edie said, her heart pounding just a little in her chest.

"I need you to listen to me. I'll treat you like a soldier, and you'll hate it, but I need to know you'll follow my command."

"Agreed," Edie said softly. "The other condition?"

Skye's eyes were hard. No hint of the gentle Skye.

"I cannot and will not pursue a relationship with you while I'm responsible for your security. It goes against logic, it goes against my training, and it goes against my ethics."

Edie held her gaze. She searched Skye's eyes for warmth or

connection. All she saw was a deep resolve. She found comfort in that, even as her heart splintered a little at the loss.

"I understand."

Skye took a moment before standing.

"I'll tell JC. We need to coordinate next steps." Skye walked to the door and then paused. She spoke without turning around.

"I will do whatever I can to protect you, Edie. But you need to know that I'm going to disappoint you."

Edie sat alone with a sore heart, trying not to hear that truth.

CHAPTER SIX

The next morning, Edie searched the loft until she found Skye free-climbing a rock wall embedded in the dark corner by the back stairs. The night had been quiet and tense for Edie. She was thankful she'd slept well in the strange environment, but she was still on edge. She needed to move.

"I'd like to go for a run."

Skye was already one flight up the wall, so Edie had to project her voice. She could just make out the pale shape of Skye's face as she turned to look down at Edie. Skye paused in her ascent, then effortlessly descended the wall. She landed lightly on her feet, her eyes bright from the exertion.

"A run?" Skye said.

"Yes, a run." Edie blew out a breath and reminded herself about her resolve to be less irritated with Skye. "I don't know how this works. Am I asking permission, is there a sign-out sheet, did you want to implant a GPS chip under my skin?"

Edie thought Skye stopped herself from smiling.

"I should be with you." Skye shook her head. "I meant I should go where you're going. Give me five minutes."

"Okay. I mean, Roger that, or whatever."

Another almost smile. As Edie turned back to the bedroom area of the loft, she smirked at making Skye smile. She wasn't entirely sure why it was so important that she remind Skye of their connection, but the pull was hard to ignore.

Edie sorted through her bag of clothes and toiletries she'd brought from her apartment and found her running gear. She felt a little sick as she remembered what Skye had found there after their meeting with Dr. Wallace. A small video camera had been installed in the pot light above her doorway, and four other audio transmitters were in the apartment. Skye had immediately updated JC, who advised her to leave all the bugs in place. Skye had also found a ghost program running in the background of Edie's phone which monitored Edie's email, social media, texts, and calls. It had also enabled location tracking. So Skye had shaken her head when Edie went to pick it up as they left.

Edie ignored the trembling of her hands as she found a hair elastic and efficiently twisted the not quite long enough strands of her dark hair into a French braid. She walked around the privacy screen Skye had set up last night and into the living room. Skye's back was to her when she walked in. She wore shorts and a black sports bra and was just pulling down a T-shirt over her torso. The muscles flexed across Skye's back and shoulders. Edie caught a glimpse of a tattoo that covered her upper left arm, but she couldn't see it in detail. She couldn't help thinking Skye was by far one of the most beautiful women she had ever met. Though Edie hadn't made any sound, Skye turned around.

"I was thinking we could take a drive over the bridge and do a run at the base of the hills," Skye said, not acknowledging Edie having seen her half naked. Skye had been in the armed forces, Edie reminded herself. Maybe it wasn't a big deal. Edie's mind played and replayed the image of Skye's built upper body. "There are some short routes and some longer ones, depending on what you're looking for," Skye said.

"Are you worried we'll be followed around here?"

"I'm operating under the assumption that whoever is following you knows you're here, yes. I think it will be safer away from my loft."

Edie looked out one of the windows, noting the light, crisp blue sky. A run at the base of the Gatineau Hills sounded perfect. A run with Skye sounded even better. She wished with a sudden, sharp intensity that a run was all they had to think about this morning.

"I'm only up to about five kilometres these days. Is that okay?"

"Yes. It's perfect."

Skye seemed to imitate Edie's subdued, almost polite tones. Edie hated it but stood dutifully silent while Skye grabbed a small backpack from the couch.

"Ready?"

"Yes."

Traffic was slow through downtown and across the bridge, Edie having slept through her usual early morning, which put them directly into rush hour. They drove silently, an inoffensive radio station playing softly in the background. Edie felt the need to apologize: for having slept in, for taking Skye's bed, for being in her space, in her car. In her life.

"What's in it for you?" Edie blurted.

"What do you mean?"

"Why did you agree to do this? Protect me, babysit me. Whatever this is." Edie waved her hand at the space between them.

"Because I can," Skye said, gripping the steering wheel of her Jeep just a little bit tighter. She glanced quickly at Edie, then back to the road. She sighed. "And because I want to."

"So it wasn't that JC guilted you into it."

"No."

"Did I guilt you into it?"

"No."

"But you didn't want to be a part of this." Edie knew she was pushing, but she couldn't seem to stop. "At Dr. Wallace's office, you said you didn't want to."

Skye didn't answer. They were across the bridge now, winding their way through the outskirts of Hull, Quebec. Edie itched to keep throwing questions at Skye, to have her buckle under the weight of them until Skye was forced to answer. She waited, though, sensing Skye was trying to formulate a response that fit within her set of rules.

A few minutes later they pulled into a parking lot of one of the many trails that led through the Gatineau Hills. While Skye grabbed her backpack, Edie looked at the large map at the base of the entrance to the trail. She stared at it, not really taking in any of the information. She was thinking about Skye's lack of answer. Then Skye approached and stood just behind Edie.

"This is a nice route," Skye said, pointing to one of the yellow lines on the map. "No spectacular views, but the run through the forest is beautiful."

Edie nodded, hoping Skye was going to answer her question. Skye seemed to pause and everything held still just for a moment. Then Skye took a step back and adjusted her small backpack, tightening the straps across her chest and waist. Edie stole a glance at it. She wanted to ask if Skye had a weapon. She thought maybe yes. A cool trickle of wind swept uncomfortably across the back of her neck and the darkened forest seemed suddenly ominous. Edie shivered.

"Don't think about it," Skye said. "Let's run."

They entered the trail, cool damp descending on them the moment they left the open parking lot. Trees towered above them, and Edie felt the peace of the forest, the grandeur of the space, the hint of sun and sky through the branches. She took a breath and fell in step with Skye, walking to the crest of a small hill before they both started a slow run.

All of Edie's senses were heightened, from the smell of damp wood and evergreens she took in with each breath to the press of soft-packed dirt and rocks and roots beneath her feet. Skye ran beside her, all tightly coiled muscles, with the sound of her breath, the smell of her soap and sweat. Edie descended into her run, a feeling she hadn't had in a long time, a meditative space that kept her even and kept her going. That peace of mind had eluded her since the accident. The sensation made her feel hopeful, and just for a moment Edie could imagine her world was just right. Changed but right.

Three-quarters of the way through their circuit, Skye's phone alert pulled Edie from her reverie. Skye looked at her watch and silenced the alarm.

"Shit," Skye said.

"What is it?"

Skye didn't answer, but she slowed her pace and Edie automatically did the same. Skye stopped completely and scanned the path ahead of them, then off into the forest, finally turning until she'd completed a full circle. Edie's breathing sounded so loud in the relative silence, and she fought to control it.

"Skye?"

"That was my car alarm. It might be nothing. Let's go."

Edie wanted Skye to elaborate, but Skye began running to the car. Her legs protested the start and stop but Edie ignored them, keeping her eyes on the muscles that flexed and rolled across her shoulders above her pack.

As they approached the top of the small hill at the exit to the parking lot, Skye raised her arm and stopped. "Stay behind me but stay close."

As if Edie would do anything else. They walked down the hill, slowing as they reached the parking lot. Edie scanned the lot and only saw the same dusty blue SUV that had been at the opposite end of the lot when they arrived. She felt Skye stiffen and followed her gaze. Someone was walking around from the far side of the Jeep. Someone Edie recognized.

"Faina? What the hell?"

Faina stopped by the passenger door of the Jeep. She acknowledged Skye with a glance but kept her eyes on Edie.

"I need to talk to you," Faina said.

Skye spoke to Edie over her shoulder without losing sight of Faina.

"She's the one who took you to the bar?"

"Yes."

"Is she a threat?"

"She's…" Edie's automatic denial lodged in her throat. She could not evaluate risk and threat. She could not block out the sound of the drumbeat. A light flashed in her eyes. And a memory forced its way to the surface. The morning after the incident in the bar, Faina standing in Edie's apartment saying, "I didn't know."

"I can't tell."

Skye slid her right hand under her backpack and rested it there.

"Edie?" Faina took a step forward.

"Don't come any closer," Skye called. "Say what you have to say from where you are."

Faina stopped and looked around the parking lot, confused or conflicted.

"What do you want, Faina?" Edie said.

"I need to talk to you. I'm sorry…I'm sorry about the other night."

"But why are you here? How did you find me?"

"I…" Faina took another step forward. Skye took a step back, forcing Edie to do the same.

"I need to talk to you." Faina was pleading now, her voice wavering. She was trembling, her whole body shaking.

"Something's wrong," Edie said quietly to Skye.

"I need to get you out of here," Skye said.

"Just give me a minute. Please."

"One minute, then I'm launching her out of the way, getting you in the Jeep, and getting you out of here."

"Roger that, Major," Edie said before she focused back on Faina. "Did you follow me here?"

"Yes. I'm sorry for the other night."

"You said that already. Why did you follow me here?"

"I need to talk." Faina looked toward the road. Edie followed her gaze. She heard nothing, saw nothing. Faina crouched down and picked up a short stick, then stood again and began scraping at the rocks in front of her with the side of her shoe. "I made you go to the bar and I'm sorry," Faina said robotically as she scratched in the dirt with the stick. "I know it hurt you. I'm sorry." She looked up at Edie, her eyes pleading. That's when Edie noticed the faded bruising under Faina's left eye, down her jaw, and along her neck. "I'm so sorry, Edie." Faina took two steps back and pointed at whatever she'd scratched out in the dirt.

"Stay here," Skye said tersely. She took a few steps forward to peer at what Faina had written.

Skye straightened and walked backward to Edie. She hadn't removed her hand from the small of her back. "She's being monitored. She wrote 'they're listening.' I don't like this. She's not alone. I need to get you out of here."

"Jesus, she's with them." Nausea again, and Edie swayed slightly as her brain ran full tilt backward, trying to make sense of this, even as her body sagged under the weight of too much exertion and adrenaline.

"Edie, focus." Skye's voice was just at the edge of sharp, a whispered command to pull herself together. "Tell her you have to go, you'll call her later, whatever. Then follow me to the car."

"Skye, I think she's hurt." Now that she'd seen the bruises, Edie couldn't ignore them.

"She's not my concern right now, you are. Talk to her. Now."

Edie felt the edges of Skye's anger, the splintering of her patience, the desire to get her to safety.

"Faina, I'm tired and I need to go. I'll call you, okay?" Her voice didn't sound right. Her modulation was off, and she sounded unconvincing. Did it really matter? Who was listening?

"Say you'll meet me for coffee. You have to say you will." Faina was near tears, and she took a few stumbling steps toward Edie and Skye.

"We're going," Skye said loudly. She stabbed a finger at Faina. "You." She gestured sharply away from the Jeep.

Faina's shoulders slumped but she followed Skye's nonverbal command and stood a few feet away. Skye grabbed Edie by the upper arm, keeping herself between Faina and Edie. Just as Skye unlocked and opened the passenger side door of the Jeep, the sound of canned music drifted through the parking lot. Edie looked up as Skye tried to hustle her into the car. That music was familiar. Edie could see Faina's face drain of colour, her eyes wide with a horror that made no sense given the quietness of the forest, the blueness of the sky, the faint strain of strings from the music. Faina slowly reached into her pocket, and Edie felt Skye tense.

"Move, Edie. Get in the car, *now*."

But the music was playing and Edie could feel her scalp, her jaw, her neck, her shoulders as they sagged and relaxed. The music sat on her chest as the adrenaline drained away. Worry went with it, fear a confusing memory. She simply needed to sleep.

"Edie, no. Hang on…"

Skye's harsh voice was overshadowed by the music and the fog of sleep descending over Edie. It blurred Faina's look of horror as she stared at her phone in her hand, the source of the music, then back at Edie. Edie closed her eyes and let gravity pull her down, even as she felt Skye lifting her into the Jeep.

❖

Edie's body swayed with the careening Jeep. She registered speed, and bumps, and gravel spraying against the underside of the car. She could hear Skye talking.

"…may be a device, I'm going on the assumption there's not. No choice right now, I have to get out of here. Yes, I'll clear it when I get a chance…okay, send me the three closest locations to this number. No, the other number is burned. Is Sasha under? Good, I'm calling him in. Keep a line open for me and start a tab. Fine, we'll sort it out later." Skye tapped at the phone in the stand on the dash.

Edie's mind was rapidly clearing the fog. Not all of Skye's words made sense, but the intensity of her tone did. The unmistakable timbre of control.

"Skye?"

Skye glanced over at Edie, then looked back to the road, constantly scanning her mirrors.

"You okay? Hurt?"

"No." Edie sat up straighter and tried to get her bearings. They were still at the base of the hills, so she couldn't have been out for long.

"What's happening?"

"I haven't seen any cars but I'm assuming we're being followed. Either by a vehicle or GPS tracking or both. When I'm satisfied no vehicle is behind us, I'm going to clear the car of any tracking devices. I already started with my phone." Skye nodded briefly toward the console. Her iPhone was cracked open, the chip beside it in two pieces.

"Jesus," Edie mumbled. She rubbed at her temples and tried to catch up. She tried so hard to place herself in the centre of this activity. Part of her mind rebelled at the thought. The other forced her to be here and live this. And help.

"What can I do?"

Another glance from Skye. An evaluation, this time.

"Watch the mirrors for cars behind us. Write down any license plate numbers. Grab the phone and take pictures of the driver if they get close."

"Yeah, okay. I can do that."

They were clearing the hills now, cars passing them in the other direction. The silence was uncomfortable, filled with questions and unknowns. Skye drove confidently, following the directions on her screen. Edie said nothing. As they entered Hull traffic, every car and driver became suspect.

"I don't know if having so many people around is better or worse," Edie said.

"It's better. Just keep an eye out."

Every stoplight made Edie feel exposed, every sluggish acceleration felt like someone was catching up. Edie blew out a breath.

"We're fine," Skye said, obviously sensing her discomfort.

"Sure, that's why you're wound so tight," Edie mumbled.

"I'm sure we made it out of the hills without being followed, but I'll feel better when we clear the car of any tracking devices."

"How are we doing that?"

Skye turned right down a street and pointed at a gas station sign. "Right here."

Edie watched as Skye drove behind the gas pumps and the attached convenience store until they arrived at the car wash.

"Seriously?"

Skye gave Edie a quick, tight grin, her eyes bright. Skye lowered the window and worked the machine. Edie didn't get the sense that Skye was enjoying this, but she was fully engaged. Edie had always sensed Skye's intellect was incredibly vast, but she kept it under wraps. In this crisis or whatever this was, Skye was more exposed and less cautious than Edie had ever seen her.

"The combination of water, soap, and brushes should do the trick," Skye said as she eased the Jeep forward into the car wash until the sensor indicated the vehicle should stop.

Moments later, Skye put the Jeep in park and the sudden onslaught of a cascade of water made Edie jump. Soap sprayed next, the bubblegum colour doing nothing to soothe Edie's frayed nerves. More soap, then a mechanical clanking as giant brushes attacked the Jeep from all sides. The sound was deafening, the Jeep was dark, and suddenly Edie was having trouble breathing. Skye took her hand and leaned across the console. She had to speak directly in Edie's ear to be heard above the noise.

"Hey, you're okay. This only lasts five minutes. You're safe, just breathe. Edie, breathe."

Edie tried. She actively fought the panic, refusing to allow it to consume her.

"I'm okay," Edie said, not even sure if Skye could hear her.

"I know. Four minutes."

Edie turned her head slightly, wanting to see Skye. It put their faces very close together. Edie's pulse accelerated again.

"Then what?"

Skye leaned back slightly. Some of the light in her eyes had dimmed. "I think we need to get out of town." Edie shook her head. Skye put a hand up. "Wait until we can talk better. I have a plan."

Edie didn't want a plan. She didn't want to get out of town. She didn't want the light in Skye's eyes to disappear. She didn't want to argue. The sound of the water and brushes was a loud, rhythmic constant in the background, making it hard to think. So Edie didn't. She rested her head back, closed her eyes, and laid her palms flat against her thighs. Three minutes to meditate. Three minutes to think. Three minutes to catch up.

Three minutes later Skye put the Jeep in gear and emerged into the bright sunlight. She immediately tapped her phone and adjusted her earpiece.

"I'm clear. Or as clear as I'm going to get without a scan. Where's the meet?"

Edie listened to the half of the conversation as Skye maneuvered them confidently through the streets of Hull to a smaller bridge that would take them to the west side of downtown Ottawa.

"Yes. I'm ten minutes out."

Ten minutes. Edie breathed for those ten minutes. She watched the mirrors. She did not try to anticipate next steps. She had learned in Kandahar that some moments were just moments, and you simply used them to prepare yourself. To store them as a reminder that your body and mind were capable of calm. Edie had to wonder how many of those moments she had left.

Edie opened her eyes as the Jeep slowed outside a mid-level, plain-looking building. Skye pulled up to the security gate, lowered the window, and held her phone up to the screen. Something beeped, and the arm raised. Skye followed the signs to the parking garage.

"Where are we?"

"A federal building. I don't think we're being followed, but this is the safest place to get the resources and equipment we need to get you out of town."

"Equipment? Jesus, like a U-Haul? I thought that was more of a second-date thing."

Skye didn't laugh, not even a smile. She just kept driving up the enclosed garage ramps until they were at P6. Skye muttered as she peered at cars, finally backing into a spot near the exit and turning off the ignition.

"Stay here. I'll be right back." Skye quickly got out of the Jeep and disappeared from view.

Edie thought about her agreement to follow Skye's orders for a full minute. Then the silence in the Jeep became oppressive, and she was suddenly completely overwhelmed. Edie opened the car door and followed Skye.

She was three cars down, talking to a tall man with broad shoulders and a shiny, bald head. They both looked up as Edie rounded the bumper and stopped. Edie waited for a reprimand, the order to get back in the car and get out of the way. Instead, after only a moment's hesitation, Skye indicated Edie should come closer.

"Edie Black, this is Lawrence Bartali. He's the head of Protag Security and my sometimes boss."

Edie refused to be intimidated by the man's size, position, or his impressive glower. She held out her hand. "Thanks for helping me out, Mr. Bartali."

He shook her hand, his grip strong and warm. "You can call me Bart, Ms. Black. As the saying goes, any friend of Kenny's is a friend of mine." His voice was warm, too.

Edie expected to see Skye blush and could not quite explain her disappointment at its absence.

"Bart's agreed to take you on as a client, which means we've got access to as many of the security resources we need. Actually, we need you to sign a contract with Protag Security." She pulled a sheaf of papers out of one of the laptop bags in the trunk and handed it to Edie.

Edie unfurled the papers and began scanning the legalese. She looked up at Skye.

"Am I signing away any rights here? What about cost?"

"You won't be signing anything away, Ms. Black. The contract just outlines that you are securing our services."

"And cost?"

Bart flicked his eyes to Skye.

"No cost," Skye said. "But we need these papers for certain permits and to allow access."

Edie had seen right through Skye's answer. But maybe she didn't care. She gestured for a pen and signed the document, handing it back to Bart, who tucked it away.

"Good, okay. Right now we're clearing the Jeep of any bugs, establishing communication links, and then making a plan to get you out of here." She paused, as if making sure Edie wasn't overwhelmed with the information. She was, but she wasn't about to show it. "Where would Faina expect you to go if you left town?"

An easy question. "My brother and sister-in-law's chalet. It's west of Calabogie. Faina knows I go there sometimes on my own."

"Will your brother be there in the next week or two?" Bart said.

"I doubt it, but I don't know for sure."

Skye turned to Bart. "Do you have the phones?"

Bart opened the back of the dark SUV and unzipped a plain black rolling suitcase. Inside was a series of grey foam compartments. Wedged neatly into one of these looked like eight new iPhones. Bart delicately pulled one out with his thick fingers and handed it to Skye. She indicated it should go to Edie.

"Code it as Edie's. We may need it to make contact."

Edie stared at the phone in her hand. It seemed to be the same model as the one Skye had made her leave behind. Holding the phone out of its case was strange. It was too light and too slippery. Edie felt a sudden case of nerves, a frisson of anxiety coursing up through her spine and into her arms. Her hand shook. She was sure she was going to drop the phone. Skye didn't seem to notice.

"Call your brother. Tell him to stay away from the chalet for at least the next week. At this point don't tell him why." Skye turned to Bart. "We've got security detail on the Black family? Home, work, and school?"

"The whole lot. I'll have an update from the boys by this aft. We'll monitor the chalet, see if anyone shows any interest there."

Edie felt sick. She was still staring at the screen of her phone. The tremors in her arm were worse. Security and police, weapons permits, tracking. *This isn't my life. This has to be a mistake.*

"Good," Skye was saying. "There's nothing to suggest anyone has made contact, but until we know who we're dealing with, we'll keep them there."

Edie's arm jerked as another tremor passed through her body. She mechanically dialed her brother's home number, the only one she could remember off the top of her head, and asked him to give her a call, leaving the new number Bart held out to her. Edie hung up and tried to tune back into the conversation.

"Any intel on the contact from today? I take it she's your best lead," Bart was saying. *Their voices are nearly conversational,* Edie thought. *They're comfortable in this realm; every part of this is familiar.* But Edie felt like she had been dropped suddenly into another life, and the lack of familiarity bred a fear getting harder and harder to ignore. Her eyes began to hurt, and the golden haze of an aura edged into her vision. Migraine, a bad one. She had ten minutes max before it hit.

"Edie? Did you hear me?"

"No, repeat the question please." Edie kept her eyes down.

Skye seemed to catch on that something was wrong. Her voice became hesitant. "Faina's last name. Or the one she's given you, anyway."

"Kassis," Edie said and spelled it out.

"Arabic," she heard Bart mutter.

"And a Russian first name. And at least two others had a Slavic accent," Skye said. "Edie, has Faina talked about her family?"

"Her mom was from Damascus but lived in the UK. She has a brother and sister, both older. I think they have a different mother. Faina didn't like talking about her family."

"We'll start there," Bart said. "I'll need a picture if you've got one."

"On my phone," Edie said quietly, feeling the loss of too many kinds of connections.

"I'll make sure you get it before the cops do," Skye said to Bart. "In fact, I'm setting up a meet with JC when we have our final destination from Sasha. We can come at it from both sides."

"I've never worked with her," Bart said. "You trust her?"

"Absolutely. I'll give you her contact info, and I'd trust any and all information with her. No one else."

Edie's head began to splinter as Skye and Bart continued to talk. It wasn't pain yet, but her senses fractured into separate components. She didn't have ten minutes after all.

"Ms. Black, are you okay?"

"Edie?"

"Migraine," Edie whispered. "I need to lie down."

Skye and Bart half carried Edie back to Skye's Jeep. Their strength was the only comfort in a world turned to pain and confusion and nausea. Edie lay in the backseat, the seat belt buckles digging awkwardly into her side. She didn't care. She needed dark and silence, and the Jeep offered both. Edie focused on her breathing, barely aware of the now hushed conversation around her. Skye opened the door and whispered for her to lift her head. She placed something soft underneath. A sweatshirt, maybe. It smelled like Skye. Edie breathed.

"Edie," Skye whispered, her fingers gently resting against Edie's temple. "Do you have meds with you?"

"No."

"I can get them from my loft. Sasha will be here in fifteen minutes."

Pain blossomed behind her eyes and burned its way around her skull.

"Too late."

"I'm sorry."

Edie melted under the onslaught of the pain. It filled her skull, her nose and mouth, her throat. It filled her chest, her shoulders, her arms. Each finger was pain, her pelvis heavy with the hurt of her year-old injury. Her legs were immobile, her feet hot and her running shoes so tightly laced she nearly cried. Something eased the pain in her feet, minutes or hours later. The darkness became more profound, and Edie removed herself from the world as the pain ravaged her body.

CHAPTER SEVEN

Edie shuffled out of the unfamiliar bedroom, passed an unfamiliar kitchen, and stopped by a bay of windows to watch a spectacular sunrise over an unfamiliar lake. Orange and pink rippled and stretched across the water as the sun gently burned over the row of dark pines across the lake. Each colour was sharp and fluid all at once, prisms and waves that extended closer and closer until Edie felt like the colours would soon touch her skin in all their gentle vibrancy.

Surfacing from a migraine without meds always felt like learning to breathe. The world was scrubbed clean, the absence of pain a gift that made her want to cry. Her pain meds could never touch this euphoria. The combination of post-migraine, a beautiful sunrise, and safety made Edie feel hopeful for the first time in days.

"Hey, how are you feeling?"

Skye approached from the kitchen, carrying two mugs. She was wearing old sweatpants, a ratty shirt, and her beanie.

"Better. A million times better," Edie said, accepting the coffee mug with a faded pineapple and the words "Produce King" on the side. She took a sip and sighed. "God, thank you."

Skye smiled an easy, happy smile.

"So, where are we exactly?" Edie said. She had a vague memory of driving, of Skye waking her up into complete rural darkness, of a stiff neck and the incredibly loud croaks and chirps of frogs as Skye helped her into the cabin.

"Near Seeley's Bay. Not quite two hours south of Ottawa."

Edie looked around. The risen sun had lost its orange pinkness in the short time they'd been talking. Pale yellow light now reached the dark interior of the cabin. It consisted of a small living room, an open kitchen and dining room, and the hallway Edie had traveled earlier with two bedrooms and a small bathroom.

"Your place?"

"A friend's. It would be difficult, but not impossible, to trace me here."

Edie searched Skye's face. Skye took a sip of coffee and seemed to allow Edie to seek out whatever she was trying to find.

"What did I miss while I was out?" Edie said.

Skye hesitated. She sipped her coffee and regarded Edie silently over the brim. Then she indicated with her head that they should sit at the table, which was half covered with a laptop and wires and phones and blinking boxes. Edie pulled back the old-fashioned high-backed chair at the other end and sat.

"Before you answer, I have something I want to say," Edie said.

"Okay."

"I know I said I would follow your orders, and I swear I'm going to do my damnest. But I need to be involved in this. I need to know what's going on. I'm going to lose it if you keep me in the dark."

Skye sighed and took another sip of coffee. "I know. JC basically told me the same thing. You have to understand this is strange for me."

"The hanging out in pyjamas together part?" Edie said, wanting Skye to smile. She did, hiding behind her coffee mug as she took another sip. Then she lowered her mug and regarded Edie with serious eyes.

"You're not a soldier under my command, but I'm going to give you commands. You're not a client paying for my protection, but I'm here to provide protection. You're not a colleague or an employee or a…" Skye seemed to reconsider her last words. She stared at Edie, as if daring her to complete the sentence.

"Or a friend," Edie said softly.

Skye said nothing. She didn't even move. Discomfort filled the space even as the sun filled the room with brilliant light. Edie's heart hurt a little.

"JC thinks you are the most likely person to figure out who is after you. I agree. So I promise to do my best to keep you in the loop. I'm just asking…" Skye fidgeted with her coffee mug and looked out over the water for a moment. "I'm not good at this. Undefined roles. I'll do my best. Okay?"

"Okay."

"So, we've got both Bart and JC looking into Faina Kassis. The OPP are also looking into Russian connections and recent Russian activity, both provincial and federal. I've requested satellite images of the park we ran through yesterday, but JC is pretty sure that will be a no-go unless they find something pretty heavy. She'll be here after lunch to give us an update, so I'd like you and me to spend some time trying to find out who might possibly be after you and why."

"Yes," Edie said slowly, picking up every thread Skye was weaving. So many pieces and dead ends and tangles. Too many questions. "I need some paper. I need to write this down."

"I can start a Google doc," Skye said, pulling her laptop closer.

"Uh, sure," Edie said. "Do that. But I need some paper. And a pen. Please."

Skye stood and left the room, returning moments later with a large pad of paper yellowing at the edges. It seemed to be a pad of paper menus with instructions on how to break down and eat a lobster. Skye ripped off the top piece of paper and flipped it over to the blank side. She also laid down a handful of pens and markers.

"Will this do?"

"Perfect."

Edie started to write. The first paper was Faina. The second was SunNews. The third was Weird Shit. Skye barked out a short laugh at that title, reading it upside down from her spot across the table.

"Okay, I'm going to start with Faina and write down everything I know or remember. Mind if I talk this out loud?"

"Not at all. Mind if I take notes?"

Edie waved her assent and picked up a pen. This felt like her investigative journalism days. They were short-lived, the field too small and too competitive. Edie wrote and spoke in tandem, only peripherally aware Skye was listening and typing.

"Okay, I met Faina six months ago, about mid-November. It's probably in my calendar, or I could get an exact date from my physiotherapist if we needed one."

"I'll make a note."

"I bumped into her twice more at the physiotherapist's office before we made a date to go out for coffee. That would be early December, there were Christmas carols."

Skye was looking at her.

"What?"

"I just wondered…" Skye swallowed. What had made her so uncomfortable? "I have to ask…JC will ask…"

Edie finally clued in. "No. Not like that. We've only ever been friends. I think Faina's straight."

Skye nodded and ducked her head as she kept typing. Edie still found her nervousness adorable. She shook her head. No time for that.

"Content. What did we talk about? In the beginning, we talked about our commonalities. Pain and injury. Treatment. What worked and what didn't."

"How did Faina get hurt?"

"She was trampled at a religious service when she was four. She still has some spine and shoulder issues since she was never treated properly." Edie considered what she'd said and what she'd written down. "Allegedly. All of this is completely unverified. It never occurred to me to question it."

"Don't worry about that now. Keep going. This is good."

Edie took the encouragement. "Okay. Background. Faina said she was born in Damascus, lived there with her mother until she was five, then her father moved them to the UK. She lived there until she was nineteen, when she moved to Canada. I don't know why."

"Father live with them?"

"Unknown. Faina didn't like to talk about him. Or her brother and sister. All I know is her father is the reason she speaks Russian."

"It's a common theme," Skye said as she typed.

Edie nodded. "Other connections. We both love music, movie adaptations of Shakespeare plays, and chocolate."

Skye smiled, almost unconsciously, Edie thought.

"Where did you guys go? How did you communicate?"

"I wasn't very mobile back then. We communicated a lot by text, some by email. If I was up for it, she would come to my place for coffee. Never hers. She said her apartment had a lot of stairs, and I wasn't in the best shape yet. So that was our habit. When I was up for it, we'd go to the bakery, the one I was at the other day. And I'd see her at physio and at the massage place she recommended…" Edie's pulse spiked and her synapses fired. "Jesus."

"Edie?"

Edie pulled the paper titled Weird Shit closer to her. She scribbled as she spoke. "The sound, that music that was coming from Faina's phone. Yesterday. At our run. The music that made me pass out or sleep or whatever. It's the same music my massage therapist plays. I recognized it but I didn't know from where." She looked at Skye, searching for answers. "That can't be a coincidence, can it?"

"Doubtful," Skye said, her eyes hard. "Tell me about that place, whatever you know."

"It's not very interesting. Just a tiny place in a small strip mall. I paid cash for the sessions, I got a receipt. There were diplomas on the wall but it's not like I ever followed up." She shrugged, embarrassed.

"Don't worry about it. Give me the details."

Edie gave her the address and her massage therapist's name.

"Keep going, I'm going to give this to JC. It's another piece of this puzzle."

While Skye texted JC, Edie stared at the Weird Shit paper in front of her. She wrote down the info they already had on the incident at the bar and on the street outside the bakery, as well as her bugged apartment and phone. She circled the drumbeat at the bar and the music from the massage clinic. Two auditory cues that had prompted an unconscious reaction. Edie stared at the words but couldn't make a connection. She had spent the last year being disappointed by her own mind, not trusting it to capture and retain what might turn out to be critical pieces of information.

Edie let out a frustrated sigh, put down her pen, and leaned back. She took a sip from her now cold coffee and closed her eyes as the glare of the sun off the water filled her vision. It didn't hurt, but Edie could hardly feel grateful for that right now. She'd felt so energized a moment ago, like they were moving forward. And once again, she'd come to a complete and sudden stop.

"How about breakfast?" Skye said.

Edie opened her eyes. Skye was obviously trying hard not to look worried. Maybe she wasn't quite a client or a friend. Maybe they were riding a strange line. But Skye cared enough about her to feed her breakfast. That was good for now.

"I'd like to go outside first. If that's okay."

"Sure. I should show you the perimeter I've got set up."

The lawn down to the water was scrubby and rocky and seemed to mostly be a series of rock gardens and wildflower beds. Skye pointed out the boxes she'd affixed to trees around three sides of the house and even out into the lake between the dock posts, a buoy ten meters out from shore and an overhanging branch.

"It will alert any time the line is broken for anything over a certain height and weight. I had two false alarms early this morning with deer. I can't figure out how to code it differently, so I'll just have to deal with it." Skye looked around, seeming completely content.

Edie turned in a circle, a little overwhelmed with the scope of the security. And with Skye's ability to set it up so efficiently. "Jesus Christ, Skye. When did you have time to do this?"

Edie hadn't intended it as a criticism, but Skye seemed to shrink from Edie's words.

"Last night," she said shortly, still peering up into the trees.

"In the dark? By yourself?" Edie was incredulous.

Skye took a step back and shoved her hands into the pockets of her grey sweatpants. She wouldn't look at Edie. "It needed to be done."

Moments ago Skye had seemed proud to show Edie what she'd set up. Now she was almost embarrassed, like she wanted to take it all back. Edie could not figure out why she was retreating.

"Don't you sleep?"

Skye turned to Edie for a brief glance before looking out over the water. A confusing shadow of pain crossed Skye's face before she shuttered her emotions completely.

"I'm going to make us some breakfast. Then I think we should start looking through your journalism connections to see if anything comes up. JC will want to talk to you about that this afternoon."

Skye turned and walked back up into the cabin, not waiting for a response. Edie followed slowly, trying to figure out what she'd said that had hurt Skye. She wished she understood. The thought of inflicting pain on Skye made Edie ache.

When she got back to the cabin, the kitchen was filled with the smell of bacon, and Skye was pouring some frozen potato cubes into a skillet. She looked up briefly when Edie leaned against the counter.

"I hope you like bacon and hash browns," Skye said. "JC's bringing us some groceries this afternoon."

"I love bacon and hash browns." Edie wondered if she should

mention Skye's sudden distance, if she was allowed to acknowledge that something had happened. Her mentor would tell her to put it on the table if she thought there would be returns from the interviewee in the end. If not, keep it close to your chest. Breakfast was ready before Edie had come to any conclusion.

They sat together at the dining room table. As Skye handed Edie her plate, Edie couldn't help but feel the intimacy of the moment. When she looked up, she knew Skye felt it, too.

"Thank you."

"It's not much, but…"

"Not just for breakfast. For every single thing you've done to make sure I'm okay from the moment we met. Thank you."

Skye blushed. Edie knew she was crossing the line Skye had so clearly drawn, but it needed to be said. Maybe it would clear the awkwardness out of the air. Maybe it would make up for whatever hurt she'd accidentally inflicted on Skye.

Skye looked up. "You're welcome."

The silence was easier as they ate in the sunlight. Edie did the dishes while Skye worked on her laptop. When she was finished with the dishes, Edie went over to see what Skye was working on. It was a simple chart with the dates of Edie's freelance assignments, contacts she made, and possible connections.

"I've Googled some of your work, but obviously you'll have a better memory for the work you've done in the past few years."

Edie snorted. "Don't count on it," she said bitterly. "Can I have access to my laptop at my apartment? A lot of it is on there."

"Yes, but not until it gets cleared by Bart's guys. I don't trust that it won't be bugged."

Edie closed her eyes. Right. Because she'd been monitored in her own home. Eyes and ears. Tracked and followed. Manipulated and manhandled. Fuck.

"Come on," Skye said gently and stood up. "I'll get you set up on the couch and bring you some coffee. I'd bake you something to go with it, but…" Skye smiled and shrugged.

"But they didn't teach you to make scones in Basic Training?"

Skye laughed. "I'm afraid not."

Skye set Edie up with a laptop and connection to WiFi with decent signal strength. Once she'd refilled both their coffees, Skye joined her with her own laptop. Edie settled into her surroundings and her task.

"How far back am I going?"

"I'd start with the year before your accident and keep going a year from there. Just see how far you get until JC arrives."

"Is there any reason not to access my Google Drive? I started using a cloud platform about two years ago to store my notes and drafts."

"Yeah, that's fine. That's great, actually. Go for it."

Edie logged into her account. She felt a little calmer, like she'd just walked into her own slightly chaotic but comfortable office. These were all her words, some of her very best successes. She was proud of a lot of this work. She did not like to think one of these articles could have linked her to this mess that was following her right now.

The morning passed easily, Skye and Edie working in silence until Edie felt the muscles in her hip tighten. She stood and stretched, just catching Skye as she tracked the rise of Edie's T-shirt over her abdomen.

"How long until JC gets here?"

"About an hour."

"I'm going to go shower, then."

Skye kept her eyes on her laptop. "Water pressure is crap."

"Can't be any worse than my apartment in Kandahar. My roommates and I used to joke that it only had two settings: gentle mist and East Coast fog."

Skye looked up and smiled. "We only had one setting at Basic. We called it the spine severer."

Edie laughed. She hadn't moved, didn't want to break this moment. "Must have been hell to rinse your hair."

Skye grinned. "One of the reasons I didn't have any."

"Really? I want to see pictures."

Skye looked down at her laptop, still smiling. "I should have some on here…" Skye trailed off and her fingers went still. She gave Edie a cautious look. Hesitant.

"Ah, we're breaking the rules. Right." Edie tried to sound like she was joking. But she was hurt by the reminder of their limits. "I'm going to go take that shower."

The shower pressure was shit, Edie discovered. But it was hot and good enough for her to soap and rinse and feel clean. Back in her room, she gratefully pulled on her own comfortable jeans and a hooded sweater. She felt more confident and more prepared to take on whatever updates JC had on this investigation.

Edie heard voices outside and crossed to the window to look out. JC was in the driveway, and as Skye approached, she pulled her into a kind of headlock hug. They wrestled briefly, both laughing and strong-arming the other. She could hear the timbre of voices but not the distinct words as the two tall, muscular women talked and JC pulled a laptop bag and groceries out of the car. They both stopped before the door, though, and looked toward the house. Edie shrank back, though they likely couldn't see her. JC asked a question, and Skye shook her head emphatically. JC said something, then punched her on the shoulder, and they entered the cabin.

Edie walked out to meet them, running her fingers through her dark hair. Her muscles felt better from the heat of the shower. JC greeted her warmly and deposited the groceries in the kitchen.

"How are you, Ms. Black? I hear yesterday was another difficult day."

"It's Edie, remember? And if by 'difficult' you mean it kicked my ass, then yes. But I'm better today."

"Good," JC said, seeming to make her own silent assessment of Edie's readiness. "I've got some updates, and it's going to be an info dump."

"I'm ready."

The three women collected coffee and sat back in the living room. JC sat beside Edie on the couch and Skye took the chair by the window where she'd spent most of the morning. It was strategic more than preference, Edie decided. Skye scanned the sightline every few minutes, seeming to need to satisfy herself nothing other than birds and squirrels was out there.

"The first thing you should know is that OPP has opened a file, so everything we're doing from here on out is officially sanctioned."

"Does that mean I should start calling you Constable?"

JC grinned. "Just when the uniform is on." She cleared her throat and kept going. "Officially sanctioned means this could go well above my pay grade and could even get pulled by RCMP or Canadian Border Services, depending on where the information goes."

"Fair enough," Skye said. "But we'll talk to you and only to you."

Edie bristled at the "we," and JC looked like she wanted to object.

"Let's not get into a pissing match so early in the game," JC said mildly. "We," she said, indicating the three of them sitting around the living room, "are going to talk this out. *We* are the team right now. Deal?"

Skye nodded. Edie relaxed.

"Okay, moving on." JC pulled up a file on her laptop. "I've got preliminaries on Faina Kassis. It's always best to start with a name and a history. Usually it leads us somewhere."

Edie understood this. It was exactly how she opened up a story.

"Only preliminaries? Your guys haven't gone deeper yet?" Skye said.

"I *am* the guy going deeper into this information, Kenny." JC's voice was still even but sharper. "I've been given the go-ahead but no real extra manpower here. Until I've got a better connection, I'm digging through this shit pile with a toothpick. Now, do you want to hear this or not?"

Skye clenched her jaw and nodded. Her left leg started to bounce as JC kept talking.

"Faina Kassis. Age twenty-six, Syrian born, holds passports for Syria and the UK. She's been in Canada, ostensibly studying, for the past four years. I'll be following up on that. Her mother died in England when Ms. Kassis was eighteen. Looks like there were some questions as to cause. I'll also be following up with that. Here's where things get interesting." JC leaned forward. "Faina's birth certificate lists no father, but her paperwork for her university application lists Peter Nikolay."

The name meant nothing to Edie, but Skye dumped her laptop on the table and began to pace.

"Tell me what you've got on Nikolay," Skye said tersely.

"High up in the Russian army at one time, at least two decades ago. His name pops up a lot at the end of the Cold War, particularly in connection to some questionable humanitarian practices. Seemed to have a falling-out with the Russian government and went missing ten years ago. He's presumed dead by our government, but no one has been able to verify."

"And this is Faina's father?" Edie said as Skye continued to pace. "Why did she put his name on her application?"

"My guess is to lend her some credibility," JC answered. "She is supposedly here studying Slavic languages at the University of Ottawa. Maybe she thought his name would never be connected to anything else. Did she ever mention anything like that? Did she ever talk about her father?"

"No, she never talked about being a student or taking courses. She mentioned she'd love to study literature and writing, but it seemed like a far-off dream. And the only thing that she ever mentioned about her father was that he spoke Russian, among other languages. I didn't get the sense she was close to him."

"What about the siblings?" Skye said, ceasing her pacing and gripping the back of her chair.

"Alex and Yana Nikolay," JC confirmed. "I was just starting to dig into their backgrounds this morning. All I have is that Alex is thirty-nine, lives in Kiev, and works for a military arms manufacturer. So far seems legit. Yana is forty-one and an academic, all I can figure out is that she's some kind of scientist."

Skye made an impatient sound and resumed her pacing.

"Dude, chill. Google Translate is a bitch, okay?"

"Jesus, Caldwell. We live in the nation's fucking capital. Tell me you don't have eighty translators at your disposal."

JC tensed at the clear insult but kept her voice calm. "You're not listening. I don't have anything at my disposal. I'm doing what I can with the information I've got, the leeway I've basically begged for, and the time that I steal from my kids. So I don't care if you need to wear a line in the floor over there, I'm not yours to command in this situation, Major, so shut the fuck up about my shortcomings and let me get on with this."

Skye's tension was palpable. Edie wasn't entirely sure what had prompted Skye to lash out at her friend. Impatience, the unknown, her inability to do anything, too many restrictions.

"We're still moving forward," Edie said into the tense silence. Skye shot her a quick look, her eyes hard. "We know more than we did this morning. As long as that keep being true, we're doing okay." Skye said nothing and kept pacing. "Skye. Okay?"

Skye sat suddenly. "Yes. Okay." She flexed her hands. She looked at JC. "Sorry."

JC waved it away easily. "Next up. The parking lot at the base of the hills. No surprise, I didn't get approval for satellite or a flyover, so

I checked it out myself." JC pulled out her phone and started swiping through screens. "I don't think there's been a ton of traffic since you guys were out there, but enough that identifying tires and make and model of cars would be next to impossible. I did find this, though. I wondered what you thought."

JC passed her phone to Edie. Skye came over and crouched beside her so they could look at it together. It was an image of the gravel of the parking lot, edged by some of the cedars that lined the entrance to the trail. Edie could see scratch marks in the gravel, but the image was too close.

"Keep swiping. I climbed on my car to get an overhead view. I don't know if it's anything, but when Skye told me about Ms. Kassis communicating by drawing in the dirt, I kept looking until I found this."

Edie swiped, the pictures getting farther back until there was a wide angle.

"Does it mean anything to you?" Skye said, her voice very close to Edie's ear.

"I don't know," Edie said. She turned the phone to see it from another angle, but the image automatically flipped back.

"Here," Skye said. She held it still and faced Edie. "Now look at it."

Their knees were touching and Skye rested her phone hand lightly against Edie's leg. The contact sent a shock up through Edie's chest, even as she registered the sweet warmth of her touch. *Unintended*, Edie reminded herself. Skye was focused and so should Edie be. She looked at the swirls and lines until they registered something familiar in her brain.

"It's Arabic," Edie said. "I'm sure of it."

"Can you read it?"

Edie stared at the screen. Her Arabic was incredibly shaky. "No, I don't recognize any of the words. I can try to copy out the characters, though. Then maybe someone else can translate it?"

"Do it," JC said. "I'll find someone to help us out."

As JC tapped on her laptop, Edie took the phone and flipped between images. She wrote down her best guess at the Arabic characters, double-checking them. Whatever Faina was trying to communicate could be pivotal. She swiped the image again and a picture of two kids, maybe ten years old, popped up on the screen. The girl had straight hair tucked behind her ears and seemed to be rolling her eyes at her brother, who was making faces at the camera.

"Sorry," Edie said and automatically swiped back. "I didn't mean to do that."

JC looked up from her typing and glanced at her phone. "Did you find a picture of my kids? Don't worry about it. I hope it wasn't the series of them trying to out gross each other."

Edie laughed. "No, just making faces. How old are your kids?"

"Ten. Charlie and Tatum are twins. And a royal pain in my ass."

"Can I take a look?" Skye said.

"Sure."

Skye swiped back until the pics of the kids came up again. "God, they're so big," she murmured.

"Yeah. It's been over a year since you've seen them," JC said. "They keep growing."

Skye said nothing, just flipped through the photos. She sighed as she gave the phone back. Then she stood and scanned the area out the window. "What's next?" she said to JC.

"I'm hoping to hear back from someone about the Arabic message. It's the best thing we've got so far." She looked between Skye standing at the window and Edie curled into the corner of the couch. "We need a break. Lunch? A hike? Canoe ride? Didn't we play an epic game of lawn darts last time we were here?"

"We're not at camp," Skye said with a snort, some of her earlier tension clearly gone. "And we're damn sure not going to play any drinking games with pointy objects."

"Basher will be disappointed," JC said, grinning. Then the smile fell away, as if she realized what she'd said.

Edie watched as Skye froze at the name, then gave a quick shake of her head.

"I'll pull some lunch together. We can eat outside," Skye said.

Skye left Edie and JC sitting in the living room. JC sighed and closed her eyes briefly. Edie gave her a questioning look but JC just shook her head slightly, obviously unwilling or unable to share whatever had sent Skye running.

The late April sun was warm, but the breeze was cold in the shade of the porch awning when the three women brought their plates of food outside to eat. They spoke quietly and politely, covering topics of no consequence, a huge departure from the heated, intense discussions they'd had together so far.

Edie missed the connection with both of them but sensed some kind of healing was taking place. She understood you needed to create space sometimes. With her belly full and the sounds of the wind in the still winter-bare trees, Edie closed her eyes and listened to the now easy exchange between Skye and JC. She drifted in a made-up world where they were friends just spending time together. She spun out the tale for a little while longer, even knowing how much it would hurt when she opened her eyes again. She imagined following JC's suggestion of a hike, pictured them returning to the cabin, tired and laughing to make dinner while sharing a drink. A fire in the fireplace, feeling sleepy against Skye's shoulder on the couch. Skye's hand in hers, leading them through the dark, cold cabin into the bedroom…

"Did we lose you?"

Edie opened her eyes. Both JC and Skye were watching her. The day was beautiful, but it was not the day she wanted. Edie sat up and willed the lingering image to dissipate. It didn't.

"I'm here. Just resting."

"I was just asking Skye if you'd found any connections through work. Any weird interviews stick out, contacts who had boundary issues, stories that would have generated controversy or an exceptional amount of attention. Anything."

"Nothing so far. My work in the past few years wouldn't have warranted that kind of attention. You can check with my boss at SunNews to see what stories generated the most attention or hate mail, but I'm pretty sure he would have shared any red flags with me."

"It's on the list to follow up on. Skye says you were in Afghanistan for two years. Did you piss anyone off, make any enemies, sleep with the wrong soldier?"

Edie could tell JC was trying to keep it light, and she appreciated the effort.

"No," Edie said, keeping her voice even. "Nothing like that."

"I need to ask a few personal questions," JC said. Her gaze was steady on Edie. "My superiors are going to need the basics covered if they're going to take any of this seriously."

"I understand," Edie said. "Go ahead."

JC glanced at Skye.

"I'll go inside," Skye said quickly, pushing back her chair. Her voice had deadened.

Edie considered letting her go. With JC, she could remain neutral, pretend that she was simply handing over pieces of information. She sighed. "Stay."

"Are you sure?"

"Yes."

Skye sat. Edie turned her attention back to JC. "What do you want to know?"

"As you probably know, most cases of violence are instigated by someone known to the victim. Usually an intimate partner."

Edie focused on the cadence of JC's voice. Though she had retreated to more formal language, she had not lost any of the connection with Edie. She was very good.

"You want to know my sexual history," Edie stated. Skye flinched across the table.

"No, not entirely. I am asking you to tell me who you have had a relationship with, an intimate relationship, in the last three years."

"Well, I'm gay, let's start there," Edie said with a straight face.

"Kissing Kenny clued me in on that one."

Edie grinned. Skye muttered curses at them.

"The last significant relationship I had was two years ago in Kandahar. Hanna Fleischer, she's German. We were together about six or seven months. She's the lead liaison with their Red Cross team."

"Who instigated the breakup?"

Edie shrugged. "We both did. It was amicable. We both knew it was never going to be long-term."

"Are you still in contact?"

"Not regularly, but we usually check in every couple of months. I'd say we're still friends."

JC wrote a note in her phone. "Anyone else?"

Edie shook her head and wished she wasn't blushing. Was it better or worse that her romantic history was so scant? Less to have to draw out and share publicly but what did Skye think of her?

"I concentrated on my new teaching gig at the university when I got back from Afghanistan. And then I had my accident and haven't been ready to try and meet anyone."

The words *until now* hung heavily in the air. Edie refused to look at

Skye, sitting so stiffly across the table. JC clearly had no compunction as she swung her gaze meaningfully to her friend before looking back to Edie.

"Thanks for that. Sorry this all sucks so much."

Edie laughed, and a little of the tension left her body. "Understatement, Constable Caldwell."

Just then JC's phone rang and she picked it up, her face transforming from easy to laser focus in a heartbeat. She was a trained soldier, Edie reminded herself. Like Skye.

"Update," JC said, her voice tense. "The message from Ms. Kassis seems to be a meet, but the message is confusing. Does laundry cat mean anything to you?"

"No," Edie said. Confusion clouded her brain. A familiar fog she had absolutely no time for.

"Yes," Skye said immediately. "LaundroCat. It's a coin-op laundry, café, and cat rescue centre. There's one on the edge of downtown, bordering the Glebe neighbourhood."

"Did Ms. Kassis ever mention anything like that? Is it near where she lives?"

"I've never heard of it. And I don't know her address, just somewhere west of downtown," Edie said. Her thoughts felt useless, her brain and body seeming to slow as JC and Skye's sped up.

"Is that the whole message?" Skye said.

"No. The rest of the message says Monday and eleven morning."

"That's tomorrow," Skye said, her voice hard.

"Yes, it is."

"She's not going."

JC said nothing. Edie felt a step behind.

"What's happening?" Edie said.

JC and Skye seemed to be having a silent argument. Neither answered.

"Please," Edie said and rubbed her head. Nothing helped with fog but rest. And even then sometimes it took days for it to clear. "I can't figure this out on my own. Please tell me what's happening."

"We think Ms. Kassis wants to meet you tomorrow at this LaundroCat place," JC said. "At eleven tomorrow morning. She's our best lead, and we need to take it."

"It's too risky," Skye replied. "Faina may be the best lead, but she's also the most likely to lure Edie into a trap. Until we know her motivation, Faina equals danger. So she's not going. End of story."

Particles of sound and vision and fact and memory layered themselves into a gently tilting haze that separated Edie from the rest of the world. She fought it, trying to stay connected to Skye's words.

"Faina might not talk to anyone else," Edie said quietly, keeping her eyes closed. "We might only get one chance. You can come with me, Skye, you can keep me safe. But I should go. I'm going."

Edie was certain she was making sense, but she had no tools to evaluate that thought. JC and Skye immediately started to argue. Their words meshed into a wall of sound Edie did not bother trying to sort through. She was done. She stood slowly.

"You two fight. Then make arrangements for tomorrow. I'm going to lie down."

Edie's body felt drained, like she'd completed a marathon or spent the day in the Afghanistan sun moving boxes of rations. She'd done neither. Her weakness was simply that. Frailty.

Lying down on the couch, Edie could still hear Skye and JC arguing through the screen of the patio door. She let the words wash over her.

"You asked for the police to be involved and now I'm involved. You can't direct this the way you want just because you care about—"

"Don't. This isn't about that. I've got a contract to protect this client, and that's what I'm doing."

"Right," JC said with evident sarcasm. "This is about a contract."

"I said let it go, Caldwell."

"Fuck that. You want to pretend that's what it's about, go ahead, but I'm not playing along."

Edie felt the wind from the lake on her skin, raising goose bumps along her arm as the breeze pushed into the cabin.

"Look, we're not on opposite sides of this," JC said, her voice gentler. "So stop treating me like I am."

Skye had no response Edie could hear.

JC sighed. "I need to know if you're armed."

"Yes."

"Permit?"

"Jesus, Caldwell. Yes."

"Good. Bring it with you tomorrow. And the contract. This needs to be aboveboard all the way around, got it?"

"Yes." Skye's voice grated.

"We'll work out a plan in the morning. We'll keep her safe. And hopefully we'll get some information so we can figure out what's going on, bring these bastards in, and let Edie get back to her life."

Silence.

"Yeah."

"And then maybe you two can—"

Edie flinched at the loud sound of a metal chair being pushed back against the deck boards.

"Can you stay for an hour? I need a run."

"Kenny…"

"I need this. Will you stay with her?"

"Yes. Go."

Edie kept her eyes closed as Skye opened the patio door and stepped quietly inside. She felt Skye stop by the back of the sofa and place a soft blanket over her. Edie nestled into the comfort, in that moment simply grateful Skye had somehow known exactly what she needed.

CHAPTER EIGHT

"D on't you have to glue it or tape it or something? That's what they do on TV."

Edie's attempt at humour betrayed her nerves. She was sitting in an office in the OPP headquarters just outside downtown Ottawa. Skye stood stiffly by the door. JC had just handed Edie a set of regular-looking ear buds that were supposedly mic and transceiver. She would wear it to meet with Faina in two hours.

JC snorted. "We'll sit and chat someday about all the way media gets police work wrong. Right now I need you to focus."

It was a lot to ask. The fog from yesterday lingered in Edie's head, not heavy or thick, just present enough that she was aware of it. And irritated by it.

"Okay."

"This is going to attach to your phone, which will act as Bluetooth so we hear the conversation in real time but also will record it for evidence. You don't need to do anything, just stick it in your pocket with the ear buds around your shoulders. Got it?"

"Got it," Edie confirmed.

"All right. Skye and Bart have arranged to have one of their guys inside the laundromat." JC looked at her watch. "He should be there in an hour. Skye, do you want to describe Sasha for Edie?"

"Tall, thin, brown hair. Right now he's got a beard and a man bun. He'll be wearing a plaid shirt."

"Going for the hipster look, is he?" JC said.

"His last assignment had him in a lot of coffee shops. Sash is good at blending in."

"Try not to make eye contact with him but don't worry about it if you do," JC said to Edie. "I'll be at the side alley entrance. Questions?"

Yes, so many questions.

"What have I done exactly to warrant all this attention? Security and wire taps and secret meets. What have I done?"

JC and Skye stared at her. Apparently neither knew what to say.

"That's what we're trying to figure out," Skye said. "Hopefully we get some answers today."

Edie rubbed at her forehead, then looked up. "Okay. Fine. But what the hell am I actually doing when I go in today?"

JC grinned. In any other circumstance, Edie would be flirting with the bright, easygoing cop. She was gorgeous and strong, she loved her kids, she was dedicated and caring. But it was the sharply edged, difficult to get to know, glowering, awkward, painfully intelligent, sweet and fiercely loyal ex-soldier who stood stiffly and silently by the door that had captured and held Edie's attention.

"Wherever you are, it looks wonderful. But I need you back for this."

Edie blushed. "Sorry."

"Don't be. Since Skye is going to be the one inside with you, I'm going to let her tell you the plan for this meet."

Skye pushed off from the door and sat across from Edie. She grabbed a pad of paper and sketched a quick floor plan. Her green-yellow eyes were focused. Action sat well on Skye Kenny.

"We'll walk in to the laundromat together at eleven. You'll be carrying a basket of laundry."

"Because you need your hands free," Edie said.

"Yes. There's a row of washers on your left, here. Find one and put your basket down. Don't go past this counter. We should have word from Sasha if Faina is there before we head in. We're just going to have to wait and see what Faina has planned and react the best way we can."

"Sounds like a plan," Edie said.

Skye grimaced. "I know. I'm sorry." She indicated the floor plan with her pen. "JC will have the back, Sasha will be on the far side by the dryers, and I can get you out the front. I have no intention of allowing them to box you in."

Edie considered the hastily drawn floor plan. She re-listened to

Skye's words. She had already noticed the light jacket Skye had pulled on over her back holster.

"You expect an ambush," Edie said.

"We are treating it as an ambush because Faina is an unknown quantity. We are prepared to extricate you at any moment. The plan is to get the information we can, possibly set up for another meet if we need to, and get the hell out of there."

Edie took a breath and held it. She let it out slowly. She turned to JC. "What information do you need? Specifically. What should I ask, if I get a chance?"

Skye and JC exchanged a quick look.

"Kenny and I discussed that last night," JC responded. "You're good at getting information. You're trained in getting information. And you know as much or more than we do about this whole situation. Go with your gut. We trust you."

An icy anxiety cramped Edie's stomach and shot up through her chest. Instinct had been her life's motto, her touchstone, her compass as she navigated the wide world of people, cultures, jobs, and relationships. But the compass had been knocked off course, the needle sometimes wavered, and Edie did not trust it to always find due north. She looked at Skye and JC. Skye's gaze was fierce and intense. JC looked confident. They trusted Edie.

"I'm in. I've got this."

"Then let's go."

❖

Edie gripped the laundry basket full of clothes tightly to her chest as Skye opened the door of the LaundroCat. The sound of washers and dryers droned as terrible pop music streamed through speakers in the corner. The far right wall was glassed-in, evidence of the new North American craze of combining cat rescue with cafés and bars and bookstores.

She caught sight of a few people sitting in mismatched chairs as lithe feline forms leapt or slept on an elaborate, carpeted cat jungle. Edie swept her gaze through the whole place, hoping she looked casual. They knew from Sasha, presumably the guy sitting on a bench hunched over his phone in the far corner, that Faina had not been spotted inside. Other than a tired-looking older man slowly folding clothes in the centre of the shop, the place was empty.

Beside her, Skye had opened one of the washing machines. Edie blinked and put down the basket. The door opened behind her, and she saw Skye stiffen. Faina wore dark sunglasses over her eyes, and her hair had been cut dramatically short. New bruises showed under her collar. She approached Skye and Edie quickly. Skye kept herself between them, her hands loose at her sides.

"Alley entrance. I only have a few minutes. Please."

Faina didn't wait for an answer, she just kept walking back through the laundromat until she disappeared. Skye tracked her movement, even as she texted out a message, presumably to JC.

"We'll go around," Skye said tersely.

Edie slammed the door of the washing machine and followed Skye back out onto the street.

"JC has eyes on Faina," Skye said, reading her phone and scanning the area. "She seems to be alone. Let's go. Stay behind me."

Faina was propping open a door halfway down the open alley. She had her head turned away, ostensibly trying to get a read on JC, who stood alert but impassive at the far end. Faina turned as Skye and Edie approached. She clenched her sunglasses in one hand, showing the reddish-purple bruise that had swollen one eye completely shut.

"Jesus fucking Christ," Edie breathed out.

Skye walked directly up to Faina and peered into the half-open door. Then she signaled to JC at the end of the alley, who gave her a quick nod.

"Go ahead," Skye said, but only took a partial step back to allow Edie to come face-to-face with Faina.

"I only have a few minutes. I'll tell you what I know, but it is not very much. They want something you have. Some kind of information you were given or have hidden. I don't understand. They keep using the word *udalit*. Take. I didn't know I was helping them hurt you. I didn't know, Edie. I'm guarded. He'll be back in not many more minutes."

Faina was breathless, her fear palpable. She looked over her shoulder every few seconds.

"Who, Faina?"

"My brother and sister. Alex is here. He goes by Alex Rada now. He wants to bring you in, I think. He says he's done with this phase. They know you are gone. They think it is my fault." Faina swallowed and touched the bruise on her neck. "It is my fault. I didn't know."

"Are you being held against your will?" Skye said.

Faina regarded Skye silently. Then she looked at Edie. "This one. She is your—"

"Security," Edie finished. "Skye. She's here to help."

"The soldier. They know of you. You have them worried."

"Faina, are you being held against your will?" Edie repeated Skye's question.

Faina focused her pained brown eyes back on Edie. "Yes. For two years now. I am never without a guard. I have no access to a phone or computer. They told me to befriend you, but I didn't know they wanted to hurt you. I'm sorry."

Skye looked down the alley again, silently conferring with JC, who could hear the conversation through the ear buds around Edie's neck. JC gave a curt nod of her head, some kind of signal for Skye.

"You can come with us," Skye said to Faina. "We may be able to offer police protection in exchange for information. Even protective custody would be safer than this."

Faina shook her head. "No. I will clean up my mess first. I got Edie into this. I will get her out. I cannot contact you again, but I am here once a week. Max, my guard, has gotten his girlfriend pregnant. She works in a store around the corner. He leaves me here and goes and fights with her."

Faina was starting to babble. Her understanding, calm, and reserved friend was babbling. She was being held prisoner. She had a black eye. Edie peered closer. So many bruises. Had she always had them? Edie felt sick.

"Just come with me," Edie said to Faina. "Right now. We'll work it out."

Faina looked like she was fighting tears. She blinked and shook her head. "I only have a minute. You should go. Do not go back out the front. Come back Wednesday. This time. I will have more."

Before Skye or Edie could say or do anything more to convince the woman to come with them, Faina had stepped back through the door and let it shut. Edie could only stare at the blank door, wondering what had just happened. Skye took Edie gently but firmly by the upper arm.

"Let's go."

Skye directed Edie silently down the street, into JC's car. She sat in the backseat while JC talked and Skye argued about clues, leads, and the bigger picture just beginning to form. But all Edie could see were the bruises on Faina's neck, the blood of her swollen eye, the chipped paint of the grey metal door as it closed it between them. *Who is Faina really?*

"I believe her," Edie said out loud. Conversation in the front seat stopped.

"Faina?" JC said.

"Yes. I believe her when she said she didn't know what was going on. And I believe that she's on our side now. My side."

"There are a lot of holes in her story, Edie," JC said carefully.

"I know. And I know you can't trust her. I just wanted you to know that I believe her. And any of my actions going forward will be based on that premise. I just thought you two should know."

JC and Skye exchanged a glance but said nothing.

By the time they arrived at headquarters, Edie had become big news. They were swarmed with suits and uniforms the second they entered the building. JC stepped confidently into the fray, and once again Edie found Skye steering her by putting her hand on Edie's lower back.

"Come on, we'll let Constable Caldwell handle this."

No one seemed to notice Skye was secreting Edie away, though she saw JC give a quick, appreciative nod in Skye's direction before squaring her shoulders, lifting her chin, and shouting over the noise for quiet.

The hallways were nearly empty and Skye navigated them quickly toward the tiny, empty office they'd used earlier. Edie sat in a barely comfortable office chair, grateful when Skye closed the door and the noise outside decreased to a distant hum.

"Okay?" Skye said. She paced around the office with jerky movements, long strides cut off by the small space. Edie wanted to stand and run her hands up and down Skye's arms, to hold her in place until some of the excess energy left her body.

"I'm okay." She was. The fog had lifted at some point, and she could not be more grateful for the timing. "What's happening out there? I thought JC said no one was really interested in this."

"Someone must have found something of interest. If what is happening to you becomes connected to a bigger case, everyone is going to want a piece of it."

"Great," Edie said. "I wish I knew why I was suddenly so important. But I guess JC did warn us."

"She did. She knows what she's doing."

"I trust her," Edie said. "And you."

"And Faina."

"And Faina," Edie agreed calmly.

"You know that doesn't make sense, right?" Skye sounded almost angry.

"It doesn't make sense to you, Skye. I'm going with my gut on this."

Skye opened her mouth to protest, but JC entered the office.

"Hey. How's everyone doing in here?" JC's voice was strained, the stress making her question sound more rote than interested.

"We're fine. What's happening?" Skye said.

"Immigration is what's happening," JC said and threw herself into a chair. "Border security and RCMP combined forces is what's happening."

"And what do they want?"

"Control over this investigation. They want to exploit Faina's obviously dangerous situation. They want to dig up Edie's past and strip her for whatever information she has."

Edie froze and Skye stalked toward JC. The cop immediately stood and put her hands up in a conciliatory gesture.

"I didn't mean it like that. I'm sorry. I didn't mean that."

Skye stopped just in front of JC. Edie could feel the palpable tension, the waves of anger emanating from Skye's tightly coiled body, the stress and power evident in JC's wide stance as she faced her friend and fire buddy.

"That's not going to happen," Skye said darkly.

"You're right," JC said. "It's not going to happen because you and I are not going to let it happen. Okay?"

Skye didn't answer, but she did step back and resume her pacing. Edie waved a hand.

"I'm over here, if anyone's wondering. You know, the centre of this shit storm."

JC rubbed a hand over her eyes, then sat again. "I'm really sorry, Edie. Let me tell you what's going on. There are four division heads out there who want to talk to you. The name Alex Rada, Faina's half brother, has raised numerous red flags, including illegal arms trading. The other issue is that Faina places Rada in Ottawa when border patrol is saying he has never been to Canada."

"What about the information Faina mentioned," Skye said. "That Edie supposedly has. Anyone have any idea what she was talking about?"

JC shook her head. "No, and that's where things are about to get dicey. Everyone wants to know what you know or what you have. There's already a team heading to your apartment to strip it. Your computer and phone have been searched, but you need to be prepared for a deeper background check. Family, friends, and neighbours will be interviewed. Your boss will be asked questions about your contacts, your work will be scrutinized. I've already heard theories about your connections in Afghanistan as well as some idiot questioning whether or not you knew Yaz Khalid, the impaired driver who hit you a year ago."

"For fuck's sake, Caldwell!" Skye nearly exploded from her spot near the door. The sound made Edie jump, but JC never took her eyes off Edie.

"I don't know what's happening here, Edie. I really don't. I'll tell you what I do know. This is going to suck. This will feel like an invasion. But I promise you that Skye and I will be here to protect you from the worst parts of it. I promise you that you can handle this. And I promise you that we will get your life back."

"I trust you. But I want to be clear that I won't leave Skye," Edie said to JC, then turned to Skye. "If you'll still have me. As a client, I mean."

"I'll see you through this, Edie." Skye's eyes sparked with tension and heat. The combination made Edie's heart rocket around in her chest.

"Thank you," Edie replied quietly before turning back to JC. But the cop was still looking at her friend. She didn't seem very happy.

"This is going to be a problem," JC said to Skye.

Skye sat in the chair next to Edie.

"No, it's not. My presence is simply a fact that the department heads will have to accept. I will be in on any interviews with Edie, I will continue to secure her at the safe house, and I will be read in on any of the meets or missions that involve Edie."

JC clenched her jaw, the only real sign that Edie could determine that JC was unhappy. "You're overstepping."

Skye shrugged. "Call it what you want. I'm not going anywhere."

Silence. Edie considered speaking up, but she got the sense these two needed to stake their territory.

"You're such a fucking pain in the ass," JC said. "You're lucky the RCMP still owes you for that incident with the princess from a few years ago. That's the only reason you're not being tossed on your ass right now."

Skye grinned. Edie relaxed.

"Okay, enough of this. Edie, I'm going to get Superintendent Donaldson. He's the liaison with the RCMP's combined forces, and he's going to ask you questions about Faina and any connections you have to Russian military, arms deals, and the illegal arms trade." When Edie began to protest, JC cut her off. "I know. The prevailing theory right now is that you know something that you don't know." Edie couldn't exactly argue with that. "Just answer the questions the best you can." JC leaned forward and whispered, "And just try to pretend these guys aren't a bunch of douche bags, okay?"

Edie smiled at JC's attempt at levity. As JC left the room, she turned to Skye, who had remained sitting next to her.

"The princess incident?"

Unexpectedly, Skye gave a short laugh. "Yeah. It's a long story."

"Sounds interesting. I'd love to hear it."

Skye looked through the half wall of windows. JC was talking to a man in a dark suit. He looked serious. And pissed.

"Another time. Prepare for round one, Ms. Black." Skye stood, and as she did, Edie felt the briefest brush of Skye's fingers against her knee.

JC entered the room and introduced her to Superintendent Ryan Donaldson. He was middle-aged and fit, and he seemed to look through

Edie as he talked. He did not even acknowledge Skye. Edie disliked him immediately. She tried to remind herself he was part of a team trying to solve this case.

"Ms. Black, I understand Constable Caldwell has read you in on our interest in your case. I have some questions for you about your relationship with Faina Kassis."

"Go ahead, Mr. Donaldson. I'll tell you anything you need to know."

Donaldson had two hours of questions. Edie repeated what she knew about Faina, not even flinching as he tried to divine a deeper meaning in their friendship. He became obviously frustrated by her short responses to his questions about Russian arms dealers. She had no connection there, as far as she knew. At some point, JC brought her a tepid, terrible coffee and Donaldson was replaced by Singh, from immigration. His questioning was more direct, and he thanked her before he left. JC brought in a box of donuts with the third and last interrogator for the day, a woman named Dr. Crask. JC was decidedly stiff during that introduction for no reason Edie could fathom.

"Ms. Black, I appreciate that you've already been through several rounds of interviews already. I have only a few questions for you, if I may."

Edie considered the politeness of the woman's tone. She was dressed conservatively in grey and white, dark blonde highlighted hair pulled back in a half clip. Her eyes were dark and difficult to read.

"Go ahead, Dr. Crask," Edie said with a similarly polite tone. She felt vaguely on edge but chalked it up to being tired.

"I'd like to know why the Russians chose you to carry information for them."

The edgy feeling rocketed to anxiety in a heartbeat.

"Di, come on," JC protested. Edie could feel Skye's tension across the room but she remained silent, as she'd been through the other interrogations. Edie admired her ability to be present and invisible at the same time.

"Constable Caldwell, you may wait outside," Crask said without taking her eyes off Edie.

"No fucking way," JC said and all of a sudden she was the fierce soldier, her size somehow heightened by her anger.

"Now, Constable Caldwell." Crask's tone was ice.

"I'd like her to stay," Edie said. She had no idea what was going on.

"I'm afraid that's not possible," Dr. Crask said.

Edie looked imploringly at JC, but she just shot Skye a look and left the room, leaving a heaviness in the air. Dr. Crask looked impassively at Edie, as if waiting for her to simply pick up the thread of a dropped conversation.

"I missed your title and role with the OPP, Dr. Crask. Maybe we can start there."

Again with that tight, polite smile. "Certainly. I'm a psychiatrist with the behavioral sciences unit. I specialize in interrogation and information verification."

Edie toyed with that phrase. "I'm curious about interrogation and information verification," she said. "Does that mean you assist the OPP in ferreting out information and then evaluating its veracity?"

Dr. Crask didn't blink. "That's paraphrasing at best. But yes."

Edie wondered what Crask made of the smile she gave her. She suddenly felt strong enough to take her on. "Could you repeat your original question, please?"

"I'd like to know why the Russians chose you to carry information for them."

"Is that the prevailing theory, then? Are we treating hypothesis as fact?"

"That's my assessment, yes."

"Let's go with the *theory*, then. I'd like to clarify your question. Are you asking me to read the mind of a person or group of people that I have not met?"

"Or that you are unaware of meeting."

Edie considered challenging her on the point, but she must have had a reason to use the word *unaware*. Her accident, her questionable memory of the months after, the fogged gaps, whatever weakness was being exploited by sensory overload, her thoughts and dreams, music that made her sleep, questions in her ear and the answers, those lilting words…

Edie blinked rapidly. Crask, obviously attuned to nuances in body language, smiled triumphantly.

"You remember someone. Meeting someone. Tell me." Her eyes were bright.

Music still played faintly through Edie's mind. She felt the tug of sleepiness but shrugged it off. No way was she giving this woman anything. Edie didn't trust her enough to open up about the lurking suspicions and pieces of information floating around in her head.

"Dr. Crask, I am being completely honest with you when I say I have zero recollection of meeting or talking to or discussing anything with a Russian national. Absolutely none."

"But you *thought* of something," Dr. Crask said. "I'd like to know what it is. It could be critical and you are unaware."

Edie somehow kept from rolling her eyes. She hated condescension. "I'm considering all the things I may be unaware of, Dr. Crask. I will let you know if I think of anything that may be helpful. Right now, though, I think I need to call it a day. I'm no longer thinking clearly, which is obviously a problem given the import of what we're discussing, isn't it?"

"I'd like to reschedule," Dr. Crask said quickly. "For a time that is convenient for you, so we may have more time to discuss those aspects of your memory that are…tenuous."

It all sounded so easy. And Dr. Crask sounded conciliatory. But Edie trusted her even less than when she walked in the door twenty minutes before.

"Yes, that's fine," Edie said.

Dr. Crask stood and walked to the door. JC appeared on the other side immediately, and they had a short, intense conversation before Dr. Crask walked away. JC stood still, staring down at the floor.

Edie, feeling like she was witnessing something private, looked instead at Skye. She still hadn't moved, but her eyes were beginning to come alive again. They warmed and brightened, deepened and opened. Edie stared transfixed as Skye morphed in front of her. Skye unfurled herself from her position at the back wall and walked toward Edie, finally dropping into the seat beside her. She seemed to be struggling with something.

"What?" Edie said.

"You're amazing," Skye murmured, almost too low for Edie to hear, almost as if she had whispered the words in her own head and hadn't intended for them to escape.

JC walked back into the office, her eyes stormy. Skye snapped her head up.

"Who the hell was that?" Skye said.

"Dr. Diana Crask," JC said bitterly. "She's the gleeful acquisition of the superintendents. Cops hate working with her, but she gets results."

"Her tactics are brutal. Like she has military training."

JC managed to look even more miserable. "She does."

"What?" Skye seemed taken aback. "Fucking hell, Caldwell. Is that *your* Diana?"

"She's not *my* anything." She looked furious. Then she seemed to rein herself in and she sat heavily in the chair. "Sorry, Edie."

"Nothing to apologize for."

"Full disclosure," JC said, straightening in her chair. "Since we'll all likely have to work together again on this. I had a brief and ill-advised relationship with Diana Crask a number of years ago. We're still not particularly good at occupying the same space."

"Ah, a terrible ex. That stinks."

JC cracked a smile. "Understatement, Ms. Black."

"Want me to kick her in the shins next time I see her?"

JC leaned back and laughed, and even Skye chuckled.

"No, but thank you for the offer." JC adjusted herself in her seat. "Okay, I'm guessing you've exceeded your quota of questions today, and the higher-ups seem satisfied, for now at least, with the leads they've got. How about you guys hit the road, and I'll come out and meet you tomorrow once I've got my kids off to school?"

"Yes," Edie said. "That would be great. I have some thoughts I want to share with you guys." JC looked interested and Edie held up a forestalling hand. "Let me manage your expectations a little. I have some bits and pieces I want to try and string together. Something my gut is trying to tell me. I'm hoping you two can help."

"It's a plan. We can also talk tomorrow about meeting with Ms. Kassis again."

Skye clenched her jaw.

"We'll work it out," JC said as she stood. "I need to go sit in on a debrief. See you guys tomorrow." She paused by the door. "Good work today, both of you."

The office was silent, and a tricky kind of tired rose up in Edie. Energy and exhaustion, brightness and haze. She met Skye's eyes.

"Ready to go, Ms. Black?"

"Ready to go, Major Kenny."

CHAPTER NINE

Edie kept her eyes closed as Skye drove out of the city, onto the traffic-jammed Queensway, and finally out onto the rural highway. Skye coordinated with Sasha, ensuring they got out of the city without being followed, but Edie didn't want to hear it. She drifted instead. She didn't sleep, just processed the day in a way that hopefully meant her brain would lay down a clear memory she could retrieve again. Considering everything that had happened today, Edie felt like she was doing pretty well. This feeling of wellness was a revelation. Tired was simply tired, not a message from her body screaming she was not capable.

"I'm worried about Faina," Edie said, opening her eyes to the grey highway and the deepening dusk.

"I know. So am I."

"You are?"

"Yes. I'm worried she's being held against her will. I'm worried about her bruises. I'm worried we shouldn't have left her there today. I'm worried she's in danger, and we could have done something about it."

Edie didn't know what to say.

"I'm also worried," Skye continued, "that she's not exactly what she seems. I'm worried she's part of an ambush, whether she knows it or not. I'm worried because she still presents danger to you. And my whole job right now is to control your exposure to harm."

Control your exposure to harm. Edie hated when Skye disappeared behind this vaguely military talk. She covered herself up in it like camouflage.

Skye's phone, propped on the front console of the Jeep, began to vibrate. The screen flashed the number of the person trying to video call.

"Shit." Skye glanced at the screen. "I should take this. She doesn't get to call very often." She looked nervously at Edie. "Sorry but..." The buzzing phone kept distracting Skye and with one quick, nearly panicked looked to Edie, she hit the connect button.

Immediately the screen flashed with the tilting, pixelated view of a woman's face. Edie got a sense of wild, curly black hair, high cheekbones in a rounded face, and laughing, bright brown eyes. The woman was wearing fatigues, suddenly filling the car with a loud, off-key version of "Happy Birthday."

"Happy birthday, Thrush! Fucking God damnit, woman, you should be here celebrating with me. Where are you? Why is it so fucking dark?"

Edie had seen Skye angry, awkward, happy, and even worried. She'd never seen her quite this uncomfortable.

"Hey, Bash. I'm in the car. And I'm not alone, so..."

"You've got a date?" she yelled at full volume.

Bash stood and began doing a kind of shimmy, the androgynous green military uniform in no way hiding the suggestion of her dancing hips. Skye rubbed at her forehead, though Edie could see her smile surfacing. Edie covered a laugh.

The woman sat down in front of the camera again. "Lemme see her."

"Basher, no. She's kind of a client."

The woman's dark eyes went comically wide. "*Kind of* a client? There's a whole long fucking story here, Thrush. But I've only got three minutes, so let me meet this woman who's clearly more than a client."

Skye sighed, and with an apologetic look to Edie, she pushed the phone to the right so Edie was in the view.

"Edie, this is my friend, Renee Bashell. Basher, this is Edie."

Edie felt herself being evaluated through time and space. "Nice to meet you."

"You, too, Edie," Basher said suggestively, wiggling her dark eyebrows. Edie laughed. She could not believe how wildly different this woman was from the reserved, careful Skye. "So how do you know my Skye?"

It was a friendly possessive, Edie decided, given how excited the woman had been at the idea Skye had a date. Edie thought she might have an ally, so she went with her gut. "We had a date not too long ago. But then I got into some trouble and now Skye is watching out for me."

"Let's focus on the date part," Basher said, looking intently into the screen. "When you say date, are you talking popcorn and a movie or like sweaty, late-night, steamy—"

"That's enough," Skye said mildly, tilting the phone away from Edie. She sounded more embarrassed than upset.

"Not nearly enough, Thrushy. I can't believe you had a date and didn't tell me. Some fucking friend."

"Fuck right off," Skye said mildly, keeping her eyes on the road. She was smiling.

"I'd love to!" Basher yelled and Skye laughed. "But I've got to go, there's a long queue waiting to log on. Seriously, happy birthday. You're the best." Basher's voice seemed to waver.

"Thanks for calling, Bash," Skye said. "You good?" The question was short but Edie detected a kind of desperation in the two short words.

"I'm the best," Basher said, laughing again. "But yes, I'm good." There was a noise in the background, and Basher gave the middle finger to someone behind her without turning around. "We miss you. Happy birthday. Peace out."

The call ended, the brightness of the screen immediately dimming, the sound of Basher's laughter echoing in the car. Skye exited off the main highway to begin the half-hour trek through the countryside to get to their cabin.

"It's really your birthday today?"

"Yeah," Skye said, sounding subdued.

"Well then, happy birthday."

"Thanks."

Edie wondered if she should push. Skye had retreated, but Edie didn't know if it was the lines she'd drawn between herself and Edie or the phone call.

"Let me guess how old you are," Edie said, hoping to draw Skye out. "You've definitely hit thirty but maybe not so long ago."

Skye smiled. "I'm thirty-four today."

"Thirty-four. You've accomplished a lot in that time, Skye Kenny." Skye didn't answer.

"I take it you don't like birthdays?"

Skye glanced at her quickly. "No, that's not it. It's just…" Skye hesitated. "I'm just a little thrown off by the call, that's all."

"Basher," Edie said. "The nickname suits her somehow."

Finally, Skye laughed affectionately. "You have no idea. You should see her in hand-to-hand. She thinks she's Xena, Warrior Princess."

Edie laughed with her. "And…Thrush?"

"Ah, yeah," Skye said. "I got that nickname at military college."

"I'd like the story of Thrush. And the story of the princess, too."

"You're demanding tonight," Skye said, laughing.

"Start with Thrush."

"It was the first couple days at RMC," Skye said. "I was eighteen, and I thought I was ready for it. The drill sergeant's whole job is to prove you're not."

"Break you down before they build you back up again."

"Right. But at eighteen, I thought it meant outsmarting them. I was very wrong."

Skye pulled off the main county line onto a gravel and dirt road. They only had a few minutes left.

"One day I was the target at inspection. We were in the quad, and the drill sergeant screamed questions at me about my kit, the lavatory rules, the history of the building we were standing in."

"And you kept answering."

"Like an idiot. The drill sergeant was getting more and more worked up with every answer I gave until he screamed out, 'What is the fucking name of that fucking bird that won't stop fucking singing?' And I answered, 'It's a thrush, sir!' The inspection stopped and he made me run laps. After that, I was Thrush."

Skye eased the Jeep into the gravel driveway at the cabin. A lone porch light lit the area. Skye turned off the ignition but made no move to get out of the car.

"So you've been Thrush now for what, sixteen years?"

Skye looked out the window toward the door of the cabin. "I haven't been Thrush for a few years. It's my military name, and that part of my life is over. Sometimes Basher has a hard time with that."

"Because…"

"Because…" Skye paused. "Because she had trouble with re-entry to civilian life. She re-upped a year ago, even though she probably shouldn't have. Using my nickname is a way of keeping me with her, I guess."

"Basher is the reason you help out Dr. Wallace."

Skye sighed. "Yes. Her unit…" Skye clenched her jaw. "Basher saw a lot when she was deployed. She's damn good at her job, but it's really messed with her. And she can't seem to find her way out." Skye shook her head. "I don't want to talk about this."

While Skye looked out the window, Edie studied her. The porch light bleached her face of any colour; she was contrasts of light and dark. Edie reached across the seat and touched Skye's cheek, then traced a light line down her jaw. Skye shuddered faintly under her touch. The heat in Edie's body swooped and spread.

"What are you doing?" Skye's voice was hoarse.

Edie said nothing. She retraced the line back up Skye's neck until her fingers rested against Skye's cheek. She wanted so much more, her wanting burning away the lingering questions and the dirtiness of the day.

Skye pulled away from Edie's touch. Edie let her hand fall.

"Let's get inside," Skye said and opened the door of the Jeep.

Edie waited only a heartbeat, hoping to get the moment back. Then she sighed and followed. Skye went into security guard mode, leading Edie inside the cabin and asking her to wait in the entry while she checked the house and secured the alarms. Edie breathed in the smell of cedar wood and wet rubber boots.

An achy tired was catching up to her. She wanted to outrun it. She saw bruises in the dim light, Skye reaching for her holstered gun, felt the breath of a muttered Russian curse on the back of her neck, heard the drumbeat. Edie shook her head, and it was all gone. She was tired of having her own brain hijacked.

"You can come in," Skye said from the doorway. Her tone was completely neutral. "It's safe."

Edie followed her into the cabin.

"Are you hungry?" Skye said, stopping in the kitchen and opening the fridge. "I can make us some eggs. Or JC brought some cans of soup."

"Sure," Edie said, mostly just wanting to draw out the moment. "Eggs sound good."

Skye silently began assembling a meal. Edie leaned against the counter and watched her move easily in the small space. Skye seemed capable of putting the moments in the car behind them. Edie was not.

"This is Basher's cabin, isn't it?"

Skye looked up from whipping eggs in a glass bowl. "Yes."

"You and Basher and JC served together."

"Yes."

They were back to one-word answers, just like the night they met. While Skye finished cooking the meal, Edie tried to find a way through. She'd done it before.

Skye silently handed her a plate of scrambled eggs and toast. Edie stayed where she was as Skye leaned against the counter in the kitchen with her own plate and quickly and efficiently finished off the food. She grabbed a clean glass out of the cupboard, filled it with water, and drank it down, no idea of the effect her movement was having on Edie. She occupied space like she owned it and would defend it.

When Skye had washed her dishes and stuck them in the drying rack, she turned to see Edie still standing perfectly still with the untouched plate of food in her hand. Skye looked at the plate, then back up at Edie.

"What's wrong?"

Everything was wrong, of course. Every single thing. Edie put her plate down on the counter and walked slowly toward Skye. Skye's eyes widened, and she took a step back. But she was trapped in the small space.

"Edie," Skye said. Pleading or warning, Edie wasn't sure. She wasn't really interested in finding out.

Edie took the last step, crossing the clearly drawn line. Skye sucked in a breath. Edie wanted to taste her. She touched Skye's shirt, tracing light lines against the hard resistance of her abdominal muscles. Then she stretched up to find Skye's lips. Skye's mouth was warm and Edie tumbled into the kiss, losing herself almost instantly as Skye moaned quietly. Edie sought more, pressing her fingers more firmly, her mouth needing to consume and obliterate, her head needing to quiet and to forget.

"No."

Skye trapped Edie's hand against her stomach. There was the

stutter of a heartbeat when Edie thought she'd give in again, but then Skye gently but deliberately moved Edie's hand away and stepped around her.

"You agreed to the conditions. I've already explained why. I won't be distracted." Skye's voice was impassive, but she was still close enough that Edie could see the wild pulse beating in her neck.

"But you want this," Edie said.

Skye shook her head. "I have a job to do. I need to stay focused."

"Maybe I want you unfocused." Edie hated the petulant sound of her voice. This was not a position of strength. She hated the power imbalance, the distance between them. The wanting. "Maybe I need a distraction."

It was the wrong thing to say. Skye's jaw tightened, her eyes went dark, and her expression completely closed down. The finality made Edie flinch.

"I'm here to make sure you're secure, Edie. Not to flirt with you and offer a distraction."

Edie held Skye's gaze. Desire still curled in her belly, but it was overpowered by the guilt and the ache sitting on her chest. She hated all those feelings. Anger rose up, unwanted and inexplicable.

"I'm certain even you are capable of being wrong sometimes."

Edie regretted her words immediately. Skye didn't flinch, though. She held Edie's eyes for a moment, then two, before she looked down at her watch.

"I'm going to check the perimeter. I'll be outside at least an hour. I won't be far."

It was a status report, nothing more. As she walked away, Skye wasn't angry. Merely controlled. The night swallowed Skye like she had never existed in the first place.

Edie moved robotically. She grabbed the plate of cold eggs and took them to the living room. She ate slowly, not thinking of anything at all. Her plate clear, Edie sat in the living room with her feet on the coffee table, simply breathing. Then she slowly, very slowly, opened herself up to what had happened.

In a moment of clarity, far too late to undo the damage, Edie knew Skye was both right and wrong. Edie *was* pushing her needs on Skye. But there was so much more to how she felt about Skye. Edie only hoped she would have a chance at some point to make amends. Considering how badly she'd messed up tonight, she wasn't sure that was possible. She pushed her hands against her eyes, pretending she didn't feel the tears against her palm.

Edie thought maybe an hour had gone by when she heard the sliding door open and close again behind her. A soldier and her clockwork. She wondered if Skye would be able to see she had been crying. She wondered if Skye would leave her sitting there in the dark. At this point, she wouldn't have blamed her.

But Skye moved into the living room, stopping briefly to turn on a small lamp in the corner. Edie blinked into the light and looked at Skye. She was sweaty and still breathing hard, and the knees of her jeans were damp and dirty. Skye stood across from Edie, like she wanted to say something. Edie looked around and realized she was in Skye's space, where Skye usually spent the night.

"Sorry, I'll move." Edie stood up, embarrassed. But as she passed, Skye grabbed her wrist.

"Wait. Please."

Edie could smell the sweat on Skye's skin, the fresh night air.

"I've found something more distracting than you flirting with me," Skye said.

"What's that?"

Skye tugged her gently closer.

"You being upset." And then Edie was in Skye's arms and she had never, not once in her whole life, felt anything that good. The feeling broke Edie, and she started to cry. Skye held her tighter, tucking Edie's face into the crook of her neck, like they'd done this a hundred times before. The feeling in Edie's chest threatened to knock her breath out and Edie gulped for air, fisting her hand into Skye's shirt as the tears continued unabated. Skye gently maneuvered them back down onto the couch, tucking Edie into her side and letting her cry.

"I'm sorry," Edie said between sobs.

Skye shushed her gently and held her. Edie closed her eyes, listened to the soothing beat of Skye's heart beneath her cheek, and slowly, so very slowly, calmed her breathing until the only place she had to go was to sleep.

❖

Edie woke alone on the couch, covered with a blanket. It had been a restless night. She'd woken when Skye had eased herself out of their embrace and gently laid Edie down. And again, in the deep hours of night, she'd opened her eyes to see Skye sitting in the chair across from her, laptop propped open in her lap, looking out the window. Skye, obviously sensing Edie's awakeness, had smiled reassuringly and Edie had drifted back to sleep.

Edie pushed back the blanket and stood stiffly, carefully stretching her aching hip. She headed straight for the bathroom, staring at her haggard expression in the mirror. She considered showering but decided coffee was more of a priority.

With a full mug of coffee warming her fingers, Edie looked out the windows down toward the lake and saw Skye. She was dressed in shorts and a hoodie, running across the length of the lawn, jumping onto the rocks of the garden in a sequence obviously known only to her, before she ran straight at a tree, jumping into the air and grabbing on with both hands and feet. Edie, astonished at her pure physicality, watched as she shimmied up with apparent ease, grabbed a branch, did ten chin-ups, then dropped an alarming distance to the ground, rolled, stood, and sprinted back across the lawn.

Edie realized she'd been holding her breath. She let it out shakily, laughing at her own response to Skye's uninhibited display of strength. Skye was a joy to watch in her element. Edie sipped her coffee, not feeling the slightest bit of shame at her voyeurism as Skye ran back onto the lawn and completed another two circuits.

Then she stopped, hands on her hips, shoulders rising and falling with her rapid intake of breath, and looked out at the lake. Edie could just see the intense look of freedom and pleasure on her face. She wondered which Skye would walk back into the cabin. What had changed?

Skye walked back across the lawn and caught sight of Edie framed in the window. She raised a hand as she approached. Edie returned the gesture, then went to the kitchen and poured Skye a cup of coffee. She met her at the door. Skye's eyes were bright and clear and she murmured her thanks to Edie as she took a sip of coffee. Skye smelled like she had last night, of sweat and fresh air. Edie was beginning to love that scent.

"Good morning, Edie." Skye's words were formal. Her tone wasn't.

"Good morning, Skye."

"I should shower," Skye said. "JC will be here any minute."

"My turn to make breakfast, then."

"Sounds good."

Skye didn't move, and neither did Edie. She wanted to preserve the tension of that moment. Skye ducked her head shyly, as if hiding her thoughts, then walked to the back of cabin. Edie let her breath out as she walked away, unwilling and unable to hide her smile.

They were talking quietly and finishing breakfast when JC arrived, reminding her why they were all together.

"Okay, update," JC said, making a space for herself at the table. She pulled out her laptop and spun it around so everyone could see. She clicked through until a picture of a man Edie didn't recognize came up on the screen. "We've got eyes on Alex Rada, and we've isolated the apartment building where Faina is being held."

Tension permeated the room. Edie went with the shift. "Any idea how he got into the country?" she said. "And why he's here?"

JC clicked her trackpad, and the image changed to a photo of a passport with Alex Rada's face. "He's traveling under the name Sergei Sokolov, a Russian businessman with legit local contacts. Obviously a stolen identity. As to why, that's still a guessing game," JC said. "Our boys at the RCMP have picked up some chatter in the last few months about arms deals running through North and South America, but nothing solid."

"And no ties to me," Edie said.

"Not a one. No one knows one reason you would come to the attention of a Russian arms dealer. Which is kind of pissing everyone off. It would be a hell of a lot easier if you were more suspicious," JC said, grinning.

"Sorry about that."

"You're cleared on the Khalid front as well, the driver of the car that hit you. No contact with His Royal Doucheness either before or since the accident. Another dead end that kept a whole team of people up until the wee hours. That was quite the shit storm. How did you weather that?"

"I was in the hospital for a lot of it. I had two surgeries and was on pain meds for the first few weeks. My memory of those first months is pretty sketchy. My brother and my boss at SunNews pretty much handled all the requests for interviews and the media attention. I didn't know I'd been in the centre of a conflict until it was pretty much over. Even then, it wasn't so much about me."

"It was more about the varying opinions on the lengths that diplomatic immunity should extend," JC added. "I certainly got that sense scanning the file this morning."

Edie nodded. "A tricky conflict to navigate in a city full of diplomats. But it sold papers at the time, and eventually the argument died down."

"But not before tearing through your life and publicizing a difficult time," JC said, sounding offended on Edie's behalf.

"True," Edie said with a shrug. "But as I said, I wasn't aware of most of it. And as a journalist, I understand you have to follow the story."

"But you'd never tear into someone's life like that, would you?" JC said.

"No, I wouldn't. It's one of the reasons I started freelancing. I could control the expectations a hell of a lot better."

Edie took a sip of her second cup of coffee. The media frenzy around her accident had placed the details of her life in full view. She felt a familiar shifting in her stomach and chest, and her thoughts sped up.

"What if that *is* the connection? The attention. The media." Edie spoke slowly, treading lightly.

"What do you mean?" Skye said.

"What if the media coverage is how I came to the attention of the Russians? I didn't meet Faina until after that, when I also started feeling like I was being followed."

"You *were* followed," Skye said. "That wasn't a trick your mind was playing on you."

"Yes, you're right," Edie said softly, glad to hear the possessive note in Skye's tone. "So what if the fact that my accident, my injury, and my life were in the national media for a few weeks is what caught the Russians's interest?"

"The timing certainly fits," JC said. "But we need a why, or it doesn't really help us."

Edie nodded absently and toyed with the handle on her mug. She was thinking about the interview yesterday with Dr. Crask.

"I have gaps in my memory," Edie said as she pulled a piece of paper toward her and picked up a pen. As she talked, she sketched a box that she divided into quarters.

"The gaps are from the accident. From the concussion." JC said, clearly not entirely sure where Edie was going with this.

"Right." She shaded in three of the boxes with her pen and pointed at the one empty box. "But what if the other gaps in my memory are not from the concussion. What if someone…what if someone did something that caused some of the gaps. Something that reacts to light and rhythm and music."

JC leaned forward even as Skye began to pace. Edie absorbed Skye's tension but kept her thoughts on the paper.

JC pointed at Edie's sketch. "And you think that's what this is."

Edie looked at the blank box before answering. Her instinct told her she was close. But this wasn't about a lack of or an absence or a gap. This was about something she had. *Take*, Faina had said. She picked up the pen with a shaking hand. She drew horizontal stripes across the blank box.

"What if they made a hole…No, what if they used a gap that already existed, so they could fill it with something else."

The words hung suspended. Skye stopped pacing and whirled around. Edie's heart rate increased and panic blossomed. *What is in my head? What do I know? What did they plant?* Edie dropped the pen and ran shaking fingers along her skull, nails digging through her hair and into her scalp, the pressure of her palms slowly increasing against her temples until she thought she would scream.

She heard JC's voice, but Skye's touch pulled her back.

"Easy, Edie. Take it easy. Nothing is happening right now. Easy."

Skye stood behind Edie and rested her hands on her shoulders. Her touch was firm and warm, and Edie focused on the feel of her hands. Skye pressed down with her palms against the top of Edie's shoulders, then eased her hands up over the back of Edie's neck. She kept her hands there, a calming heat and pressure, then she gently pushed her fingers into Edie's hair, forcing Edie's hands down and away. Too soon, Skye had retraced her fingers through Edie's hair, trailing down the vertebrae in her neck before skimming lightly off her shoulders. Skye sat down beside her.

"Okay," she said shakily. "This is a possibility, right? I'm not crazy?"

Skye took her hand. She seemed incapable of speaking.

"No, you're definitely not crazy," JC said. "It's a theory without legs, though. We need some way to test it."

"You're talking about her brain," Skye said. "Not a science experiment."

"I know that," JC said. "We're just talking here, trying to figure this out. Team, remember?"

Edie felt Skye's tension through their joined fingers. She squeezed Skye's hand.

"I know this question is ridiculous, but I need to ask," JC said to Edie. "Is there anything in your head that seems odd or out of place? Anything suspicious, or that doesn't fit. Numbers, maybe. Thoughts or facts that don't seem attached to anything."

Edie knew what JC was trying to do, gently guide herself through her own synapses and neurons. Like a doctor on the hunt for illness, sorting healthy tissue from damaged, or isolating a virus in a bloodstream. Edie thought of a book she and her brother had as kids, an illustrated journey into the human body. Edie had loved the unlikely adventure of it. Shawn had loved the medicine.

"Edie?"

Shit, now I'm drifting. "Sorry. No, there's nothing I can think of like that."

"What about dreams? Anything recurring in the last few months? A face, maybe. A conversation. A place in your dream you keep going back to."

"I..." Edie stopped. "Nothing recurring, no..."

"Anything," JC urged. "Try not to edit for logic right now."

"The only thing that sticks out is the night after the bar incident. It was like I was having a conversation in my dream. And there were lyrics, but maybe that was the band. And I've heard lyrics since then."

"Any specific words you can remember?" JC was obviously trying not to sound too excited.

Edie pressed her palm to her eye and tried to sink into memory. Nothing surfaced. "No, just this...sense of lyrics. Of rhythm." She shrugged helplessly.

"You're doing great," Skye said and rubbed her thumb briefly over Edie's knuckles.

"You're doing great," JC confirmed. "Have you ever been hypnotized?"

"Once, yes."

"Let me guess. For a story?" Skye said with a half smile.

"Yes, for a story. There was a craze on the West Coast a few years ago. Students were trying hypnotherapy to help them retain information for their exams. They'd study in a hypnotic state, then attempt to induce a similar state prior to their exam. It wasn't as widespread here, but it sent faculty and staff at the University of Ottawa into a tailspin one semester as students tried to induce hypnotic states in each other at the beginning of an exam. It didn't quite fit anyone's existing definitions of cheating, so there was a lot of running around changing policies and procedures."

Edie felt a shift in her thoughts, a tenuous connection.

"Were you susceptible to hypnosis?" JC said. "I've heard some people aren't."

Edie ignored the question, trying to attach meaning to the bit of intuition that swirled in her belly and her thoughts.

"That sounds familiar, doesn't it?" Edie said. "That idea of hypnotic induction, using phrases or sensory elements to stimulate a neurologic response. That sounds familiar. That's been happening to me."

Not just familiar, Edie thought. *This idea feels solid.*

"I need to get hypnotized. I need to find out what's in there."

No one spoke for a moment.

"Hypnosis has a shaky scientific history, Edie. It's never been reliably validated as a therapeutic approach," Skye said. Edie suspected Skye was working very hard to keep her voice even.

"I know. I did the research for my article."

"Way to mansplain to your girlfriend, Kenny," JC muttered. It was a halfhearted dig, but it broke some of the tension.

Edie stood up and went into the kitchen. As much as she craved Skye's touch, she needed to sit in her own head and body for a moment. She grabbed the coffee carafe and walked back to the table, refilling all three mugs. No one spoke beyond a murmured thanks. When she returned, Edie evaluated the two women. JC looked thoughtful, Skye doubtful.

"This is the first solid hypothesis we have. I want to pursue it."

Skye shook her head, then held up a placating hand when Edie glared at her. "I think we need to be cautious, that's all I'm saying."

"*We* can discuss all we want, but *I* will make the decision."

From the set of her jaw and the way she flexed her fingers, Skye clearly wanted to argue. And her quick glance outside meant she wanted to escape and run and burn off the excess of whatever it was she was feeling.

"I know that," Skye said, still looking out the window. "I agree. I'm sorry."

Edie silently accepted the apology, knowing it was different than Skye's approval.

"Is this hypothesis enough to take to your supervisors?" Edie said to JC.

"Yes, I think so."

"And what will they do with this idea that I am possibly wandering around with unknown information in my brain embedded by Russians with links to arms deals?"

A moment of silence as they all absorbed the scope of the hypothesis they were putting forward.

"They'll want it out," JC said. Her eyes were hard. She looked like Skye in that moment. Her protective soldiers.

"Exactly," Edie said, with a slightly detached calmness. This was what she wanted, wasn't it? To excise this piece of her. To put this all behind her. She could submit to whatever test or hypnotic state the police wanted if it meant leaving this all behind.

"God bless it," JC breathed out suddenly. "Fuck." She sounded edgy and miserable.

"What?" Skye said. "What's wrong?"

"They'll want Crask on this," JC said.

"No," Skye said, her vehemence trailing off with a look of desperation to Edie.

Edie could see Skye struggling. Skye wanted to make the decision for Edie. She couldn't. She wanted to issue a command, but she couldn't. She wanted to take control of this situation. She couldn't.

"Fuck." Skye ran a hand through her hair.

"When can we take this forward?" Edie said. "Are you going to talk to someone today? Maybe tomorrow, after the meet with Faina. Or before." Edie was ramping up, her thoughts on fire.

"Let's hang on a minute," JC said. "I think we need to take a break. Clear our heads before we talk about next steps. And before we talk about the meet tomorrow."

Edie was about to voice her own objection when Skye suddenly stood.

"I'm going to check the perimeter." She stalked through the cabin with long strides and was out the door in seconds.

Edie looked at JC. "I don't need a break. We're finally getting somewhere. I want to keep going." They didn't need Skye for this, not her flurry of objections and her barriers of caution.

"I know you don't need a break," JC said wearily. She put her head in her hands for a moment, rapidly scrubbing at her face before looking up at Edie. "But she does." JC jerked her thumb toward the front window where Skye was launching herself into a tree, reaching with one arm to adjust a sensor.

Edie didn't say anything. She wanted to protect her new connection with Skye, but she'd always been independent. And it felt too good to let go of, even for Skye.

"I can do this on my own. I don't need Skye controlling every aspect of this."

"None of us can do it on our own, Edie. And before you object, I'm going to take off my cop hat for a moment and put on my friend hat. This," she said, indicating Skye's flurry of activity outside, "is not evidence of Skye struggling with her lack of control over decisions."

JC stopped and grinned at Edie. "Well, not entirely anyway. This is Skye coming to terms with the fact that there is not one blessed thing she can do to protect you against your own brain. None of her strength, her brilliance with strategy, or her off the charts intelligence can protect you. And that is scaring the shit out of her."

Edie felt some of the fight go out of her. She sat down. It had never occurred to her that Skye could be scared.

"This is why Skye didn't want to be my security," she said.

"Yep."

"But she agreed."

"She did."

Edie looked at JC. "You weren't surprised."

"Not in the slightest. She has a strong sense of duty, that one. The army loved her for it and didn't want to let her go."

"Duty," Edie said, hating the word. She saw the honour in it, the loyalty and the bravery. But she didn't want the word applied to whatever was between them.

"That's only part of why she's here," JC said. "The two of you are going to have to figure out the rest on your own."

Edie sighed. "If we ever get the time."

"Yeah. We're working on that." JC stood and picked up her phone. "On that note, I'm going to go check in with the suits. Then I'll grab your reluctant but valiant security guard and we'll talk about next steps and what's happening with the meet tomorrow. Deal?"

Edie kept her eyes on the coffee mug in front of her. "Yeah. Deal."

She wondered what she was really agreeing to, but she stood and put on another pot of coffee. The three of them were going to make a plan.

CHAPTER TEN

Faina was late, and the alley was damp and smelled like cat pee. Edie shifted her weight slightly, trying to relieve the ache in her hip from that night she'd slept on the couch. Skye glanced at her from her position covering the street end of the alley and the back door of the laundromat. JC was standing just up the alley, and two other plainclothes cops were just out of sight and inside. A big team.

Skye hadn't been happy. She and JC had fought at headquarters about the deployment of the team and about the fact that Skye had failed to mention Sasha would be in the neighbourhood. The phrase "lack of cooperation" had been thrown around, and they'd made Edie tense.

She tried to concentrate on what she was going to say to Faina, how she was going to convince her to come with them. She didn't know. Her lack of confidence, her heightened tension, and some other unnamable anxiety felt like a fierce thing in her chest. She shook her head and closed her eyes. She had no time for this.

The door of the laundromat banged open. Skye immediately moved in, closing the angle and the access to Edie. Faina stepped outside, looking scared.

"It's not safe, you have to go," Faina said.

"Come with us."

Faina shook her head vehemently, her dark hair whirling, but she stopped the movement suddenly and put a hand to her neck, obviously hurting.

"I've got a minute only. It's not safe here. They are closing down.

Shutting down. The operation." Faina's words were short, frantic bullets of information. She was terrified.

"Walk away from it," Skye said quietly and fiercely. "Step away from the door and walk with Edie down this alley. We'll protect you."

"I can't." Faina's voice was choked. "I've done everything wrong. If I stay, maybe I can stop them or warn you. Take Edie away. Please."

"You're only putting yourself in danger," Edie said. "If you really want to help me, come with us right now. If you don't, we are in the dark and you remain a suspect with questionable motives."

It was the truth, laid out plainly in the dim alley. Faina's expression registered shock and then blankness as she all but disappeared.

"They killed your massage therapist, Pino," Faina said. "They are hunting you. The only reason you are safe is because you disappeared. You have to disappear again."

Edie heard "hunting" with a repetitive, uncomfortable clarity in her skull. Someone shoved the door behind Faina wide open, sending her sprawling into Skye. Edie reached out to steady them both as the man who emerged from the back door reached for her, his expression murderous. He yanked Faina back by her hair. Faina screamed and Edie launched herself toward them, but Skye caught her around the waist and spun her around, pushing her up the alley.

"Let me go!"

"Move Edie." Skye kept shoving her away from Faina.

JC ran past them with her weapon drawn, shouting instructions. Skye pulled Edie to the side and pinned her up against the wall. The rough brick scratched at her back through her shirt, but she had no time to think as a man and a woman converged on her and Skye. Skye launched a kick at the man's knees, then elbowed the back of his neck as he doubled over. She was just seconds too late to block the blow to her midsection from the woman. Edie felt the impact of it against the wall, helpless and struggling to breathe.

Then suddenly Skye was gone and Edie sagged under her own weight.

"Edie, run! Get out of here."

Skye had the woman by the shoulders, spinning and dragging her back down the alley where Edie could see a confusing melee of bodies, weapons, and shouting. Edie wanted to follow Skye's instructions, she even looked up at the alley, toward escape.

Then the woman Skye was wrestling somehow managed to wiggle out of Skye's grasp and launched herself at Edie again before Skye could react. Edie took three steps back, but not fast enough. The woman tackled Edie, sending her flying back into the wall, her head hitting the bricks with a thud that sent shocks through her neck and back and stomach. Edie felt instantly sick, the weight of the woman against her stomach, the feel of her hands tearing into her T-shirt. Then the weight was gone as Skye reached down and picked the woman up, her face a mask of controlled rage.

"Edie, get the fuck out of here. Find Sasha. Now!"

Scrambling, scared, Edie got her feet under her and ran down one alley. Hearing voices, she turned down another. Whose voice? How many were there? She emerged out onto the side street. Better to blend in with the pedestrians, people focused on their phones or their destination? Better to hide in the side streets and alleys, not knowing who was coming at you or from where? Her head pounded, a faint but consistent reverberation that seemed to keep pace with her heart. Or maybe it was a drumbeat. Edie ran from that, too.

Each step sent a pulse up through her legs, through her hips into her torso. It traveled up her neck and throbbed through her head, but it brought clarity with it. She was farther away, closer to downtown. Dodging pedestrians was getting harder, and she was drawing attention to herself. Edie slowed and got her bearings.

Business district. She breathed and let her heart rate settle, surprised when the pain in her head ratcheted down almost immediately. Stopping at an intersection, she looked over her shoulder. Just people intent on getting to their next destination, keeping appointments, talking with colleagues or kids. No pursuit. No one hunting that she could see.

Edie gripped her phone. Where was Skye? What had she said? *Find Sasha.* The light changed, and Edie let the mass of pedestrians swallow her up as they crossed. She wasn't sure how she was supposed to find Sasha. She'd only seen him once and wasn't convinced she remembered what he looked like. Edie wanted Skye, but Skye was busy fighting her way out of an alley. A frisson of anxiety made Edie stumble, and she leaned up against the nearest building. Skye would be okay. She was a soldier and a fighter. She was strong.

Edie looked around at the banks and office buildings and storefronts. But this was the nation's capital, so there were also dozens of embassies and diplomatic missions. Some were massive, like the stone fortress of the US embassy six blocks away, and some were smaller. But each had some security presence.

Edie needed to find a populated area near an embassy and wait for Skye to contact her. She found it half a block later, a tiny courtyard full of men and women on their lunch breaks, with two bank buildings on one side and an office building with ten African embassies and commissions in the other. Perfect. Edie found a vacant stone edge of a planter box, sat down, and pulled out her phone.

Edie stared blankly at the screen. She wanted to evaluate the lump on the back of her head, though she knew full well the damage inside could far outweigh any swelling of her scalp. Enough. She would think her way through this. She would wait for Skye to contact her. She would get information about JC and Faina. There must be people in custody by now, the woman who had attacked her. She'd attacked Edie. Pursued. Take. They were coming after her, just as Faina had said.

The phone vibrated in Edie's hand, startling her out of her rising panic. A text from Skye, and the relief Edie felt threatened to undo her completely.

Where are you?

Edie began to type back a response. Her gut told her to wait, a red flag of caution. Edie considered the information she had. A text from Skye. *No, be more specific.* A text from Skye's phone. Asking for her location.

Take.

Edie, where are you?

Edie typed. *I'm safe.*

Tell me where you are. I'll send Sasha.

Another piece of information. Edie remembered Skye yelling at her to go find Sasha. So not exclusive information. More than one side had access to that name. It wasn't good enough.

I'm calling, Skye typed.

Seconds after the text came through, the phone began vibrating insistently. Edie's finger hovered over the green accept button. She wanted to hear Skye's voice, her reassurance, her single-minded goal to keep Edie safe. But what she pictured was Faina's look of horror as her phone played music that seeped into Edie's brain, that twisted her synapses into sleep and unconsciousness. She heard drumbeats. Edie let the phone keep ringing. It wasn't good enough.

Answer me, Edie.

Edie typed. *I'm scared of what I'll hear.* Safe enough words. She hoped Skye would understand, and she hadn't given anything away if it wasn't Skye at the other end.

Right. Okay. Keep breathing, Edie.

Tears pricked her eyes. That sounded like Skye. Moments later two more texts came up in rapid succession. The first one was a hyperlink. The second said *Meet me at the Twelve. You know username and password.*

Edie clicked the link, typed and retyped as her fingers shook. So close to Skye. She could trust this. The image on her phone was a tiny version of what she'd seen on the laptop on their first date, but Edie immediately recognized the Twelve. It took her a moment to figure out how to navigate it on her phone. Tiny figures walked through the office space, their names hovering over their heads. Edie didn't see Skye. She checked the giant clock on the wall. Just before noon, a meeting was about to start.

The private chat window opened. Gordon was typing.

Friend or foe?

Edie recognized Gordon's name, the employee who jumped on the trampoline and practically lived at the Twelve.

Friend, Edie typed. *I'm looking for Skye.*

Another figure dropped into the room, and when Edie zoomed in, she could see Skye's character with her camo hat. The chat screen flashed.

I'm here. I've got this, Gordon. Thanks.

Gordon's name flashed off the chat.

Edie, are you okay?

Yes, I'm okay.

Where are you?

Metcalfe Street. In a courtyard. By a parking garage.

I'm sending Sasha. He's not far. Do you remember what he looks like?

I think so.

Look at the whiteboard.

Edie navigated over until she could see the whiteboard. A white square like a projector light showed up and then a photo of Sasha appeared.

Okay?

Yes. Okay. Are you hurt? Faina? JC?

All good. Sasha is only two minutes out. He will bring you to me. Need to get your head checked out.

I'm fine.

It wasn't a request.

Edie shook her head. That sounded exactly like Skye.

Fine.

A voice intruded on her digital conversation.

"Hey, there you are."

Edie looked up as Sasha approached, an easy smile on his face. He seemed utterly relaxed, wearing a T-shirt and jeans and looking like any other person on the street. Edie stood and walked toward him. Unexpectedly, he pulled her in lightly and kissed her cheek. An easy, friendly gesture. He also whispered in her ear.

"Did you see anyone following?" he said, pulling back again, that easygoing smile still on his face.

Edie shook her head, unable to speak.

"Come on. Your ride awaits."

Edie fell in step beside him, Sasha keeping the conversation light as he guided Edie by a brief touch on the arm. They were walking back toward the laundromat, and Edie's stomach clenched.

"It's okay," Sasha said, obviously reading her distress. "The place is swarming with cops. And we're not heading there anyway. Strict instructions from the boss to take you directly to the hospital."

"Where's Skye?" Edie said.

"She'll meet us there." Sasha indicated a grey Honda Accord parked outside a low apartment building. "Hop in."

Edie got in the car, fastened her seat belt, and Sasha eased them into traffic, through the downtown streets and onto the Queensway. Something wasn't quite sitting right, the information wasn't falling into place the way it should.

"Where is Skye right now?" Edie said again. "Right this second."

Sasha tried flashing a smile at her. For a lot of reasons, that wasn't going to work. Edie waited with the patience of a journalist after information.

Sasha sighed. "She's at the hospital."

Nausea. No time. "Tell me what happened."

"Let's start with the part where she's okay. Everyone is. Well, some of those Russian dudes aren't doing so hot. Okay?"

"Yeah. Okay."

"Faina is in custody and needs clearance by a doctor before the OPP could bring her in and question her. SOP."

Standard operating procedure. Like any of this could be considered standard.

"Go on," Edie said.

"Skye and Constable Caldwell were both cut in the process of apprehending the suspects."

"Cut." That word had too many connotations. A scratch that ripped at skin, blood trembling to the surface. The clean, shallow slice of a blade. An incision. The violent invasion of a blade into flesh.

"Cut," Sasha said. This time his voice had edge. "One of the suspects, the woman, had a blade. Neither one is life-threatening. I promise."

Edie trusted him.

They didn't speak again until they got to the hospital. Sasha confidently pulled into a spot right out front that clearly stated No Parking. He grinned at Edie.

"I'm trying to beat last month's parking ticket total. Bart loves it."

Sasha talked his way through the secure Emergency Department, his easygoing attitude and some type of security badge paving the way. Edie followed blindly, trying to block out the smell of hospital. It was all familiar: the intrusion of the hospital intercom, the press of bodies in the busy hallway, the inexplicable combination of misery and work place.

"Edie."

As Skye walked toward Edie, she noticed two things. First, Skye was holding the left side of her body carefully angled away from Edie. Second, as Edie was searching Skye's expression for evidence of their connection, Skye seemed equally intent on hiding it.

"You need to be triaged," Skye said, a commander issuing orders to her troop.

"You're hurt," Edie said.

Skye looked down at her left arm briefly. The white bandage under the edge of her shirt was innocuous, capable of hiding any number of injuries.

"I'm fine. Tell me about your head. Have you seen a nurse?" Skye hadn't moved, but she was retreating nonetheless. Her voice was brittle with precision.

"Not yet," Sasha said. "I brought her right here, boss."

"You need to get checked out, too," Edie insisted.

"Your head is more important."

A nurse, an Asian man about Edie's height with broad shoulders, black hair, a stern expression, and a definite twinkle in his eyes interceded. "You both need to sit down and be quiet and follow orders," he said. "That's the only way whatever police drama you have going on here is going to end. I'm Nurse Brian, and I've got orders to treat you troublemakers and clear you out of here. So who's first?"

Edie pointed at Skye. "She's bleeding."

Skye gave Edie a disbelieving look. "Nice try. Tell him or I will."

"Yes, tell me. I do love a reluctant history." Nurse Brian crossed his arms in a show of extreme patience.

Edie sighed. "I have a history of severe concussion, a year ago, and about an hour ago I hit my head."

Brian uncrossed his arms and took a step closer to Edie. She felt his evaluation of her pupils.

"I've had no blurriness or double vision, at no point was I unconscious, and I can remember everything that happened since I hit my head," Edie added.

"How hard did you hit?"

"I heard it," Skye said and she sounded just a little bit sick. "She hit a brick wall and I heard it."

The nurse glanced quickly at Skye, then returned his gaze to Edie. "Any nausea or vomiting?"

"Some nausea," Edie said.

Skye looked like she was going to break something.

"I'm fine," Edie said quietly.

"Yeah," said Nurse Brian. "Actually, I get to be the one who decides that. So, you," he said to Skye, "need to get back to the treatment area from whence you came, and you need to come with me so I can put you in the system and get you on the list for CT."

Skye crossed her arms over her chest. Edie took note of the hospital bracelet around her right wrist. "I go where she goes."

Nurse Brian rolled his eyes. "Great. That's super sweet. I'm so glad you guys are going to make this easy on me." He looked up at Sasha, who had been standing very still. "What about you? What are we treating you for today?"

Sasha merely shook his head at the nurse, seemingly incapable of speech.

"Sash, why don't you go check on JC and Faina and come back with an update," Skye said.

"Yeah, okay." Sasha took off down the hall.

Edie and Skye followed Nurse Brian back to Skye's vacated treatment area. He grabbed a tablet from the nurse's desk on the way.

"Both of you sit. I don't care where. We'll start with head injury's history."

Edie sat on the chair by the bed and gave her history. The nurse took her pulse and blood pressure and checked her temperature, and then he very gently and confidently palpated the small knot at the back of Edie's skull. Skye, sitting stiffly on the gurney, could not quite hide her worry behind her security mask. Edie took heart at this. It made her headache and her worry ease up just a little.

"Okay, you're on the list for CT," the nurse said as he expertly wrapped a hospital bracelet around Edie's wrist. "It's just a precaution, given your history. It will be a couple of hours, so get comfortable. And no, you don't get a choice."

Edie sighed and nodded.

"Great. First intelligent thing you've said so far." He turned to Skye. "Now you. You're waiting to get stitched up. Pretty sure that means sit here and don't move. Have I been clear?"

"Crystal," Skye responded.

"Roger that, Commander," Edie said.

With another eloquent and well-practiced eye roll, Nurse Brian swept out of the curtained treatment area.

Edie craved Skye's closeness and wished she could ease the look of worry Skye couldn't hide. Wished they were anywhere other than this hospital waiting for a CT scan and stitches.

Edie watched Skye scan the small treatment area, assessing the staff and patients in the hallway before landing on Edie and starting the sweep all over again.

"JC and Faina? What happened?" Edie said.

"They're both okay. Getting checked out. We can't talk here. Debrief later."

Fierceness and deadness, such an odd combination, Edie decided. Skye was so clearly angry, still on alert. Nearly hypervigilant.

"Skye," Edie said quietly.

Skye didn't answer, just kept scanning.

"I'm okay, you know."

Edie could almost hear Skye's teeth clash together as she clenched her jaw. So much anger. But where was it directed?

"Are you angry I wouldn't answer my phone?"

Skye's eyes were stormy, all turbulence and upset. "No."

"Why are you so angry?"

Skye shook her head. "Not at you. I was impressed," she said, almost reluctantly. "It was a smart decision not to trust who was on the other end. You've got good instincts."

Their conversation was interrupted by the physician's assistant, a woman with dark hair and a disinterested expression. She wheeled a cart into the treatment area, set up, and began unwrapping Skye's bandage in a manner that rode the line between efficient and careless.

Edie got out of her chair and stood by Skye's shoulder. Skye only glanced up briefly, then looked down at where the PA was exposing the injury. Edie looked closely at the cut on the outside of Skye's lower bicep. The slice was clean, less than an inch long, and lightly crusted with blood.

"It's frozen already?" the PA said, prodding it with her finger. That didn't quite seem professional to Edie.

"Yes," Skye said, looking down at the cut.

The PA grunted. "Should only take a few stitches, it's not very big."

She sounded disgruntled, as if Skye had failed to make her night more interesting. Edie's dislike for the woman increased exponentially and she tensed, ready to say something.

"It's fine," Skye said. "Leave it."

Edie growled quietly, and Skye seemed to be holding back a grin. She twitched on the gurney.

"Stop moving, please."

Edie shot Skye an apologetic look, and Skye's dark eyes danced with laughter and confusion. Edie wanted to reassure Skye, maybe make her laugh again. Instead, she took the time to examine Skye's tattoo, the cap sleeve that disappeared into her T-shirt tucked over her shoulder. Its eight black bands circled her arm, spaced half an inch apart. Woven between the bands was a red and gold dragon, its tail and wings and neck twisting around on itself in a knot of scales and wings and claws. The colours were incredibly vibrant.

Skye seemed to track Edie's gaze and she looked down briefly at her arm, just above where the PA was making short work of the stitches.

"I got it when I left the army," Skye said.

"Eight bands for eight years?"

Skye nodded.

"And the dragon?"

"Story for another time."

A young man in navy blue scrubs opened the curtain and looked in.

"Edith Black?" When Edie nodded, he stepped in closer, took a look at the hospital bracelet, and checked his tablet. "Come with me, I'll take you down to CT."

Skye tried to sit up.

"Don't move, please," the PA said, never taking her eyes off Skye's arm.

"Are you almost done?"

The PA didn't answer. Then she efficiently snipped the dark, stiff thread, slapped the bandage back on Skye's arm, and carted herself out.

Edie shook her head. Those stitches had better be good.

"It's fine, let's go," Skye said, tugging down her shirt and standing up.

They followed the man in blue scrubs down multiple hallways. Each step brought an increasing sense of dread that Edie tried very hard to ignore. But the anxiety gained on her as they entered the Radiology section. *I've been in a CT scanner lots of times before.* She wasn't claustrophobic. It had never really bothered her before. In fact, it was mostly boring trying to lie still and hold your breath at the right moments. So why this time?

Edie went through the procedure in her head. Hospital gown,

injection of contrast dye which made her slightly nauseous, enter scanner room, lie on bed, disappear into machine, close eyes, listen to instructions, hold breath, hear clicking and whirring, hold still, lights flashing…

Edie's stomach dropped. Flashing lights.

"I don't think I can do this," Edie said, but her faint words were lost in the sudden flurry of activity and instruction. The man in blue scrubs stopped in front of a curtained change area, handed Edie two gowns as he reeled off instructions about how to put them on, asked about jewelry on her body, then closed the curtain between them.

Edie removed her clothes, listening to the discussion between the tech and Skye about where she could wait. The two were negotiating terms, and Skye was winning. Dropping JC's name and rank into the conversation seemed to help. When Edie was double-gowned, she pulled the curtain aside, her bare legs cold but not the cause of the shivers in her body.

She didn't say anything, just followed the tech to the next room where he went through his pre-checklist questionnaire: dentures, pregnancy, surgical staples, piercings, implants. Another man in blue scrubs waited with the contrast dye already pulled up into a syringe. Maybe it was better this was moving so fast, Edie thought, as she closed her eyes and felt the sting of the injection. It would be over faster.

Instructions and movements and Edie was somehow already on the narrow black bed with the thin, plastic covered mattress. She tried to take a deep breath to decrease the shivering.

"Are you cold?" one of the techs said. "You can't move during the scan."

"Yes." Edie gave the easiest, though not most truthful, answer.

She heard the tech leave the room and stared straight up at the ceiling, counting the tiles and vents until she felt a welcome, warm weight covering her. The heated blanket decreased the shivering a little, but as soon as the tech continued with his instructions, the shaking returned. Edie knew she'd lost control. She couldn't calm her nervous system.

"This isn't going to work," she heard the tech say.

Edie felt a moment of shame, and she kept staring up at the ceiling, her thoughts rapidly spiraling as she began counting her faults instead of tiles.

"Get another blanket and give us a minute."

Skye's voice. Edie closed her eyes. She wasn't sure she had ever felt this exposed.

She could feel Skye standing by the edge of the bed. Edie continued to breathe, her body shaking with uncontrolled irregularity under the rapidly cooling hospital blanket.

"Do you want the princess story or the tattoo story?"

Edie opened her eyes. Skye was looking expectantly down at her. "Both?"

Skye's expression of amusement was enough for Edie. Her body started to calm.

"Nice try, Ms. Black. Choose one and I'll tell it to you over the intercom while you're getting your scan. Interrupted by instructions from the techs, of course."

Edie considered her options. "Will you tell me both eventually, or is this my one and only chance?"

Skye's eyes darkened. "I think you know the answer to that already." Her voice was just at the edge of rough, and the warmth that spread through Edie's body had nothing to do with the heated hospital blanket.

"Then I'd like the princess story now. And the tattoo story later."

The tech came back into the room carrying another blanket, which he spread over Edie. "How are you doing?" he said, sounding more concerned with the schedule than Edie.

"I'm good," Edie said and smiled at Skye. "I'm ready."

The tech gave the last few instructions, and he and Skye disappeared back behind the glassed-in wall. Edie closed her eyes, warmed by the blankets. She listened to the tech's instructions as the machine slowly drew her inside. When the nausea made small ripples through her stomach, she breathed through it, knowing it likely wouldn't get much worse. She'd actually never felt this okay getting a CT scan. Her body had always been more battered, her concussion always worse.

"Can you hear me?" Skye's tinny voice through the speakers.

"Yes," Edie said faintly, keeping her eyes closed and focusing on not moving.

"Okay, so, about six months after I moved back to Ottawa from the UAE, Bart asked me to be part of the security detail for a visiting princess from Dubai and her entourage. We spent a lot of time at tiny boutiques while she shopped and exclusive clubs while she partied."

Edie thought Skye sounded a little nervous. She imagined it wasn't easy for the deeply introverted Skye to tell complete strangers a story about her life. In that moment, refusing to shy away from the feeling, Edie loved her for it.

"Anyway, Bart was coordinating security with the RCMP, and I was just following orders and keeping an eye on the somewhat flighty princess as she complained about the boring Ottawa night life. One night I'm leading the perimeter team on a gala event at a downtown hotel, and I see a guy I recognize from the UAE.

"I knew damn well he was on American and Canadian hit lists for political espionage, ferrying information between the UAE and the rest of Europe. I see this guy meet up with the head of the princess's security outside the hotel, and I immediately alert Bart, who immediately alerts the RCMP. Who, for whatever bureaucratic reason, doesn't have a clue what to do with this info.

"Since I'm the only one with eyes on him, I end up coordinating what amounts to an international takedown outside this gala event. All while maintaining security on the princess and without creating a scene that would draw international attention. At least the RCMP took on the job of telling the princess her head of security was now in custody."

Skye's voice was interrupted by the beeping of the machine and the tech's voice came over the intercom.

"You're done. Bringing you out now."

Edie opened her eyes as she re-emerged into the scan room. She was slightly disoriented, having spent the last fifteen minutes living in Skye's story. Edie got up when she was instructed and led back to the change area. Moments later she was dressed and Skye was waiting in the hallway.

"So, how does it end? Pissed-off princess or grateful princess?"

Skye blushed and Edie laughed. "Grateful princess. Which was fine until she tried to seduce me when we took her back to the hotel. I'm pretty sure she thought I was a man. I still hadn't grown my hair back, but she didn't seem concerned either way. Bart had to send in another team leader so I could escape without causing a different kind of international scene."

Edie laughed. "That was a great story." She touched Skye's arm lightly. "Thanks."

Skye made no movement away or toward. "You're welcome."

They stood in the hallway as the world moved around them. It was Skye, on task Skye, focus on the mission Skye, eye on the prize Skye, who broke the silence.

"We need to go check in with JC and see where the investigation stands. While we're waiting for your test results."

Soldier Skye may have spoken, but gentle Skye gazed back at her. As they made their way silently down the hallway together, that was enough for Edie.

CHAPTER ELEVEN

JC looked harried, talking on the phone outside a private room on the fourth-floor medical unit. She had a light bandage around her right wrist. A uniformed cop stood on the opposite corner. As they approached, Edie could almost feel Skye pulling herself in, drawing on whatever vast amount of energy reserves she had to readjust to her singular focus. Edie didn't hate the feeling of Skye drawing away from her. She merely accepted it for what it was.

"Good, you're here," JC said as she caught sight of them and hung up. "We've got a debrief back at headquarters in an hour. I've just had three heads of department literally screaming at me for the last hour. Like I'm the one slowing down Ms. Kassis's medical discharge."

"How is Faina?" Edie said. She'd had no update beyond the assurance that everyone was fine. "Can I see her?"

"First, she's okay. Given her recent history, she's being monitored for signs of shock or trauma." JC's eyes went cold. "She's obviously been used as a punching bag in the last week or so, but Ms. Kassis is insisting this wasn't true of her entire two-year captivity. She's also insisting she's well enough to be discharged and questioned."

"She wants to be questioned?" Skye said.

JC shrugged. "She wants to help."

"Even knowing she might be implicated? Charged, even?"

"Even then."

One some level, Faina's insistence on doing the right thing, regardless of the cost to herself, relieved Edie. She recognized this concerned and supportive Faina. Not secretive and disloyal.

"Can I see her?"

"Yes, but I and a uniform will have to be present. She's a person of interest, and her connection to what happened to you has not yet been established. Everything will be monitored. Okay?"

"Yes, okay."

JC seemed to hesitate, and then she pushed the door open into the private room. Edie had expected Faina to be gowned and in bed, but she was standing by the window, looking out over the parking lot in the same jeans and hoodie she'd been wearing in the alley. The light through the window cast her in dark relief, and even though she turned at the sound of their entry, Edie could not make out her expression.

"Faina?"

JC and Skye both hung back by the door. Edie stepped in closer to Faina before she registered a woman in uniform standing in the corner of the room.

Faina's expression tore at Edie's heart. The bruises were just as awful as they'd been this morning, now accentuated by three red lines on the side of her neck. Finger marks. Edie felt a surge of anger and guilt. Edie's undoing was the expression in Faina's eyes. Not meek or cowed, but fierce.

"God, Faina. I'm so sorry." Edie's guilt spoke first.

Faina took a nearly shocked step back and raised a trembling hand to her mouth. She shook her head.

"Don't say that." Faina's voice trembled. "Don't say that to me."

Edie took a step toward her, and Faina's tears spilled over.

"I didn't know what was happening to you. All this time and I didn't know." Edie needed to say it as much as she wanted Faina to hear it. She put her arms around Faina.

At first Faina was stiff, refusing to give in, but she finally let out a choked, strangled sob, her hands pressed to her mouth. Too much had been done to them. Both of them. And as she held her friend, one person who had seen her at her worst and still believed in her core strength, Edie felt a new kind of resolve. They would fight this, all of them. She turned to look over her shoulder, never letting go. JC and Skye stood like the silent, protective soldiers they were, and Edie sensed their support. Maybe they didn't know Faina yet the same way Edie did, but they were no happier with the way Faina had been treated.

It took a few minutes for Faina's sobs to gentle. She turned away, obviously embarrassed, and walked into the bathroom. She emerged moments later with puffy eyes that seemed clearer for the recent storm.

"I'd like to know what's next, Constable Caldwell. I understand people want to speak to me."

JC approached before answering the question. "Once you get medical clearance, then yes, we'll take you down to—"

"I am ready to go right now. I don't need to wait for medical clearance, unless there are questionable test results that have not yet been shared." Her bearing was almost regal, Edie decided. Even with the bruises, strength looked good on Faina.

"No," JC admitted. "But the doctors wanted to wait and see—"

Once again, Faina cut her off. "The doctors are waiting for me to fall apart," she said calmly. "I just did. You witnessed it. It did not precipitate a medical emergency. So I'm ready to leave."

JC seemed to be at a loss for words, a fact both Skye and Edie clearly found amusing. Edie covered her smile as Skye shot her a half grin, her eyes dancing. JC caught the look and narrowed her eyes.

"Both of you can just stuff it. Honestly," JC muttered. She turned back to Faina. "Ms. Kassis, I'll let the doctor know you're ready to leave. I'll ask that you wait for any last minute instruction regarding any of the injuries you received today. Then I'll take you down to headquarters myself."

Faina glanced at Edie.

"I'll be there," Edie said. "They won't let me in the room with you, but I'll be there."

"As will I," Skye said quietly.

"Me, too," JC said.

Faina looked between the women forming a barrier between her and the rest of the world.

"Thank you."

❖

It was late at night and pouring rain by the time every department in the building questioned Faina, deemed her a continued person of interest, and finally released her into JC's custody. Though she was no longer a suspect, her familial connection and her own unwilling connection to Edie's situation meant she couldn't leave under her own recognizance. The RCMP had given her the choice of house arrest with an officer or a detention centre. Faina had chosen house arrest, and the powers that be had chosen JC.

After a mad scramble to call in her ex-wife to take her kids, JC signed the paperwork delivering Faina into her care, and the four of them left the police department where they'd spent the last eleven hours. Skye suggested they all crash at her place. The cabin was too far, they were all too tired, and Faina's protective custody meant she had to have at least two other officers with her at all times. They needed to be somewhere secure. Somewhere inaccessible. Skye's formidable and comfortable loft was perfect.

As Edie entered, she thought about the first night she'd been here, sitting with Skye on the couch and sharing her thoughts, her space, and her work. Skye had held her hand so sweetly.

"Mind if I make some tea?" she said to Skye, who was conversing quietly with JC while Faina looked tentatively around the loft space.

"No, go ahead. I don't have much, but you're welcome to whatever is in the kitchen."

Edie walked to the kitchen and filled the kettle with water, opening cupboards until she found tins of loose tea and some mugs. One navy blue mug had a faded Star Wars logo and the faint etchings of Storm Troopers. Edie smiled and left it in the cupboard. She heard a sound behind her as Faina walked in.

"I thought you'd like some tea," Edie said. "Have a seat."

Faina sat on a stool at the kitchen island while Edie twisted the knob on the gas stove until the blue flame caught. Edie noticed Faina flinch. While she waited for the kettle to boil, she leaned against the counter and looked into Faina's tired, bruised eyes.

"You're safe here, you know," Edie said, reaching over and taking her hand. "You're safe with JC and Skye. With me."

Faina glanced at JC and Skye, who were bent over their phones. Edie guessed Skye was giving JC full access to the extensive security system for her loft. Faina sighed. Edie realized she couldn't say anything to make it all okay. She finished making the tea, put a steaming mug in front of Faina, and sat down beside her.

"What did they tell you about my interrogation today?" Faina said, no bitterness in her tone.

"Only that JC's superiors are satisfied you are not complicit in what has happened. I heard the word 'duress.' I know your immigration status is in question. I know JC has taken you into protective custody. That's pretty much it."

Faina nodded thoughtfully and stared down into her tea. Edie had so many questions, but she didn't want to batter Faina with them right now.

"I think I will spend a long time apologizing to you," Faina said quietly, without looking up. Before Edie could respond she added, "Please allow it, Edie. I know it is a lot to ask. Please allow it."

"Can you tell me what you think you're apologizing for?"

"I was willingly misled by my brother and sister. When my mother died and Alex and Yana sought me out in London, I thought they were coming to me as family. I was young, I was lost, and I had no one. Still…" Faina took a moment before she continued. "They brought me to Canada and told me I would be able to study here, but they had to wait for certain visa approval. I believed them. In the meantime, I needed to do my part to pay for the rent of the flat I shared with several of Alex's colleagues. It didn't take me long to figure out they were employees, not colleagues, and whatever business Alex was conducting wasn't legitimate.

"I was allowed out for the first year or so, although Alex made it clear I shouldn't get to know anyone until my visa papers were sorted. But I could go to the library and a coffee shop. I spent a lot of time reading on my own. I thought about what I would study when my visa came through. I imagined living on my own. I would watch the baristas very carefully and think maybe I could get a part-time job. Or I could be an interpreter. When Alex approached me and said he had an easy job for me, I worried. He showed me a picture of you and said you were a journalist who likely had information about the death of our father."

Edie leaned back, completely startled with this revelation.

"I know now that you didn't," Faina said quickly. "That you don't. But I had no reason to doubt Alex. And he told me you weren't aware of knowing it. You were just in the wrong place at the wrong time. He asked me to simply get to know you. Become friends. And that eventually, months and months later, I could maybe ask some questions. That was all."

Faina took a sip of her tea, and Edie did the same.

"You are the first friend I've had since I was a child in Syria," Faina said quietly. "When Alex told me you were recovering from an accident, I felt a kinship with you. The day I met you, I could see how hard you were fighting to be independent. To be okay. It made me feel strong to help you. And then after that, we had so many things to talk about. Endless things to talk about. I could make you laugh. You treated me like my own person capable of interesting thoughts and ideas. I knew Alex had set up our friendship, and he was monitoring our texts and emails. But I thought we were becoming proper friends. I could ignore the part where Alex was targeting you, stalking you. He knew which physiotherapist you were seeing and sent me there. I ignored all of it.

"And then when Alex asked me to get you to go to a certain massage therapist, I ignored the uncomfortable feeling in my stomach. That maybe Alex wanted more than information about our father. I encouraged you to go. But I didn't know what they were doing to you. I didn't know, Edie. And I'm so sorry."

Faina's grief and guilt was heavy and uncomfortable, a soaked wool sweater against her skin. Edie wanted it off.

"What were they doing to me, Faina?"

Faina looked up, and her eyes were pure misery. "They've hidden information inside your head. Implanted it there. My sister Yana is a neuroscientist in Kiev. She has developed a way of embedding encrypted information into the human brain. I don't know how. I'd tell you if I did. They targeted you because of your head injury. Your accident was all over the news. They knew you had one, and they exploited it. And I helped. In this I am complicit. And I am so sorry."

Faina seemed to lose any vestige of control over her emotions at this point. She put her head in her hands and her shoulders shook. Edie moved closer and put her arm around Faina's shoulders. But Faina was too close to a physical collapse. Edie looked up as Skye and JC approached.

"She needs to rest. She's completely spent," Edie said.

"I'll clear out the apartment above the garage," Skye said. "Faina and JC can stay up there."

"Yeah, okay." Edie looked up at JC. "You'll take care of her?"

"I will. I promise," JC said.

Skye and Edie stood in the kitchen as JC and Faina made their way upstairs. Edie glanced at Skye.

"Did you hear all that?"

"Yeah. JC filled me in on some as well."

It was hard to think. She was so tired. But one thing was perfectly clear.

"We were right. There's information in there. We need to get it out."

Edie knew she should have been upset. Scared or angry. Violated. But right now, she just felt tired. Safe but tired.

"I thought the upstairs apartment was just storage," Edie said. "Why did you let me take your bed the night I stayed here?"

"Because I wanted you near me," Skye said. Her eyes snapped back into focus, like she'd just heard what she'd said and couldn't believe she'd spoken the words aloud. Her eyes were vulnerable, and she looked helplessly at Edie. Edie was grateful she did not take back the words.

"I should go help them get set up," Skye said.

"And I'm going to have a shower and crash."

"Yeah, okay. Good idea. You know where to find everything."

Skye left Edie alone in the kitchen. She sipped her rapidly cooling tea and listened to the echoes of commotion above her. She would sleep, and Skye and JC and Faina would be nearby tonight. And tomorrow, no matter what Skye said, Edie planned to talk to Dr. Diana Crask. She needed answers.

❖

Edie woke in the middle of the night to pain in the back of her head. She turned quickly on her side and took the pressure off her bump. She took a moment to be grateful for the absence of headache and a clear CT scan before stretching in the soft, satiny grey sheets of Skye's bed. Skye's bedroom was simple greys and blues, understated but just a little luxurious with the feel of the sheets and the thickness of the blanket.

Edie listened for any sounds of movement from the living room.

The loft seemed utterly still, just the thrum of the slow-moving overhead fans high up in the ceiling. The glow of at least one light from the living room shone around the edges of the privacy barrier to the bedroom. Knowing she would take some time to get back to sleep, Edie decided to get up.

Skye was sitting in one of the chairs opposite the couch, her beanie slouched on the back of her head, laptop open in her lap. Her eyes were closed, her fingers resting lightly against the keyboard. It was the first time Edie had seen her sleep, or even look the slightest bit tired.

Before Edie could decide if she should wake her up, Skye opened her eyes. Edie felt caught, pulled in by her naked expression, the sense of having been captured and drawn in. The sense of having been seen. Skye blinked, refocused, and sat up.

"Hey," Skye said, clearing her throat. She checked her watch. "Why are you up?"

Edie sat down on the couch. She was ever so slightly dizzy but didn't want to admit it. She didn't want Skye to worry that it had to do with her earlier blow to the head.

"Couldn't sleep?" Skye said, obviously concerned with Edie's lack of response. "Is it your head?"

"No, it's fine," Edie said, trying desperately to focus on Skye and calm her body at the same time. "I just woke up and wanted to see you."

Skye surprised her and smiled. "I'm right here."

The last time she'd flippantly made a remark about Skye's seemingly endless reserves, Skye had completely shut down like she'd been criticized. Edie wanted to proceed with caution.

"You don't seem to have to sleep very much."

As she had predicted, Skye stiffened. But she also answered. "No, I don't."

"How much?" Edie said, keeping her voice soft, willing herself to not give whatever reaction Skye so obviously feared.

"Two or three hours a night."

"Will you tell me about it?"

"My parents say I slept normally until I was about eighteen months," Skye said. "Or what they thought was normal since I was their only child. And then I just stopped. Apparently I didn't cry, I just lay in my crib and talked and sang to myself. They would bring me puzzles and books, and I'd just keep myself occupied until they got up."

"You were reading."

Skye hesitated then continued. "Baby books. But yeah, I could read." She grinned suddenly. "And then I learned to get out of my crib."

Edie laughed at Skye's triumphant expression, as if her crib was the first obstacle course she could remember defeating.

"What was school like for you?" Edie said.

Skye's expression faltered. "Never great. I mean, it was fine. I..." Skye hesitated. "I was reading at a fourth-grade level by the time I started kindergarten. I had an excess of energy, and very few of my teachers understood that. I knew from a very early age my brain didn't work like the other kids'. I didn't know how to change it. I wasn't sure if I wanted to.

"I remember very clearly being in the third grade. I was supposed to be outside for recess but I had gotten distracted by the plumbing to the sink in the back of the room. It was an old school, and the pipes banged in the walls and I wanted to know why. So I wedged myself in behind the supply cupboard and started climbing."

"Of course you did," Edie murmured. Skye grinned.

"Two teachers came into the room and they were griping about the principal, the workload, their students. I knew I wasn't supposed to be in the class, so I just hung suspended from the pipe and listened. I heard my teacher call me a know-it-all. She used the word 'special' like it was dirty. She predicted I would trip over my own brain one day and no one would be there to help me up because I hadn't made any friends. They said I was too smart but then laughed and said I wasn't really smart enough when it counted."

"Holy hell, Skye. That's awful."

Skye nodded. "It was. And I tried for a lot of years to fit in. I spoke even less in class, I took my time finishing worksheets, I was never the first one done. I mastered the art of looking like I was paying attention, but really I was making elaborate circuit switchboards in my head. But nothing seemed to work. All I knew was that I was too much of some things and not enough of others." Skye snorted.

"*That* has been an ongoing theme in my life," she said darkly before shaking her head. "Anyway, I started running religiously, and that helped. By junior high school, I had set up an obstacle course in the woods behind the park near our house, and I'd be out there running it at three in the morning. My parents were furious when they found out. Because I lied. So they signed me up for karate to learn self-defense and laid down some rules. My mom and dad took turns going out with me to the woods at four thirty every morning. But I wasn't allowed to go by myself."

"Your parents sound like good people."

"They are. I think I was a total puzzle to them from the very beginning. But they never made me feel like I was a burden. They offered to home-school me, but I was too intent on fitting in. And by the time I was thirteen, I planned to finish high school early and go to RMC to study computer science."

"And that's what you did."

"And that's what I did. I still had a lot of growing up to do. The army helped with that. I still didn't entirely fit in, but I made friends. Friends like family," Skye finished quietly.

"JC and Basher."

"Yes. And I accomplished my goals. I graduated top honours and pursued officer training. And I..." Skye hesitated again, then sighed. "And while I was in training, I knew what it felt like to be tired. For the first time in my life I knew what that felt like. I felt normal."

The silence and the lateness of the hour enveloped them.

"Thank you," Edie said.

"For what?"

"Telling me all that. I think it wasn't easy."

Skye held very still, then pushed her hand through her hair under her beanie, seeming to give herself a mental shake before putting her laptop down on the coffee table and sitting up. "I wanted to."

"Even though it breaks the rules."

Skye sighed. "Yes." She leaned back again in her chair and looked up into the loft space above them. "You understand why, don't you? That we can't...I can't...If I get distracted and something happens..." Her voice was jumpy now, stressed. Like she'd just remembered the mission, the threat, all the unknowns that suddenly crowded the air and the space between them.

"I know. It's okay. I get it."

"Thank you, Edie."

Her name on Skye's lips was the lightest touch, the understanding in her voice like a moment of connection or benediction. As if this moment was blessed, to be held reverently. And the physical distance between them was the only evidence that they had agreed, for now, to remain apart. Edie closed her eyes as Skye had. For now, she thought. Just for now.

CHAPTER TWELVE

Y ou *want* me to hypnotize you?"
Edie controlled her expression at Dr. Crask's condescending incredulity. She evaluated the response. It wasn't an information-seeking question, obviously. Edie had been quite clear in her explanation and request. She got the sense that Dr. Crask was thrown by the suggestion. That was fine. Edie could wait. She cast a very quick glance at JC, who sat stiffly in the chair beside her, and then at Skye, who stood with arms crossed against the back wall, her face impassive.

"Can you?" Edie said.

Dr. Crask's pencil-thin eyebrows drew down in a look of scorn.

"That's the wrong question, Ms. Black. Hypnosis is a base form of neurobiological exploration paired with the mere suggestion of psychotherapy. It's unproven and unscientific."

"So you're saying it's beneath you." Edie knew perfectly well she was baiting Crask. Prodding and poking to elicit the response she was seeking.

"I'm saying I have an ethical obligation to provide only medically sound, evidence-based therapies. Whatever you think of me, Ms. Black, you should know I will adhere stringently to these tenets of my profession."

She was making a good point, but it wasn't the answer Edie wanted.

"But we have proof, thanks to Ms. Kassis, that some form of hypnosis was used to embed information inside my head. We know that a variety of sensory tools have since been used, possibly in an attempt to extract that information. You are saying that, as a psychiatrist, you are refusing to aid me in accessing whatever is in my own head?"

"I'm saying a careful review of all the information needs to be evaluated and rigorous scientific standard needs to be applied."

Crask was hiding behind scientific jargon, hoping to throw her off. That was fine. Edie was sure of herself, too.

"I'll find someone else, then. If you're unwilling or unable to hypnotize me."

"No, you won't," Crask said with an air of triumphant superiority. "Whatever information is allegedly embedded in your head is now an issue of national security. No way will Donaldson or anyone else let you talk to a charlatan with a two-year college degree."

This was news to Edie. She broke eye contact with Crask and looked to JC, who was leaning forward with her elbows on her knees, obviously trying to stay relaxed.

"Is that true?" Edie said.

"Yes."

"So I'm stuck with this until…what? Until the federal government decides how they're going to carve it out of me?" Nobody answered. There wasn't an answer. "I want it out," Edie said forcefully. Looking first at Crask then at JC. "I want to be hypnotized, and I want it out. Now."

Edie's ultimatum was met with silence.

Dr. Crask seemed to be regarding her with a trace of grudging respect. She turned and addressed JC for the first time since they'd all sat down in the office.

"Constable Caldwell, I think we need to meet as a team and discuss Ms. Black's request. I admit her request has merit, but I want my professional objections clearly documented."

"You're right. The team is re-questioning Ms. Kassis now, verifying yesterday's statements and following up with new lines of questioning. We'll pull everyone together." She turned to Edie. "We need some time to do this right, Edie. Just give us some time."

Edie sat back in her chair, hearing the sense in JC's words but hating the inaction.

"Yes, fine."

The two women left. Edie regarded Skye, who hadn't moved from the back of the room.

"I'm guessing you agree with Dr. Crask," Edie said, sounding more petulant than she liked. She had no reason to be annoyed, not at Skye or JC, not even at Dr. Crask. Edie was off balance. She felt weighed down by the information in her head.

Skye pushed off from the wall and came to sit beside Edie. "Some of it, yes. I also think you should do it."

"Really? I thought you wanted to wrap me in bubble wrap and pack me away in Styrofoam peanuts."

Skye laughed. It was her real laugh, Edie thought. Uninhibited. It was a perfect sound.

"Well, that, too," Skye said. "But I also know you can handle yourself. You're the one who needs to make the decisions about your life, Edie. I'm sorry if I ever made you doubt that."

This, right here, would be the perfect time to kiss her. The door opened. Skye leaned away from Edie and fixed her eyes on JC and Crask as they walked in.

"It's a go," JC said. "The team was already most of the way to that decision. They were trying to figure out how to talk you into it, actually. Kenny, there was some talk of not allowing you in the room. Something about a level of clearance."

"I want her there, JC," Edie said.

"I know," JC said. "That's what I told them, and I think they've taken that into account." She didn't seem completely convinced.

"I have some conditions," Dr. Crask said. "Given your car accident and subsequent head injury, I want clearance from your neurologist."

"Okay, fine," Edie said. "Dr. Elsweth is my neurologist. I can sign consent for you to speak to him. What else?"

"You'll sign a release clearing me and the OPP from any wrongdoing and to guard against any future lawsuits."

"Yes, I'll sign. When can we get started?" Edie really didn't want to dwell on this.

"We need a smaller room, somewhere quiet," Crask said. "Free of distractions. Since I have no idea what preliminary instruction was originally used for the hypnotic induction, I will be starting from scratch."

Skye leaned forward. "Are you qualified for this?"

"Yes," Crask replied haughtily. "It may not be the most reliable form of information retrieval, but it was part of my training."

"When?" Skye said. "When was the last time you performed hypnosis?"

Dr. Crask's expression became mean. "I believe you are the muscle here, Ms. Kenny. Leave the more analytical decisions to the rest of us."

Skye never changed expressions, but JC laughed harshly. "You're not even close on this one, Di. I won't embarrass Kenny with the stats, but look up her file sometime. It makes for interesting reading."

"We're wasting time here," Crask snapped. "Caldwell, find us a room. Ms. Kenny, you can wait here."

"No." Edie and Skye spoke at the exact same time. Crask looked startled and then annoyed.

"Fine!" she said. "You want your bodyguard in the room, that's fine. Just stay out of my way," she said, storming out of the room.

"She's nervous," JC said when the door had swung shut. She looked at Edie. "Kenny wasn't out of line when she asked about her credentials. It came up at the meeting, and Crask admitted it's been ten years since she was trained in hypnosis as information retrieval and about eight since she performed one. Diana Crask does not like to be considered incompetent."

"But she can do it?" Edie said. "Is it safe?"

"She says she can."

"Do you trust her?" Skye said.

JC sighed and leaned against the corner of the desk, folding her arms over her chest. She briefly looked down the hallway where Crask had disappeared before focusing on Edie.

"Dr. Diana Crask is a woman on the way to the top in her field. She's incredibly bright and completely driven. I believe her drive to succeed is balanced by a strict adherence to an ethical code." JC grimaced. "At work, at least. So, my advice to you, Edie Black, is that if you want to proceed with the hypnosis, you should go ahead and you will be safe. But under no circumstances do I recommend dating her."

Edie laughed some of her anxiety away as JC grinned. Skye simply rolled her eyes.

"I appreciate the advice on both fronts," Edie said.

"Now, if you are looking for dating advice, I've got this old army buddy—"

"Leave it alone, Caldwell."

"All right, kids," Edie said. "Let's go dig around in my brain and see what's in there."

The words put an end to any of the lightness of the moment. Skye and JC both looked at her carefully. Edie prayed they wouldn't ask if she was sure.

"Okay," Skye said evenly. "Let's do it."

"Let's do it," JC echoed, heading toward the door. "I'll bring you the release forms and figure out the sudden objection to Kenny." She paused and looked back. "We'll both be there with you, Edie. You've got this."

Edie took a breath. She hoped JC was right.

❖

The empty office had beige walls, a small conference table with chairs shoved against one wall, and slatted blinds over the window. A one-way mirror was set into another wall, and Edie knew JC and at least two of the heads of the department were behind that glass. A padded dark blue leather chair had been procured at Crask's request and muscled into the small space. Edie tried to put the audience out of her mind.

Dr. Crask was already seated in the office. Her sharp-eyed sureness soothed some of Edie's nerves as she and Skye walked into the room.

"Ms. Black, take a seat," she said, indicating the recliner. "Ms. Kenny, I'll need you to remain out of Ms. Black's eyesight, and I will caution you now that if you interfere in any way, I'll stop the procedure and ask you to leave the room."

Skye pulled up a chair near the door, directly behind Edie and directly in Crask's line of sight.

Edie adjusted herself in the chair and took in a deep breath. Crask was a tool, a means to an end.

"I'll start by outlining the goal and the procedure," Dr. Crask said. "As you've been made aware, this session is being recorded. I will be using relaxation methods and a guided optical fixation technique. The goal is to induce an altered state of consciousness whereby I guide you, through suggestion, to access memories you are unaware, or only peripherally aware, that you have. Do you understand, Ms. Black?"

"Yes," Edie said. "Could you call me Edie? I'll find it easier."

"Of course. The scope of my questions will relate to information we believe was placed, by suggestion, into your memory during a purported massage appointment. I will ask questions regarding the physical setup of the room, the people you were with, as well as conversations that you have had. I may need to ask personal questions that you would otherwise be uncomfortable sharing." Dr. Crask paused. "Are you willing to proceed, Edie?"

"Yes."

"Then let's begin. I'll ask you to recline in your chair and close your eyes. I will guide you through a relaxation technique, but feel free to use any techniques you have found helpful in the past."

Edie tried to allow Crask's voice to dominate her thoughts. It wasn't exactly soothing, but it was even and modulated with no bumps or divots to snag Edie's thoughts. More than once Edie caught herself as her brain and body began to relax, the unconscious flinch of thinking she was falling asleep. She concentrated again on Crask's voice, on the weight of her own body in the chair. And she listened, almost unconsciously, for Skye's breathing.

"Okay, Edie, with your eyes closed, I'd like you to slowly look left and then right. Left and then right. Let your eyes feel heavy and slow as they move. Left and then right. Left and then right."

The sensation was odd and not unwelcome, this heaviness in her eyes, as if her whole body swayed in a ponderous, rhythmic dance as she looked left and then right. Left and then right. Was it her voice in her head? Or was it Crask's? It wasn't a time for questions. Left and then right. Heavy. Left and then right.

"In a moment, I'm going to take you down into your own thoughts. You will feel calm and still and safe. You will be able to hear my questions, and they will guide some of your thoughts. Soon I will snap my fingers and you will sleep and listen."

Left and then right. Heavier still.

Snap.

Weightless.

"Edie, tell me where you are. Describe it."

"I'm in my apartment. It's so beautiful." Words were effortless things. "Everything is white, and it's sunny. And there's so much dust."

"Why is there dust, Edie?"

Edie laughed, a reverberation in her chest. "Because it's Afghanistan."

"Edie, I want you to stand in your apartment and close your eyes. I'm going to ask you to take me to somewhere specific now. Can you do that?"

"Yes." She could do anything.

"I want you to stand in your apartment in Ottawa with your eyes closed. I want you to be there right before you went to your first massage appointment. Tell me when you're there, Edie."

Greens and blues instead of whites and light. The air was cold instead of warm but still sunny. Edie felt herself flinch and draw back. "The sun hurts my eyes. Hurts my head. It's hurting."

"Put on your sunglasses, Edie. The pain goes away."

Of course. Relief in her chest at such a simple solution. No sense of movement, but the pain died down. The pain was gone. She sighed.

"Who is with you, Edie? Who is going with you to the appointment?"

"Faina is coming to pick me up. She can't drive. We're going to take a cab together."

"Faina Kassis?"

"Yes."

"Is there anyone else in the apartment with you?"

"No."

"Is there anyone else in the cab with you?"

The cab swayed around the corner. "The driver."

"Okay, Edie. You're at your massage appointment. You've checked in at the desk, you've waited. Now tell me where they take you."

"The room is small and grey. The carpet is grey. The massage table is covered in sheets. There is a wood desk with a computer. It's off. An iPod on a docking station with a speaker. Papers in a folder. A plant in the corner. It's fake."

"Who is in the room with you, Edie?"

"Pino."

"Where is Faina Kassis?"

"I don't know."

"Tell me where you are during the massage."

"Lying facedown on the massage table. I'm not wearing a shirt or bra. My body is covered with a sheet. It smells like lavender. Everything smells like lavender. There is music. Sound. Water over rocks. Flute."

"Are you relaxed?"

"Yes."

"Good. Okay, Edie. You are going to stay relaxed and breathe. You are going to listen to your breathing and to the water over rocks and the flute. I am going to ask you next about the massage. First, other sounds will happen around you. Movement. Talking. Shouting. You won't hear any of it. There is no need to pay attention to it. Breathe, listen to the music, smell the lavender. Pay attention to my voice and your voice. Only my voice and your voice. Can you do that, Edie?"

Easy. So easy. Pain was nonexistent. Concern had not come with her into this room.

"Yes."

Breathe. Water over rocks, the lilt of a flute as it climbed and descended. Arms fell free, weightless and easy. Breathe.

"No, I'm not going anywhere."

That voice didn't exist. Edie wanted it to, the elusiveness of dreams.

"Ms. Kenny, I need you to come with us now."

"No."

Voices were not there. Not in this room. The scuffle, a fight, was happening somewhere else. Edie's stomach dropped, worry wormed its way through her stomach.

"I want to get up," she said.

"You can get up anytime you want, Edie. Nothing is holding you. Can you try something first?"

She was afraid. Something was missing. "Yes."

"Describe the water over rocks. Is it fast or slow?"

"Slow. Bubbling. High notes and low notes. It never stops."

"That's good. Remember, you hear only my voice and your voice right now."

"Edie—"

"My voice and your voice, Edie. No need to pay attention to anything else right now."

She wanted to. That voice was in her chest as she breathed. It was in her chest. A warmth and a weight, a touch and a reassurance. Edie did not pay attention to the door closing, but worry spiked and she put her hand over her chest to hold the voice in. She relaxed again.

"How are you feeling, Edie?"

"Calm."

"Good. Tell me what happens next?"

"Pino comes into the room. He is quiet and serious. Shy maybe. He tells me he will massage only shoulders and neck today. He changes the music. I..." Edie finds only blankness. A darkness. A gap.

"What's wrong?"

"I don't remember." The words were a whimper.

"Tell me about the music."

"Strings this time. Quite beautiful. Not a composer I recognize."

"Is there anything else different?"

A haze of light, a kind of glow. "Yes, there's a pink light. I can see it through my closed eyes. But not really. It moves slowly, and it's hard not to see it. I follow it. I feel sleepy."

"Feel sleepy like that now, Edie. It's safe."

Strings started high and drifted in smooth precision up and down the scale. The glow seemed to follow. Edie watched and slept. New voices.

"I hear voices. Words. Can I hear the voices in my head?"

"Yes, Edie. You can hear the voices in your head. Tell me what they are saying."

"No."

"Can you still hear the voices?"

"Yes."

"Good. You can tell me what they are saying."

"I can't."

"Edie, what are they saying?"

Her head hurt. She pressed her hand to her chest. Where was she?

"Edie, you are going to breathe in while you count to four, then breathe out as you count to four."

That voice was not the warm voice in her chest, but she paid attention to it. She followed the command.

"Where are you, Edie?"

"Lying on the massage table."

"Good. What are you hearing?"

"Music. And poetry."

"Do you like poetry?"

"Yes. I used to read it a long time ago."

"Did you ever memorize poetry?"

"Yes."

"Tell me the poem you're hearing, Edie."

She wanted to speak but struggled.

"The strings are playing, aren't they, Edie?"

"Yes."

"Listen to the strings and tell me the poem."

They went together. That was okay. "The savageness of man lies not in the actions but in the echoes of silent history."

"Very good. Tell me the rest."

"Fortune has no will where flowers refuse the fertile soil of deliberate thought."

"Keep going, Edie."

"Waves can tell lies as oceans undermine the sanctity of every natural law."

"Excellent. Keep going."

"Men who do not falter as they lie know not the hearts of a truth-speaking nation."

"Well done, Edie. Tell me the rest."

A blank. A break. A greyness.

"There is nothing else."

"Is there a key to the poem?"

"I don't know."

"Is there a way to unlock it?"

"I don't know."

"Did the voice tell you anything else?"

The blankness and greyness. Fog. "No."

"Is the voice still there?"

"No."

"What do you feel?"

"The sheet covering my shoulders."

"Is there anyone else in the room?"

"No, I'm alone."

"Okay, Edie. When I snap my fingers, you are going to wake a different part of your brain. You will remember everything that happened. You will remember that you have been safe. All your memories are still your own."

Snap.

Edie opened her eyes. The light in the room seemed dimmer. She had an odd sense of time having passed without her being aware of it. But her thoughts were clear and sharp. Then a wave of anxiety hit her in the chest and she locked eyes with Dr. Crask before looking behind her. Skye's chair was empty.

"Where's Skye?" she said.

Crask put up a hand.

"Let me complete the session, Ms. Black. Can you tell me where you are?"

Her modulated voice was a smoothness that made Edie suddenly angry. "I'm in the fucking OPP Headquarters, my name is Edie Black, you are Dr. Diana Crask, it is Thursday afternoon, and I want to know where Skye Kenny is right this instant."

Dr. Crask's looked quickly at the one-way mirror and then back to Edie. She seemed oddly subdued. Uncertain.

"You shouldn't have been able to hear that. When she left. I successfully induced an altered state, you were responding to suggestion. We retrieved...something. But you shouldn't have been able to hear that."

Edie said nothing. She sat very still. It was stillness or screaming right now.

Dr. Crask looked back at the window. "We're done."

Edie turned to the door when it opened, needing to see Skye's tousled, messy hair, her long stride as she crossed the room, the laser focus of her gaze. But Superintendent Donaldson walked into the room.

"We have some questions for you regarding the information you just shared under hypnosis. Are you well enough now, or do you need a break?"

The conciliatory tone, the vague assumption of frailty, the condescending look was nearly more than Edie could stomach. She swallowed the torrent of anger and accusations and channeled the energy into what she needed. Information.

"I am perfectly well, thank you. I am not, however, open to being questioned after you broke our agreement for Ms. Kenny to remain with me anytime I was being questioned."

Donaldson was clearly unhappy with her language. "There was no official agreement, Ms. Black."

Edie smiled. It was cold. "Hide behind that if it makes you feel better. It was an agreement. You broke it. I have nothing to say."

Donaldson flicked his gaze to the one-way mirror and back again. Edie tried not to think about the number of eyes and camera lenses directed at her right now.

"Ms. Kenny has not been cleared at this level of the investigation—"

"That's your problem, not mine. And it existed when you agreed to allow her to be part of this."

"The information is a matter of national security, Ms. Black." Donaldson was clearly losing his patience.

"Yes, I believe it is," Edie said calmly. As he escalated, she relaxed. She could handle obstinate all day. "And unless you can find a specific, plausible, and ironclad reason why Skye Kenny should be barred from continuing to do the job I have hired her to do, this matter of national security is getting no help from me."

She was gambling. As Donaldson stewed over her ultimatum, Edie considered the fact that maybe she had very little else to contribute to this investigation. She got the sense Dr. Crask had guided her through revealing everything she knew. But Donaldson didn't know that.

"I'll be back," Donaldson said tersely, and he left the room.

Dr. Crask still had the look of uncertainty as she regarded Edie. Edie held her gaze but didn't speak.

"I would not have agreed to them removing Ms. Kenny if I believed it would cause you stress. I truly did not anticipate that reaction. I should have. I hope you will accept my apology."

Strict ethics, that's what JC had said. Edie appreciated Crask taking responsibility for an error and her public, even documented, apology. But she wasn't sure she was ready to forgive.

"I would have pulled you out if you'd continued to show an elevated stress level," Crask continued. "Regardless of what I was asked to do. But you were able to calm down, and I made the professional judgment to continue."

Edie recognized how skillfully Crask had guided her through the hypnosis. She was left with the clarity of a dream and an odd awareness of having been present and not. Even with Crask's skill, it was sensing Skye that had helped her descend. It was the feel of Skye in her chest that she'd held on to, the voice that had become breath along with her breath as she'd twisted through panic in her hypnotic state. She'd felt her inside. Edie put her hand to her chest, mimicking the motion she'd made while she was under. Right there. Skye was right there. How? How had she let her in, so close, already? A mistake, maybe. Among so many mistakes. Was this simply a reaction to stress? A lifeline, not love.

Edie stood quickly and walked to the covered windows. With a quick, jerky movement she pulled up the blinds, searching the cloudy sky and cityscape for an answer. She didn't see one.

"You said 'regardless of what you were asked to do,'" Edie said, turning to Crask. She needed to refocus, solve a solvable problem. "I'd like you to tell me what they asked you to do."

"I informed you at the beginning of our session the goal of the hypnotic induction," Crask said, a little authority returning to her tone and posture. "All questions were directed at that goal."

"It was recorded."

"Yes."

"I'd like to see it," Edie said. "Beginning to end."

"You'll have to ask Donaldson."

Edie's gut said Crask was skillfully maneuvering her around something. Sleight of hand, the suggestion to look elsewhere.

"Just before you pulled me out, you said I would remember everything. That my memories would still be my own."

Crask nodded.

"You didn't have to do that. You could have removed the whole episode."

"Absolutely not," Crask said, clearly affronted. "I could not ethically remove memories from you without your permission. Even *with* your permission."

"But you were asked to, weren't you? By Donaldson or someone else." She waved vaguely toward the mirror without looking at it. She didn't care who heard.

Crask's lips thinned, and she said nothing. Edie hadn't really expected her to, but her body language was confirmation enough. Edie looked back out the window, and the two women waited in complete silence.

Nearly ten minutes later, the door opened again. Donaldson

stood in the doorway and indicated with a jerk of his head that Crask should exit. She made no acknowledgement of Edie as she left. Then Donaldson stood aside and allowed Skye to enter the room before closing the door behind her.

Skye looked murderous. From the spark of fury in her eyes and the set of her shoulders to the way she moved across the room as if hunting prey. Edie held up a trembling hand. She didn't want Skye to come any closer. She needed distance, recognizing how easy she found it to be pulled into the force field of Skye's protective energy. Wasn't that all it was?

Skye stopped in the middle of the room at Edie's nonverbal request.

"They took me out. I didn't know how much I should fight. You were already agitated, and I didn't want to make it worse." Skye poured out words like a confession.

"I know. It's all right."

"It's not," Skye said darkly.

"Where did they take you?" Edie said. Stick to facts. Seek information.

"Down the hall. JC was back there," Skye said, indicating the mirror. "I had to trust she'd watch out for you. I'm sorry, Edie. I should have fought. I should have anticipated the fuckers would do this."

"I've asked to see the video footage, but if JC witnessed the whole session, then that's good enough for me." Edie needed confirmation from JC that she remembered everything. Her gut said Crask had told her the truth, that she would not have taken any of Edie's memory of the hypnosis session. But Edie needed to be certain.

"Are you okay?"

"I'd like to see JC." She turned to the mirror and raised her voice. "I'd like to see Constable Caldwell."

"Edie?" Skye took a step closer.

Edie shook her head and took a step back. Skye looked bewildered, hurt, and then her expression closed down. Soldier Skye. Alert and impassive. Immovable.

A moment later, JC stepped into the room. She looked pissed. "Edie, I'm sorry. I didn't know they were going—"

"It doesn't matter." Edie was sick to death of apologies. "Did you witness the entire hypnosis session? From the time I entered the room until Dr. Crask brought me out again. Did you see it?"

"Yes. I saw it all."

"Good. Then I'd like to sit down with Donaldson. Or whoever is calling the shots. I'm ready to talk about what we just figured out I've been carrying around and what we're going to do with it."

JC and Skye both observed her with calculating expressions. Edie refused to shrink under their combined gazes. She felt strong, maybe a little shaky at her core, but she had the will and the presence of mind and the energy to move forward. As JC looked at Skye, shrugged, then led the way out of the office, Edie rested in her conviction that nothing was going to stop her.

CHAPTER THIRTEEN

I'm going to stop you right there, Ms. Black."

Edie sighed. Whatever three-day course Donaldson had taken twenty years ago on how to resolve a conflict situation wasn't working, and his inefficiency aggravated Edie almost as much as his condescension.

"What are you objecting to this time?" Edie said.

They'd already been at this for an hour. Donaldson from the RCMP combined forces, Petrie from the Canadian Firearms Program, JC, Crask, and Edie. Skye, who had said absolutely nothing, just hovered like a dark cloud at the back of the room, both threatening and comforting. They were trying to discern the meaning to the lines of verse Edie had delivered during her hypnosis. The team was convinced Edie had also been given a key to the code, or had been in the presence of said key.

"We have to make absolutely certain we have retrieved all information, Ms. Black. We cannot move forward without that understanding."

"But why not move forward with what you've got?"

She was fully serious, but Donaldson and Petrie were looking at her like she was dense.

Edie sighed and tried again. "Look, I gave you those lines of verse, but I don't know what they mean. And I really don't think I have the key."

"I think Ms. Black is right," JC said, sitting forward in her seat. "It's shitty security to keep the key with the lock."

"Then we're stuck," Petrie said, throwing his pen on the desk and leaning back. "Until our guys can crack this code with what we've got."

They wanted different things, that was clear. Now that Edie had the information out of her head, she wanted whoever put it there captured. She wanted freedom. For herself and for Faina.

If the lines of verse were really linked to illegal arms trade, law enforcement wanted dates, times, and locations of a drop. They wanted quantity and types of arms.

Something didn't make sense. The information was linked to Alex Rada. The people who had attacked them in the alley were linked to Alex Rada. But he was the one who had put the information in Edie's head in the first place. Which meant they didn't need Edie to get the information back. They needed Edie to protect the lock and key.

"They're protecting the technology," Edie said, speaking mostly to herself. "The concept of embedding information in the human brain. It's proprietary. And next to useless if law officials are aware of its existence."

"Aware of its existence, maybe," Dr. Crask said, picking up Edie's thread. "But that's not helpful when no one knows who may be carrying information. You didn't know for months." It sounded like an accusation, but Edie ignored the tone.

"True. It's the benefit of the technology, isn't it? It could be anyone."

"But they need hypnosis to embed it and retrieve it?" Crask said.

"I don't know about that," Edie said. "Embed it, yes. *We* used hypnosis to retrieve it. But maybe…" She trailed off, unsure where her thoughts were taking her.

"They wanted to know how else the data could be retrieved," Skye said from across the room. She hadn't moved, still leaning against the wall with her arms crossed over her chest. But her eyes were alight, sparked by a problem to be solved. "The sensory tests—the lights and the drumbeat at the bar—they weren't keys to understand the code, they were testing keys to see which would unlock the safe. And it worked. You heard those words in some form after the incident at the bar. They unlocked it using that drumbeat."

Keys and locks. And treasure. If you were hiding treasure in a safe, it made sense to know who could duplicate the key. But what did the Russian want with her? Why *take*?

Edie's stomach dropped. She felt suddenly cold, and the brightness of the room dimmed briefly before lighting up again in a disorienting pulse of sensation.

"They don't need me for information."

"What do you mean, Edie?" JC said.

Edie was having trouble pulling the thought and words together. Linking her brain to locks and keys. To being followed. The drumbeat was a heavy bass thunder no one else seemed to hear.

"Take it easy," JC said. "Whatever you just figured out, take it easy. Take a full breath. When you're ready, let us know what you're thinking."

Edie wanted the words out, she wanted proof. She wanted this over. Edie looked back over her shoulder at Skye, who had taken a step away from the wall but seemed frozen in place. Edie pushed down the ache in her chest. This was very nearly too much. She closed her eyes, felt the pull of the words she wanted to say, rearranged them, then opened her eyes again.

"We know Alex Rada is not after me to get the information in my head because he put it there. He is after me to prevent your locksmiths from inspecting the lock and discovering the safe technology that he's developed. He wants to keep the lock out of your hands. He doesn't intend to let me live."

Her theory was met with silence. Donaldson and Petrie exchanged glances. JC looked at her with a concerned and calculating expression, Dr. Crask with a grudging approval. Edie could not bear to look at Skye.

"So, if you want to continue to crack the code of what the verse means, be my guest. You'll excuse me if my focus remains on how to extricate myself from this situation unscathed."

Edie stood, proud her voice had remained steady and her hands didn't visibly tremble.

"Is there somewhere I can go?" She looked at JC. "I just need a break. Outside?"

"Good idea, come on," JC said, standing and leading Edie out of the room. Skye quickly followed, and they made their way through headquarters. JC took them up three flights of stairs at the back of the building, and then she pushed open a door with a neon yellow sign that warned them to keep out.

Edie welcomed the wash of air over her face as she stepped onto the graveled, dirty surface of the half roof. Fans whirred and generators hummed through the thick smell of city and oil. Edie didn't care. She wasn't inside the office. Wasn't inside *that* office, trapped with the knowledge that someone wanted her dead.

"God." Edie doubled over and tried not to throw up.

JC got to her first, putting a reassuring hand on her back. Skye joined her seconds later, a gentle touch on the back of Edie's neck. Edie didn't move, just breathed and anchored herself in JC and Skye's strength. Their combined touch kept the panic at bay.

"Sorry," she muttered, straightening but keeping her eyes closed. A gust of wind hit her face and cleared her thoughts. The fact that Alex Rada wanted her dead was one piece of information. It had been true for weeks. It could help them move forward. That was where Edie needed to focus.

"Don't worry about it," Skye said. Her voice sounded stilted. Edie felt the distance and knew she'd created it.

Edie gently extricated herself from their grip. "Thanks. Both of you. I…just got overwhelmed."

Skye stared at the pebbled ground. JC blew out a short, frustrated breath before answering. "No problem. Really. We should have called for a break earlier." She checked her watch. "Actually, why don't I get Faina and bring her up? She's probably due for a break as well." With a meaningful glance at her fire buddy, JC took the roof access.

Edie knew neither Donaldson nor Petrie trusted Faina enough to allow her to sit in on the brainstorming sessions. Instead, Edie imagined she'd been getting a similar interrogation to Edie. Trying to find what Faina knew of poetry and the illegal arms trade. Under any other circumstances, she and Faina would laugh at that.

"What's so funny?" Skye said, obviously having heard Edie's snort.

"This whole situation. Their questions. The fact that two hours ago I spouted poetry under hypnosis. The knowledge that someone wants me dead." Edie shook her head. "There's a definite element of the ridiculous here."

"Not the word I would have chosen."

Edie hadn't expected Skye to get it. Capable Skye, the one with the skills and the intelligence to take on Russian arms dealers who wanted her dead. She could lay out a mission, collect intelligence, identify weakness, and build fortification. She could execute a plan. But that wasn't the way Edie lived her life.

She gathered information and burrowed deeper and asked questions until she understood. She connected with a story, a person, a country, an idea. She looked for the interesting, the ridiculous, the curious, the heart. And she pursued impulses, finding out where she fit, staying with a story or an event until she'd learned what she needed to learn. Until her gut told her it was time to move on.

They were so different, Edie concluded. So very, very different.

"You're angry at me, aren't you?"

Skye had launched her question into cyberspace, the cursor blinking, waiting for a response.

"No. Nothing that happened was your fault."

Skye stopped scanning the surrounding buildings. "Fault is one thing. Result is another."

It may have been the most revealing thing Skye had ever said. Edie felt the urge to ask, to dig and burrow deeper into the vulnerability Skye had just revealed. Yesterday she would have. But right now Edie felt cautious, as if she was incapable of holding on to any more pieces of Skye.

They stood in uneasy silence until the rooftop door opened again and JC emerged with Faina. JC looked between Edie and Skye, possibly evaluating their distance and their silence.

Faina looked exhausted, but she held her head high and her back straight, as if her posture could keep her from sagging under the weight of the interrogation and the suspicion. Maybe it would. Faina was still standing.

"How are you holding up?" Edie said.

"I keep trying to tell myself that my patience and consistency in responses is what will get me out of this mess. But it gets harder and harder to remember as the day wears on."

"Sorry this is so shitty," Edie said. An inadequate response, but truthful.

"Yes, shitty is the right word for it." Faina cracked a smile. "And while I was betraying my startling lack of knowledge of the illegal arms trade, I understand you were giving a poetry performance."

The explosion of laughter was exactly what Edie needed, a forced exodus of toxicity. They both grinned and laughed. Neither felt the need to explain or apologize for her response. They were simply friends sharing a weight, taking the burden of the other person's trouble and releasing their own. Everything became lighter in that split second of laughter.

The laughter died down as awareness of their situation returned.

"They're asking you about those lines of poetry, aren't they?" Edie said.

"Yes. I'm not sure they believe me when they said I don't know them. And that no one I lived with here spoke poetry, especially not English poetry, around me. I did share that it was a love of my father's, both my parents actually. I had always liked the fact that both my parents were gifted with words and language. They did not raise me together, but I felt it was something that bound us." Faina kept her eyes on Edie as she talked, none of the hunched shoulders and dropped voice of the past when she talked about her family. Still, the sadness of her loss of connection was palpable.

"What about Alex and Yana?" Edie said.

"Nothing as whimsical as poetry for Alex and Yana. Alex is military to the core, and Yana is a scientist." Faina shook her head. "They tell me Yana has disappeared. Left her post at the university in Kiev. They can find no trace of her." Faina gave herself a small shake and pulled herself away from her past. "They are very intent on this code, aren't they? These police and agents and what have you. Maybe, though…"

"Maybe what?"

"Maybe we are done?" Her hopeful tone tore at Edie's heart. Faina rushed on. "Now that the information has been retrieved, and maybe if they begin to believe that I know nothing…Maybe we are done. We can leave this behind."

Edie wanted to leave behind the knowledge that someone had taken advantage of her weakest moment, had invaded the space in her head and manipulated her memories. That they wanted her dead. And when Edie looked up into Faina's pleading, brown eyes, she wanted to leave behind the knowledge of what had been done to her friend. They'd seized her life, used their connection as family to gain advantage. Kept her hidden and scared. The evidence of her defiance was still visible on her face and neck. Edie wanted to tell Faina it was over. But she wouldn't lie.

Faina seemed to read the truth in Edie's expression. She closed her eyes and tilted her head back, as if sending up a prayer for strength or guidance or simply the will to continue. Edie expected tears from Faina, though she'd only ever broken down once. What she saw when Faina opened her eyes, however, was not defeat. It was a fervor, the long sight of a mission and the absolute belief that it would be fulfilled.

"They are asking me the wrong questions," Faina said. "Locations and dates, type of weapons and ammunitions, transportation and warehouses. These are things I do not know. But I do know where to find them. I do know how they wanted me to make a connection with you, track you even. And I do believe that before I ran, before Constable Caldwell took me away, their plan was to capture you. I was to be part of that plan."

"And your resistance cost you those bruises," Edie said evenly. They were talking, finally. They needed this.

"Yes. The presence of Skye made them desperate. They could not track you on your phone. You stopped going to your apartment. You changed all your patterns, and they had no access to you."

"I'm no use to them as a safe of information if I am aware of it."

"Or even if you are suspicious. Your behavior was suspicious."

"Right," Edie said. She didn't want Faina to come to the next conclusion. All she knew was that she wasn't strong enough to say it out loud. It didn't matter, Faina connected the pieces as Edie had done earlier.

"No," she said quietly. "This is why *take*. This is why contact became vital. Not for access. For…"

"Retrieval," Edie said. "Capture. I think they want me…gone."

"No," Faina said, her voice shaky. "Say the truth of it, Edie. They want you dead. This is the conclusion you have reached. This is something you know."

Edie swallowed against the fear that pressed onto her vocal cords, her chest. "Yes."

"This will not happen," Faina said, the tone of her fervor matching the fire in her eyes. "That may be the goal, but many barriers are in their way." She nodded toward JC and Skye, who stood talking intently only ten feet away. "We will come up with a plan. And *then* it will be over. And we will both be free."

Steps to an achievable goal. Edie focused on that. "We?" she said, letting a smile surface.

"It will have to be our team of women," Faina said, her eyes lighting up. "The boys seem intent on war games and guns. Our goals are different. I say we make a plan."

Edie looked to Skye, her protector and guardian. She would probably not approve of this plan.

"Tell me what you're thinking," Edie said.

"We need the head of the snake, and we need it now. The authorities want information. They want to catch as many as they can in their net as they pull it in. Fine, we can use that. I say we propose to meet with Alex. I should make contact."

"What are you approaching him with?" Edie said. "What's your hook?"

"What does he want from me, I wonder?" Faina said, obviously to herself. "I am no longer useful, in fact I am a liability. He wants only to silence me. But he thinks I am only scared, that I have no connection. That I have no protection. So maybe he thinks I am asking him for safety. That I will exchange what I know of the investigation for my immigration papers. My passport. The tools I need to disappear from the authorities who are treating me badly." She paused and looked at the ground, then up at Edie. "Do you think he will buy it?"

"I'm not sure it's enough," Edie said. "Realistically, he wants both of us silenced. We need to give him the opportunity to do that." At Faina's look of protest, she clarified. "We need to make him think he has the opportunity to do that. If he needs access, we give him access."

Faina nodded slowly. "Yes. But why would you approach him? What possible reason could you have?"

"We tell him I want it out. We tell him just enough to let him know we have some of the information but I want the rest out. We tell him it hurts, and that the police won't believe me. That they're treating me like I'm crazy. We tell him…"

Edie saw it then, the entire scene in her head. She arranged and rearranged it, but she was very, very sure he would fall for this. "We tell him I want to recreate the scene where it takes place. If he believes the police don't yet know everything, he might agree to this meet.

Especially if we can convince him we are doing this without their knowledge."

When Edie looked up, she could see JC and Skye watching them intently. "We should tell them," she said. "JC and Skye."

"Agreed."

"You two look like you're plotting," JC said as she and Skye joined them.

"I guess we are," Faina said. "I think I should make contact with Alex and bring him out into the open so he can be captured and this can be stopped."

Both of them met Faina's declaration with a shocked silence.

"Let me complete the thought before you give us reasons why this is not a workable plan," Faina continued. As Faina laid out their admittedly half-formed plan, Edie had to admire her friend's strength. Faina was unapologetic in her approach as she discussed the goal, the risk, and the ultimate pay-off in the end.

As Faina spoke, Edie watched as Skye became more and more agitated. She was completely unsettled by this plan. By the time Faina had summarized their plan, JC looked thoughtful and Skye was shaking.

"What's your plan for making contact?" JC said to Faina.

Before Faina had a chance to answer, Skye's restless agitation boiled over.

"You can't possibly be thinking of approving this?" Skye said. "This plan has no tactical merit. It's a terrible fucking idea."

"It does have merit," JC said evenly. "If you'd put away your feelings for Edie for just one goddamn minute, maybe you'd be able to see that this plan could achieve a number of goals. Including keeping both Faina and Edie safe. Long-term safe."

Skye clenched her jaw and flexed her hands. In that moment, she was a dangerous creature, cornered and captured, ready to bite any hand that came near her, captor or rescuer. Skye spun on her heel and stalked to the edge of the roof. Edie watched as she braced her arms on the concrete half wall and hung her head down. Everything about her was tight and stressed. Edie wished she had something to offer, but she knew with absolute certainty she did not. She turned back to find JC watching her.

"I know," Edie said, responding to JC's advice before she had a chance to give it. "She'll come around faster if we leave her alone."

JC looked surprised, then amused. "Skye has no chance against you," she said before refocusing on Faina. "We'll talk about what you're proposing, but I need you to know this has to go through the proper channels. I need authority and clearance and support on this." She looked between Edie and Faina. "And I need both of you to promise that you're not going to go rogue."

"Because you would lose your job if we did," Faina said. "We won't risk that."

JC looked startled. "No," she said. "I mean, yes, but that's not why I'm asking for your promise. We don't have enough manpower, even using Skye's security contacts, to cover a plan like you are proposing. And I won't put either of you at risk. It's either aboveboard and fully resourced, or it doesn't happen."

Edie and Faina exchanged a quick look.

"Promise," Edie said.

"Yes, I agree also."

Edie heard the soft grinding of gravel as Skye approached. She looked more in control, though no less stressed.

"I'd like to hear your plan for making contact with Alex Rada," she said.

"At the laundromat," Faina said immediately. "He knows the owner. I can have a message delivered there and explain I want to meet. Tell him I have Edie with me, that she wants him to re-hypnotize her to get the information out."

"Would you ask to meet him there?" JC said.

"No," Skye said. "The massage therapy office."

"He will remain suspicious," Faina warned, "no matter what story I give him. He will believe the police are part of it, setting this up."

"We just need to get him there," Skye said. "We just need him to believe he has the opportunity." She blinked rapidly. "You will tell him I'll be there. That I'm hired help to ensure nothing happens. He already knows about me, knows where I live, knows I'm protecting Edie. Let him think we're three women acting on our own. Let him believe you are scared."

"Exactly," Faina said, and the fervor was back in her voice again. She and Skye were nearly on the same page, figuring out how to manipulate Alex Rada, use his own ego against him.

"Okay," JC said, clapping her hands together, breaking the spell of victory before they were even off the roof. "I'm taking this down to the team. I need to spin this plan so that it targets their goal and ours. I think we might have something. Maybe we can start today."

The word "today" hung in the air. It stood for urgency, completion. There was movement and progress. Edie liked the word. It felt good. Even the thrill of fear made her feel alive and present in her own body. She looked at Faina and JC, felt their resolve and support. And she made herself look at Skye's tension and focus.

This is what we are, Edie said to herself. No matter what JC said, they were security guard and client. They were connected only by circumstance and Skye's abilities and sense of duty. She was suddenly embarrassed by the way she'd been pushing Skye to be something they weren't. To make this about more than the stress of their situation. But whatever they may have had was gone, snuffed out by the twisted plans of a criminal. And as Skye followed her from a respectful distance off the roof of the building, Edie swallowed the idea of what could have been.

CHAPTER FOURTEEN

The message was delivered to the laundromat an hour ago."
JC turned away from the window in Skye's loft, still tapping in a frenzy on her phone. She was coordinating from afar, and her stress was obvious. Or at least it was to Edie, who sat next to Faina on the couch. Two boxes of pizza, napkins, and beer dominated the table.

"I still think I should have gone," Faina said, delicately wiping her fingers on a take-out napkin.

"High risk with low reward," Skye said from across the table. She'd continued to be relatively quiet the rest of the day, adding her opinion and offering advice in her clear, direct way then retreating to her back corner of comfort. As if she really was just the hired help, as she'd referred to herself earlier. Edie was not comfortable with their distance, but she wasn't comfortable with their proximity, either. "You and Edie easily could have found a messenger. It supports our story and keeps you away from the Russians."

"Until tomorrow," Faina said quietly.

"Until tomorrow," JC confirmed, dropping her phone on the table and grabbing her first slice of pizza. "Skye's going to hook us up so we can virtually attend the team meeting early tomorrow morning. We've got a team mobilizing at the massage therapy clinic right now, so we'll know entry and exit and who's covering."

"We're assuming we're being watched right now, aren't we?" Faina said.

"We know we're being watched," Skye said. "And we're using that to our advantage."

"How?" Edie said.

Skye was remote. Present but not. Soldier Skye.

"We're going to corroborate our own story. They know we're here, they know JC has been staying here. So around two in the morning, they'll see JC leave. And a couple hours later, they'll see you and Faina and I look like we're sneaking past the two sets of cops staked out around my apartment. They'll report back to Alex Rada that we're on the move and heading toward our four o'clock meet."

"And they'll follow us to the clinic," Faina said.

"That's right," JC said, reaching for more pizza. "Where we'll already be set up."

Faina looked at Edie. "We can do this."

Edie wasn't so sure. But if Faina could take this on, so could she.

Edie tuned out as the conversation continued. The pizza was sitting like a stone in her stomach. She was tired and she was nervous. She'd been questioned and manipulated and talked down to all day. She'd been under hypnosis with someone else guiding her through her own memory. She'd had Skye in her chest, perilously close to her heart. Edie looked at Skye, who was focused on the conversation, her eyes bright with excitement over a plan that needed to be executed. This was where Skye belonged. This was where Skye wanted to be. Not finding her way into Edie's every thought. Not extricating herself from Edie's heart when Edie could not tell the difference between love and loyalty.

Edie stood and quietly began gathering the plates and pizza boxes and napkins. She needed out, some time on her own. Maybe she could find a book, get lost in someone else's world for a little while. She cleaned up their take-out meal, washed her hands in the sink, and found her way back to Skye's extensive bookcase.

It was lit with spotlights, and the darkness of the back of the vaulted loft made Edie feel closed in and protected. Even the murmuring of the continued conversation in the living room seemed muted. Edie couldn't see any order to Skye's collection. Fiction and nonfiction, worn paperbacks and stiffly bound academic texts. Coding tomes and Can Lit. A series of science-fiction novels with jewel-toned spines next to a textbook on superstructures in major US cities. *Autobiography of a para-Olympian, Jurassic Park, The Art of War, The Lord of the Rings.* Edie found herself smiling at the number and breadth of books, the sheer magnitude of Skye's intellect and interest. She could get lost here.

Edie was putting a book back on the shelf when she heard a sound behind her. Faina joined her at the bookcase.

"I'm worried about you," Faina said.

Edie snorted. "Join the club." She wanted humour to dull the edges of what she was feeling. Sleight of hand is what Dr. Wallace called it. An illusion of coping, not an actual strategy. Edie wished she could see Dr. Wallace. She'd welcome an hour of dismantling the ragged, cobbled-together shell of her self-protection right now.

"I'd like to ask about you and Skye," Faina said, ignoring Edie's sad attempt at deflecting.

Edie rubbed at her eyes. "What would you like to know?"

"You like her."

"That's not a question."

Faina raised an eyebrow. Edie sighed. "Yes. We had a date, before all this blew up. Then she made it clear nothing else was going to happen. And now it's too late, even when all this is over. If it's ever over. I can't see how we're supposed to get past knowing each other through this."

Edie and Faina both flinched as security alarms blared their warnings and monitors suddenly came to life next to them in Skye's office. Alerts and signals mixed with JC's yelling and the sound of rapid footsteps through the loft. Skye appeared suddenly out of the dark, tapping at her watch, her expression stony.

"Multiple security alerts," Skye said, her tone clipped. "Could be a breach. Follow me."

Fear spiked adrenaline through Edie's body, but she quickly obeyed the command. Skye brought them to the very back of the loft, up against the climbing wall. Part of the wall was built out, creating an overhang for free-climbing. Skye moved them in and behind this jut-out to a tiny, dark alcove. Light from the rest of the loft was cut off, and the only real illumination came from Skye's watch face, which still pulsed with alerts.

"I need you both to stay here until JC or I come to get you. Only us. I don't care who's in a uniform." Faina and Edie stood silently as Skye looked between them. "This might be nothing. Stay here. Stay quiet."

Then she left without another command or another glance. The package had been placed and secured, and the rest of the mission had to be executed. Skye was efficient and utterly in control. And now gone. Edie could not swallow the fear. The darkness pressed on her, worse once the other lights in the loft were dimmed until darkness and silence permeated the entire, massive space. The silence was more oppressive than the darkness.

Faina slipped her hand into Edie's and squeezed. Edie closed her eyes and listened to the sound of Faina breathing beside her and the steady, slow thrum of the fans overhead.

Edie barely swallowed a curse of panic at the crash above them. She pressed against Faina's shoulder as they listened to the sound of running through the loft, boots on metal stairs, another crash followed by a thud, then shouting and a gunshot that cracked so loud Edie couldn't hold back a gasp. She ducked and cowered and swore, gripping Faina's hand tighter.

Shouting above, thuds, and then beams of light that arced over the loft, yells Edie could not distinguish though she strained to hear the familiarity of a voice, a tone, a word. Soon sirens blared outside, more arced lights, more boots on the floor. But no more crashing or thuds, no more gunshots. Radios talked along with the sirens, the presence of a cavalry of officers Edie so desperately wanted to believe meant that they were safe.

But where was Skye? Who discharged the weapon they'd heard? Edie could spin and rework the story so many times in her head. So many ways her heart could break.

Lights came on in the loft, their glow barely lighting the alcove. They were still gripping each other's hands when they heard officers calling to each other, then calling to Edie and Faina. Faina shook her head. They would wait for JC or Skye.

Edie heard footsteps approaching.

"They're back here." JC's voice. "We'll bring them out."

Faina let out a ragged breath. In a moment the climbing area was lit up, then Skye appeared at the entrance to their hiding spot.

"It's clear. We're clear," Skye said. Edie didn't understand. Why didn't she say "safe"?

Skye didn't move, still blocking the entrance. Her eyes were wild. Edie had expected a steely calm from soldier Skye, but Skye looked barely under control, as if something raged inside her.

JC appeared over Skye's shoulder. She touched Skye lightly. Skye flinched, then blinked.

"Let them out, Thrush. Danger's passed."

"We need to get them out of the city."

"That's not—"

"It's not safe here." Skye bit off each word.

"Yes, it is," JC said carefully. "We'll see to that."

Skye still stood in the entry, looking back and forth between Edie and Faina.

"You need to let them out. Now." JC's voice seemed to cut through whatever haze had overtaken Skye.

Skye hesitated for another second, then moved to the side. Faina ducked out first, then Edie. Skye was stone, utterly untouchable. Edie had never been afraid of her, but she understood how others might be.

Edie followed Faina's back blindly until she heard Skye call out behind her. "Kitchen. I want them away from the windows."

Edie heard JC sigh and change course, taking them into the now brightly lit kitchen.

"What happened?" Edie asked JC.

JC was about to answer when a uniformed cop came in from the living room.

"Caldwell, we're looking for an ID on the Russian asshole upstairs, and we hear you might know someone who knows him."

Faina stiffened beside Edie.

"Take five seconds to read this scene, you piddling shit for brains, and try that again," JC said to the young cop.

"Sorry, Constable Caldwell. I didn't know the civilians…sorry."

"Try again."

"When you have a moment, the guys upstairs need you."

"Better. Two minutes."

The cop shifted his weight, looking uneasily at Skye's furious expression. "And we need the homeowner's help. We need to check all the access points, and there are a million in this old building."

JC looked at Skye, who gave a short, sharp shake of her head. JC looked annoyed but answered the cop.

"Two minutes," she repeated, dismissing him with a gesture.

"Who is it?" Faina said when they were alone.

"We don't know. Two people attempted to enter the building through the ceiling in the second story of the building next door. Skye's security alerted us in time to catch one of them as he attempted to access the upstairs apartment. He fired on us as soon as we entered the corridor. Shot went into the wall, no one was hurt. The second assailant got away, and neither of the street crews were able to pick him up."

Edie processed it all in small chunks. JC's retelling sanitized the event somehow. As if the facts could erase the image of Skye running full out toward a man with a gun. Because she knew, even without JC's account, that's exactly what had happened. Edie gripped the stainless steel countertop with both hands, staring at the brushed pattern in the metal. She forced herself to breathe and be present for this.

"Faina, I'm going to ask you to come down to the station and identify the man we have in custody." JC's voice was no longer commanding or neutral. She was careful and calm and soothing. "We need to know what you know. If you can identify the second man from the security camera image as well, that would be helpful."

"Yes, of course," Faina said immediately. "I'm ready. But does this affect the plan for tomorrow in any way?"

JC tilted her head back and forth. "It's too early to tell. One thing at a time, okay?"

"Yes, I'm sorry. Okay."

JC gave a tired smile. "Nothing to apologize for. Let me check with the guys upstairs, and I'll come and get you." JC turned her attention to Skye, who stood stiffly still in the area between the kitchen and living room. "I need you to check in with Sergeant Tremblay about securing the building."

"Fuck that," Skye spit out. "They can secure the building when we're gone. You follow your protocols, I'm getting Edie the hell out of here."

Edie looked closer at Skye, whose eyes never seemed to stop scanning and assessing for danger before moving on. She seemed deep into a kind of hypervigilance, different than any other protective mode Edie had seen her in before. JC seemed to clue in as well that something was very wrong with Skye.

"Thrush, I need you to break this down for me. Break down the security here for me, assuming you get everything online. Assuming you stay with two, no, three sets of patrols outside. Go."

It was a command, from one tactical officer to another. And it worked. Skye barked out a list of access points, security measures and potential upgrades, identifying weaknesses in the plan, grading the strength of the overall security. When she was done, she seemed to look to JC for confirmation.

"Yes, I agree. Now, can you identify any location with a reasonable distance that would meet or exceed the standards you just described?"

Skye opened her mouth and closed it. "No," she said. Her body sagged slightly before she straightened again. But it was enough for Edie, who consciously tried to relax also. It was obviously enough for JC.

"Good. Okay. So Edie stays. We've got two officers in here with her. Go find Tremblay."

Skye gave a curt nod but made no move. She searched out Edie's gaze first, and Edie was sure Skye was going to say something. But Skye simply glared at Edie with a dangerous look in her eyes before spinning on her heel and storming away.

Edie felt drained, as if Skye's energy had been holding her up. But she didn't want to sit, she didn't want to spin with her thoughts. Faina touched her hand lightly, but even that was too much. Her skin was oversensitized, electrified, and uncomfortable. She gently moved her hand away.

"Edie, are you going to be okay if I take Faina down to the station?"

"Yes," Edie answered, not quite able to look up at JC. "You'll be back later?"

"Probably much later, but yes. We may need you to look through some photos, but that can wait until tomorrow." JC ran a hand through her hair, a rare gesture of impatience. "I need Kenny to go through the lineup as well, but I'm not getting her even half a block away from you tonight."

Edie didn't know what to say. The thought of Skye half a block away made her sick.

"Edie?" Faina sounded concerned.

"I'm okay. Shaken up. You go with JC, and I'll see you back here. It's okay."

All the right words, every one. Faina looked unconvinced, but she stood and followed JC out when it was time to go. The kitchen was empty but the loft was not. Voices crowded down around her, most of them unseen. The sound of boots on the stairs was constant, as was the faint beeping of Skye's security system as they opened and closed the doors.

She could hear cops commenting on the loft, speculating on who Skye was, discussing the price of Ottawa real estate, griping about their need for coffee and the shitty task they'd been assigned. Oddly, this everyday work chatter calmed Edie the most. This recent, terrifying event was simply a series of dropped clues and evidence to be gathered. Since she could not form the conclusion to this story, Edie began making coffee. Her movements were automatic, requiring no effort. Her thoughts were on Skye, a still shot of Skye helping her make coffee in the church kitchen, a self-conscious half smile on her face.

Coffee made, Edie sat back at the island. A uniformed cop hovered just outside the light of the kitchen, occasionally calling out to someone or thumbing through his phone. Edie stared at her hands resting on the surface of the counter. The light reflecting off the shiny surface made her think of the sun in Kandahar. She heard street sounds and voices, she could smell diesel and cooking fires. A man smoking, friends laughing, the honk of a horn and tires on sand. Edie immersed herself in it, letting herself drift away from the present, escaping the way she had so many times as a child.

Eventually, Edie became aware that the loft was nearly quiet. Subdued voices now, fewer lights, and no more clanging metal of the stairs. She'd been peripherally aware of cops coming in and out of the kitchen for the last hour, some asking her questions, giving a nod of thanks for the coffee. Mostly they just let her be.

When she heard Skye's voice, still in full command, she felt her muscles tighten, a line of tension that started at the base of her spine and travelled up each vertebra until the sensation erupted as a sound wave in her skull. The sound was music, though.

The cop who had been her guard shuffled away, updating Skye on his way out. Then more footsteps, the sound of a door closing. Fading footsteps on the stairs. Silence.

Edie's breath was sharp in her chest as she waited. She could feel Skye in the air, knew she was close. She could feel her tension, the barely controlled wildness of her thoughts. Even without seeking her out in the darkness, Edie was pulled to her. This time, Edie had no intention of resisting Skye's gravitational force.

Edie walked away from the bright lights of the kitchen. Suddenly Skye was right in front of her, her body rigid. Edie's first impulse was to take a step back as Skye's fury and tension enclosed her, but she didn't. She took a step in, Skye's eyes flashing with a desire so intense it was palpable. Edie was no longer capable of making decisions. Her need for Skye overrode everything else.

Edie reached out slowly and touched Skye's throat, the pads of her fingers just resting on the vein in her neck. Skye's pulse pounded beneath her fingers and a dark, guttural sound emanated from her at Edie's touch. Edie slipped her hand around the back of Skye's neck, Skye an immovable object as Edie pulled herself in until their bodies were touching.

Skye didn't move at first, then suddenly she ran her hands through Edie's hair, cradling her skull, bringing her even closer. Skye touched her forehead to Edie's, breathing hard, her chest heaving. Edie placed her palm there, connecting with Skye's energy.

"They keep trying to take you from me." Skye's voice was rough, like nothing Edie had heard before.

"No," Edie said, rubbing the palm of her hand over Skye's breastbone, up to the hard ridges of her clavicle and back down. "I'm right here."

"Threatening you," Skye muttered, seeming distracted by the movement of Edie's hand. "Left you alone this morning. They tried to come here. To take you."

"No," Edie said sharply, needing to break through Skye's spinning, protective thoughts. She needed to prove to Skye that she was right there. She pulled Skye even closer, fingers tracing the base of Skye's skull. Then she kissed her, the pressure of her lips proof that she was there and safe. And that she wanted her.

Another guttural sound from Skye, but this time Edie felt it through her fingertips and lips. Skye's kiss was a challenge, an invitation to open up and experience the full force of her power. Edie accepted it, deepening the kiss, taking Skye inside her until they were fused and she was dizzy.

Edie felt Skye's hands drop down her back, fingers taking the shape of her spine, shoulders, ribs until her hands gripped Edie's hips. The sensation of tightness, the pressure on her pelvis was intense and Edie broke the kiss, gasping as heat engulfed her entire body. She felt strong and shaky all at once, and she began to unbutton Skye's shirt.

Edie pushed the shirt down off her shoulders and arms. Skye looked dangerous and powerful, the ridges of bone, the contours of her muscles in this dim light, the tattoo that wrapped her bicep evidence of her strength, the muscles of her abdomen as Skye strained to breathe.

"God, Skye…"

But Skye didn't need words. She pulled Edie against her, as if her touch was vital, and she fused them together again with a kiss that took all of Edie's strength to return. Skye walked them backward, guiding Edie with a hand on her hip as they kissed and breathed. Stumbling now, Edie gripped the waist of Skye's jeans.

Skye had slowed, maybe distracted by the press and flex of Edie's fingers or maybe even by her own exploration of Edie's hips and back and ass. It was all too slow for Edie, so she broke the kiss, ignoring the growl from Skye. Skye's eyes flashed a warning, but Edie just tugged at the waistband of Skye's jeans. They crossed the loft, Skye stalking her now, long powerful strides as Edie guided them to the bedroom.

They shared momentum, a combined force of desire and a lingering fear. Edie climbed onto Skye's bed and pulled Skye with her. Skye, still on her knees, resisted just long enough to pull Edie's shirt off over her head in one tug. Then Skye kissed Edie hard and pushed her down into the softness of the bed.

Edie couldn't remember how to breathe for a moment, but it no longer seemed important. All she wanted was Skye, and she gripped her hips and rolled her over, making just enough space between them to sweep her hand over Skye's abdomen, over her ribs, until the pad of her thumb skated over the hard ridge of Skye's nipple.

That growl from Skye's throat was shakier this time, and Edie suddenly wanted to be relentless with her touch. To not allow Skye to think or breathe or know anything but Edie's hands on her body. She ran her palm over Skye's breast, knowing the shape of her, the feel of heat against her skin, the sounds in Skye's throat as her body strained against Edie. Skye's lips against her jaw, then teeth, a scraping against her skin that sent Edie spinning. Skye circled Edie's shoulders and rolled them over until Skye was looking down on her with the fiercest, sweetest expression Edie had ever seen. Skye paused for just a scattered heartbeat of a moment, then she lowered her head and kissed her, and Edie was gone.

Sensation dominated every nerve in Edie's body and synapse in her brain. Skye lowered her head to kiss down Edie's neck, collarbone, breastbone, and finally enclose Edie's nipple in the heat of her mouth. Edie arched, breath an explosion of sound she couldn't shape. She pushed her hand against Skye's skull, trying to hold her there. But Skye pushed back, refusing to submit or be guided as she moved to Edie's other breast. Barely holding on to conscious thought, Edie insinuated her hands between them and unbuttoned Skye's jeans, then her own. Points of pain as Skye's teeth toyed with her nipples, as the zippers and buttons of their jeans pressed into flesh and their bodies sought connection and release.

Skye pulled back without warning, leaving Edie cold. She tugged at Edie's jeans until she lay naked, then she stripped herself bare as Edie watched. When she climbed back onto the bed, she began a slow, steady ascent of Edie's body, leaving her marked with a kiss or a bite, thumbs traveling up slowly from Edie's knees, inner thighs, the juncture of her hips until Edie thought she would scream. Skye covered Edie's body with her own, intertwining their legs. Skye thrust her hips against Edie with a force that made Edie cry out, and Edie hooked her leg around Skye's calf, holding her in place.

Edie was melting. She could not isolate points of pleasure. Their bodies were a combined force of heat and energy that could not be stopped or separated. And when Skye reached between them, the press of her fingers against Edie's flesh made them both moan, the feeling impossibly more intense as Skye stroked her with every thrust.

"Edie," Skye said, voice tight with strain. "I need…"

"Yes."

Edie couldn't be sure the words had actually passed her lips, but in the next moment, Skye filled her. Lights exploded behind Edie's eyes and together their bodies gave themselves over to the shuddering, unstoppable release.

Edie tried to push against the wonderfully heavy fog that blanketed her. She could feel Skye separate from her, though she hadn't moved. Then Skye shifted, easing out of Edie. She wanted to protest, but she couldn't form words. Edie fought the heaviness in her limbs and forced her arms around Skye's neck, entwining her shaking fingers in an attempt to hold her. But Skye continued to move away, the tension in her body getting more pronounced, her thoughts nearly loud enough for Edie to hear.

Skye easily broke Edie's hold, gathering Edie's hands together and holding them against her chest. Edie could feel her heart thudding against Skye. Then Skye lifted her head and looked into Edie's eyes. Edie saw a dawning pain in those yellow-green eyes, a glimpse of self-loathing, and a sea of unnamed regret. Skye pressed Edie's hands further against her chest as she eased away.

"I'm sorry, Edie. Christ, I'm sorry."

"No."

Skye pushed herself entirely away and stood. Her bearing and body were still powerful but diminished. Lost. Edie hated knowing she had anything to do with that. She hated knowing she was powerless to counteract whatever thoughts were circling through Skye's head right now. She had to try.

"Stay," Edie said, hoping it would be enough.

Skye bent and picked up her clothes with one hand. She was achingly beautiful, the light from the loft etching her body in stark lines of black and white.

"I'm sorry," Skye said again. This time her voice was nearly devoid of emotion. "Just…stay here." Then Skye turned and left.

Chapter Fifteen

Edie hadn't been strong enough to listen to Skye leaving. She wasn't sure how long she'd been buried beneath the pillows and blankets of Skye's bed, wishing she could sink right through and escape from the pain.

Edie pushed aside the blankets and tried not to think as she pulled soft, clean clothes from her bag and mechanically got dressed. She left the bedroom where she'd both had and lost Skye, and walked into the living room. JC and Faina were on one couch, each with a mug in their hands, talking quietly. They both looked up when Edie walked in. Edie wanted to hide, to never have surfaced and had to face the possibility she would never have a chance with Skye again.

"Hey, Edie."

The combined compassion in JC's tone and the sympathy in Faina's eyes threatened Edie's composure. She hadn't cried. She didn't intend to. But she wasn't sure she wanted to talk. She looked out onto the deserted street, the occasional car or cab making its way into the downtown core. Edie guessed it wasn't long after midnight.

"Are you okay?"

Edie considered Faina's question with as much honesty and self-reflection as she could muster.

"No," she said, still staring out the window. "Not really."

A movement caught Edie's eye as she looked down at the scene below. One of the cars parked across the street had someone inside. Edie felt a moment of fear and was about to take a step back when she realized it must be one of the surveillance teams. Three, JC had said. A lot of manpower. She caught another movement, this one almost directly below the window.

It was a brief flash of light, pale skin in the darkness. Edie couldn't make out a form let alone features, but she was suddenly very sure it was Skye. Skye wouldn't have left her unprotected. Edie wasn't sure how to feel about this being the only unbreakable connection they had right now. Possibly the only one they would ever have.

"Skye is out there, isn't she?" Edie said. When her question was met with silence, she turned around.

"Come sit down," JC said.

Edie complied. Her legs still felt shaky. And she was cold. She sat opposite JC and Faina, waiting for an answer.

"She's running," JC said but didn't explain. There really wasn't much else to say.

"How did everything go at the station?" Edie said. Gather information. Focus on tomorrow's meet. Today's meet. Solve a solvable problem.

"Good. Faina was able to identify both assailants from tonight's break-in. We had a lucky break when the second guy showed up at the ER with a long slice down his leg from broken glass about two hours after he left here."

"They're giving different information, though," Faina said. "One is saying Alex is here, the other saying he has left but doesn't know where."

"Do either of them know anything about the meet?" Edie said.

"We're not sure. They're not exactly being cooperative, and their testimony is pretty suspect at this point. Now they're both wanting lawyers, so that's slowed the process down somewhat."

"What about the timing?" Edie said. "Do you think it was in response to our request to meet? Or coincidental?"

"I think not coincidental, though I've got nothing to back that up. I think they want access to one or both of you. I think they are considering the meet later today a major risk. And I honestly don't know if they are going to take the bait."

Disappointment weighed Edie down.

"We will end this for you," JC said. "For both of you."

Edie closed her eyes. She used a relaxation technique Dr. Wallace had taught her at the beginning of their sessions together. Breathing and meditation, an exodus of thought, a release of tension and worry. She hadn't used it in a long time but was grateful it came back to her so she could filter out the continued conversation, the slow awakening of the day outside, the ringing of a phone, the sound of someone making coffee. And the awareness of Skye as she circled and hovered and fought and protected her from a distance.

❖

Just before two in the morning, Edie returned to her spot on the couch after showering, finding a coffee, and reluctantly eating the toast Faina had given her. JC cursed as she connected wires and cords to a laptop and massive computer monitor on top of a wheeled cart. Their debrief meeting was about ready to start. The meet itself was only two hours away.

Skye would be here any minute. While she'd showered, Edie had worked hard to gain some perspective. She tried to remind herself she did not actually know what was in Skye's head or heart. What she needed was an opportunity to find out. No action without data. But today was a different kind of action. A life course action. And if you wanted a good answer, you had to wait for the right time to ask the question. Edie needed to find patience.

A moment later, both Skye and Sasha entered the living room. Edie looked right at Skye, who was fierce and battle-ready in a black T-shirt and black cargo pants. She looked pale. And she wouldn't meet Edie's eyes. Instead she walked over to JC and checked the video conference hookup. Edie's heart sank just a little, but she rallied. She needed to focus.

"Okay," JC said, glancing at her phone. "We've got a minute before the meeting starts. Shouldn't take too long, then I'll get you guys hooked up before I take off." JC looked around the room, frowning when she saw Sasha lounging in one of the chairs. "Sash, you know I love you, man. But hit the road. You can check in with Skye later."

Sasha just smiled his easygoing smile and looked at Skye, who was fiddling with the monitor. Edie had a feeling the computer didn't actually need tending.

"Kenny? What's Sasha doing here?"

Skye kept her eyes on the monitor, like she was defusing a bomb. "What? Oh, he's my backup."

JC sighed the frustrated sigh of a woman whose unlimited well of patience was nearly running dry. "Kenny, how many times do we have to do this? I'm your backup."

Skye glanced at her friend. "You're my official backup. But you've got protocols to follow and a job to keep. Sasha doesn't. He stays."

"Nice of you to read me in on this, fire buddy," JC said. "Fine. Sasha, you need to stay out of camera range for this meeting. You're not here, and I know nothing about your involvement. Okay?"

Sasha gave a lazy salute and wandered back to the kitchen.

"Call's coming in," Skye said as the monitor came to life. She tilted the tablet, adjusted the setting, then stood beside the couch opposite Edie as Donaldson's face came into view.

"The clinic has been under surveillance since yesterday and teams moved into position just before the note was delivered," Donaldson said. "There's been no sign of Alex Rada or his associates. Basically, it looks like the clinic was abandoned after we shut it down during our investigation into the disappearance and suspected murder of Pino Barros."

The word "murder" dropped through cyberspace and landed in their midst with a heaviness Edie should have anticipated. Her hand shook, nearly spilling her coffee, and she quickly placed it on the table, drawing a quick glance from Skye.

"We're wired for video and sound at the location," Donaldson continued. "Constable Caldwell, you'll be running point with Ms. Kenny the second they leave the loft. You'll drive away at two thirty, drive four blocks, make a car switch, then circle back to intercept Ms. Kenny, Ms. Black, and Ms. Kassis at this intersection." Donaldson indicated a map, and Skye used her phone to expand it on her monitor.

"Roger that," JC said, peering at the map. "I'll wire them up before I go and run a check. How many teams are inside?"

Donaldson switched views to a schematic of a building. Edie forced herself to listen to team placements, officers on the roof, coverage, and sniper range. She wondered if it was all too much.

Edie realized she'd been drifting when Skye's voice intruded on her thoughts.

"Wait," Skye said. "We're not taking any time to talk to Alex Rada.

Faina and Edie are not there to collect information. We're drawing out Rada, you grab him, end of story."

Donaldson leaned toward the camera. "We also need to draw out that information, Ms. Kenny. The second we arrest Alex Rada, he is going to lawyer up and clam up. We have to expect that. Which means those dates and times are history. We need the date of that drop. This is big, national and international big. And Ms. Black in particular has a unique opportunity to draw Rada into conversation. Her motivation in this is ironclad, she doesn't care what the information is, she just wants it out."

Donaldson leaned back again and adopted a more conciliatory posture as he sought out Edie and Faina sitting on the couch for the first time. "You are both in unique positions to get information from Alex Rada. Ms. Kassis, you have the connection of family and Ms. Black, we are counting on your history as a journalist to ask questions that will yield the most information in a short period of time."

Edie was fully aware she was being manipulated. She glanced at Faina.

"Understood, Mr. Donaldson," Faina said smoothly.

"Understood," Edie echoed. JC said they would have their own debrief after this. Edie was looking forward to hearing what JC and Skye had to say.

"Our optimal cover is for the lobby and the treatment area. Beyond those rooms, you're adding time for us to get to you. It goes without saying you don't leave the building, and you don't go anywhere else. Any questions?"

Obviously, yes, thought Edie. She was about to walk into a meet with a man who embedded information in her head. Who held his half sister captive and beat her when she didn't comply. Edie had to hope his ego would make him overstep.

Donaldson's face disappeared as the video conference wrapped up. JC and Skye kept looking at the schematics, and Sasha wandered back out to join them.

"I'll take the lead," Edie said to Faina. "I think you should still play it scared. From what you've said of your brother, I think he'll like that we need something from him. It will make him feel powerful. And hopefully boastful. The sooner we get him to talk, the sooner this can be over."

"I agree," Faina said. "About his ego and feeling powerful. But he is suspicious. He's a monster, but he's smart. I just don't think he's going to fall for this." She waved her hand at the schematics of the clinic on the screen.

"He might not," JC said from across the room. "He might not be there at all. He might try to derail plans. In fact, we have to anticipate his agenda. And intervene at the right time."

Skye walked closer to Faina and Edie. She was in full planning, protective mode. "You both need to know that my agenda is to get you two out of there safely. I don't give a fuck about information or a confession or anything else. You'll listen to me, and I'll get you out. Understood?"

Faina glanced quickly at JC, who was staring pointedly in the other direction. "Yes, understood," Faina said.

Skye switched her gaze to Edie, the first time she'd looked directly at her since she'd walked back into the loft. Edie wanted to welcome her back, to remind Skye of their connection. But the Skye who would listen to that was not present.

"Yes," Edie said. "Understood."

Half an hour to debrief was no time at all. As they discussed evacuation routes, optimal positions in the room, leading questions, wireless communication, and distress signals, Edie felt a slight break from the energy around her. She felt disconnected, as if she was an observer simply trying to make sense of a scene. As everyone else ramped up, Edie slowed down.

"You ready for your tracker?" JC brought a plastic kit over to Edie on the couch. Edie blinked and realized Skye was adjusting her earpiece and Faina was slowly turning her head from side to side as if testing her range of motion.

"These look more like what they have on TV," Edie said.

JC gave a short laugh. "Let's hope they work as well as the ones on TV. I'm going to put this just inside the back of your shirt. It's tiny, you won't feel it. Just don't lose your shirt out there."

"Not a problem." Edie appreciated JC's attempt at humour, even though she was struggling.

Edie felt JC's cold fingers on the back of her neck.

"I get the sense my fire buddy over there has fucked up."

Edie didn't reply.

"If she has," JC continued, "she'll make it right. And if she doesn't..." JC laughed quietly. "I was going to say that I would kick her ass. But I believe, Ms. Black, that you will have that covered."

JC patted Edie's shirt back into place and sat back. "There, we're done. You good?"

A layered question, Edie thought. *So many ways to answer.*

"Yes," Edie said firmly.

JC put a hand on Edie's shoulder. "Ten minutes, Ms. Black. We've got this. I'll see you on the other side of this thing."

Ten minutes. Ten minutes to breathe and think and not think. Ten minutes to catapult herself forward and backward through time. To relive moments of regret, reassess her readiness, find the sparks of anger that put her in this position and fan them into a controlled, burning flame. Edie looked around the loft at her own team, placed herself firmly in this present with these people and their shared goal. Scared or not, this was happening. And Edie was ready.

❖

"Edie in the front with me. Faina, you take the back."

The two women complied without saying a word. The garage was cold and damp, the sounds of the car doors slamming were too loud. Edie shivered. Her nerves were taut, and a low-lying headache had settled at the base of her skull not long after JC had left and the whole plan had finally been set into motion. The car was uncomfortably silent, a moving tension that stretched and filled the space. Edie breathed.

Skye tapped at her phone, and the garage door opened. The sun was still a few hours from rising, but the deepness of the dark caught Edie off guard. The streets were completely empty.

"I need you both to know that I will follow the plan as outlined by Donaldson, insofar as it aligns with keeping you safe. If you can get information, get information. If you can't, I'm pulling you," Skye said in her authoritative voice. "You both have two trackers and a backup. So do I. I'm armed because they'll expect that. The Russians will likely make me give up my weapon and my phone. I have a backup of both. Get in there, ask questions, draw out Rada. Leave the rest to Donaldson's team. Any questions?"

A meet. An interview. An information exchange. That's all this was. Edie had done this countless times before.

"If Rada hasn't shown up in five minutes, then I'm calling off the—" Skye paused and tilted her head, touching her finger to her earpiece. "Go ahead." Another pause as she listened. "Just now? What does it say?" Skye cursed under her breath and yanked the steering wheel over abruptly to the curb. She looked in her rearview mirrors and scanned the area before speaking again. "Send the image to me. Faina can read it."

Skye pulled out her cell phone from one of the cargo pockets. She tapped at her earpiece as she tapped at her phone.

"Sasha, did you get that? Yes, stand down for now." Skye turned in her seat to address both Edie and Faina. "Someone just put a note on the door of the clinic. It's in Russian. Donaldson is getting his own interpreter, but I want you to take a look at it." Skye opened an image on her screen and handed the phone to Faina. "It's blurry because it's zoomed in. See what you can decode."

Faina took the phone with a steady hand and zoomed in on the image. She was frowning.

"I'm not sure I understand. I believe it says five morning and pig's back and this word could mean building or...what's the word...kiosk."

Skye took the phone back from Faina and started typing as she talked. "They want a meet at Hog's Back Pavilion, that's near the falls. At five a.m. JC, did you get that?" Skye sighed in frustration. "Yes, Donaldson, I can identify access points as well as you can. That's not my primary concern. We have no sitrep, no teams in place, and no time to get teams in place. I'm aborting." Even from the passenger seat, Edie could hear the faint buzz of noise through Skye's earpiece. "Yes, I've read them in. No, this is a completely unacceptable level of risk. Only an idiot would—"

Edie put her hand gently on Skye's forearm. "Put it on speaker," she said quietly. She and Faina needed to hear what was going on, and Skye needed to be rescued before she said something she couldn't take back.

Skye said nothing, just stared blankly down at Edie's hand as if she were evaluating an unknown object, trying to assess its function in the environment. Then she reached up and put her phone in the hands-free unit on the dash, subtly and effectively breaking their connection.

"Okay," she said and hit the icon for speaker. "Donaldson and Caldwell, you're on speaker."

Edie heard Donaldson swear. The spiraling lack of control around this situation clearly had everyone on edge.

"We can have backup teams on site in twenty minutes. Twenty-five, tops," Donaldson said. "Both sides of the falls and the bridge. I'm sending a map now."

"That's not good enough," Skye said. "We'll have no one at the pavilion other than two beat cops at the end of their shift who don't have a fucking clue what's going on."

"Ms. Kenny—"

"Don't bother, Donaldson," Skye said shortly. "Twenty-five minutes puts us past the meet time. And don't pretend these are advance teams. They're cover teams or cleanup teams, and that is unacceptable."

"We lose them if we don't make this meet," Donaldson said, his voice hard. "We lose any chance of recovering the information that will—"

"I don't give a—"

"I want to go."

Faina's voice was loud enough to be heard but calm enough that it cut through the escalating fight.

Skye and Edie both turned in their seats to face Faina. The streetlights lit up half her face with an orange tinge, the other in shadow. But her eyes had an internal fire, a zeal and purpose that made her look powerful. That made Edie ever so slightly afraid.

"I think we should listen to Skye on this," Edie said. "Donaldson's agenda is to get that meet information at any cost. It's not worth it."

Faina was shaking her head, emphatic in her denial. "I think you should stay. I will go on my own. My own risk. If I am ever going to convince the officials that I am not a threat, that I am not now and have never worked with my brother or sister on this, I need to follow through. I need to see my brother. I will bring him in, and maybe then they will believe me. Maybe then they will let me stay."

Edie's breath fled as an ache of sadness pressed against her chest. So many competing motivations, so many assessments of risk. And so much to lose.

"Not on your own." JC's voice came over the speaker. Edie had almost forgotten they were listening. "You go with backup or you don't go at all. Kenny's right about the risk. I'm leaning toward not at all."

The car was suddenly filled with noise, voices that argued and chased each other down. Edie was lost in it, and she closed her eyes, the headache ratcheting up another notch. They were losing time.

Suddenly silence filled the car again. When she opened her eyes, she saw Skye had muted the conversation.

"It's not safe," Skye said to Faina.

Faina smiled sadly. "You are not telling me anything I do not already know, Skye. But either way, I am not safe. I will be deported, likely charged with multiple offences. I am not safe." She emphasized every one of those words and Edie felt them all like hammer blows to her skull. "For the first time in a very long time, I have the opportunity to pursue a life course, to contribute something for the greater good. I see a glimpse of my own life at the end of this. I want to make that happen. If that means risking meeting my brother, I will."

More silence. Edie didn't know what to say and, clearly, neither did Skye. How to contradict Faina's logic? How to argue the pursuit of happiness in her own life?

"I will leave the car," Faina said when neither of them spoke. "Skye, you will stay with Edie. Call it in. They'll pick me up and take me to the new location." For the first time, her voice quavered. "And I'll see you at the end of this. Edie, I'll need some tea, so you can have that ready for me, okay?"

Crying was unhelpful in this moment, but Edie cried anyway. This wasn't right.

When Edie did not speak, Faina once again filled the silence. "I love you, you know. You are family to me. Skye, take good care of her."

Edie couldn't breathe or swallow. This could not be happening, everything was spiraling so quickly, and all of it was so wrong. She heard the car door open.

"Stop," she said, the word a command and a force and a directive to the world to just slow down, pause, and take a moment. She was suddenly very sure this was not where they were headed. This was not the next step in a life that had been hijacked. She would write the ending to this. As much as she could.

"We go together," she said. "We stick with the plan. Just a new location." She reached up and unmuted the speaker. A cacophony of voices. "Listen up," she said, loudly enough to be heard over the din. "We're going to the clinic as planned, assume they are watching for us. Skye will get out and pick up the note. We'll drive to Hog's Back Falls. Set up your teams. Do what you need to do." She leaned back and waved vaguely at the phone on the dash. Skye could take over and figure out the details. The certainty in her chest that going with Faina was the right move outweighed the uncertainty at the outcome. Edie could hear Dr. Wallace's voice in her head. *They are all just moments. You can handle moments.*

She felt a light touch against her arm. "Thank you, my friend." Edie squeezed Faina's hand.

Edie closed her eyes when Skye pulled her Jeep back onto the street. Voices continued unabated, Skye adding her thoughts, the anger in her voice a steady simmer Edie wasn't sure anyone else could detect.

"I'm taking the most direct route," Edie heard Skye say. She opened her eyes and oriented herself in space. "Elgin Street to Colonel By Drive. Sasha, give me an account of the route every step of the way. Caldwell, I want an update from the street cops near the falls. Donaldson, tell me how far out your teams are."

Moments. Pieces of the puzzle. Edie looked around. Traffic was bare, just the occasional car or taxi or produce truck passing them on the straightway through downtown.

"Approaching Pretoria Bridge underpass. Taxi ahead," Skye said. Still so tense. Mind on the mission. "I'll make the right onto Colonel By in one minute. Donaldson, I could use that update."

Edie could hear the cars on the Queensway above as they entered the underpass. It was the city's major artery, connecting them to Toronto, Montreal, and beyond. It never slept.

Edie heard the squealing of tires and the revving of an engine almost at the same moment as the crash from behind them sent her flying forward against her seat belt.

"Ambush!" Skye yelled. "JC, I need you. Pretoria Bridge underpass. Now!"

Skye wrenched the steering wheel of the Jeep hard left into the empty oncoming traffic lane. The taxi in front peeled around until it blocked them in and straddled the median. Skye swore and gunned the gas, trying to get around, but the taxi lurched forward, cutting her off.

Skye jammed the gear into reverse, halted by another crash as Skye hit whoever was behind them.

"I'm boxed in," Skye said, even as she tried to find a way out. "Full-sized commercial transport truck, dark paint, no logo, can't see the plates. Shit. Two, no, three assailants emerging from the truck. Anytime now, Caldwell."

Edie's heart wouldn't stop pounding, adrenaline making her shake, making everything sharp, making her fear acute. A figure emerged from the taxi and walked rapidly toward the Jeep.

"Skye, the taxi." Edie got no more warning out before men were banging at the windows and kicking at the doors.

"Fuck that. Hold on." Skye pressed her foot down on the gas, sending the men flying back as the Jeep rammed into the taxi. It skidded sideways with the awful screech of metal on metal, and then a sharp crack ricocheted through the underpass as the back window of the Jeep exploded in a shower of glass. Edie screamed and ducked, Faina cried out, and Skye swore as the window beside her exploded and arms reached in through the broken glass.

"Edie, Faina, run!"

But Edie was reaching across the centre divide and punching the hands that grabbed at Skye, wrenching a finger back until it snapped and someone yelled in Russian as Skye elbowed the unseen assailant. One of them wrenched the passenger door open, pulled Edie's seat belt away, and got her out of the car. Arms gripped her hair and around her chest, lifting her off the ground. She knew she was supposed to go limp, to make it harder to carry her away. She tried, but every muscle in her body screamed for action, to hit and kick and bite and run.

When she saw Faina being pulled from the Jeep as well, her rage and fear would not let her go. Skye emerged, kicking one of the assailants so hard in the chest he flew back and bounced against the pavement. Two more attacked, and she caught one with a blow to his throat that sent his head snapping back. But as he went down he must have swept her legs and she fell, disappearing behind the Jeep. Edie could hear the scuffle of bodies, the echo of shouts in the underpass, and her own continuous scream.

"You shut up," the man holding her yelled in her ear in a thick accent. A side door of the truck opened and the men passed Faina to another set of hands that jerked her inside. Edie tried to crane her neck around to see where Skye had ended up, but the man yanked her head around and tried to lift her.

Edie kicked back. She didn't have enough room to get much power behind it but she connected with his shin, tangled her legs with his, and he faltered. Without thinking, Edie snapped her head back and felt her skull connect with his cheekbone. The man cursed and his grip slipped. Edie fought like a wild animal and got two full steps away from her captor. Skye was being kicked on the ground, then a man knelt and pulled Skye's hands behind her back.

"No!" Just a few more steps and Edie could have reached her. She was strong enough for this. JC was seconds away. She could help Skye to her feet. They would fight.

But the grip tightened on her wrist and Edie's captor swung her around so violently that she ended up right at the entrance to the truck, where she was lifted and flung inside. She hit the metal floor, sliding with momentum until she lay still. Edie could taste blood in her mouth, and the mixture of rage and fear made her want to throw up.

"Edie." Faina's voice was very faint, almost lost in the rumble of the engine, in the lurching movement as the truck began to move.

"No," Edie moaned. This wasn't happening. She heard a thud behind her then the slam of a door, shouting, and the truck accelerated, making Edie slide a little as the truck rapidly gained speed.

"Edie? Faina?"

Skye. Relief flooded Edie's system. She pushed herself up on her arms and crawled toward Skye's voice. The truck swayed and lurched around a corner. Edie fell over, but she pushed herself back up until she touched Skye's boot with her hand. She kept moving until she had crawled up beside Skye, who was half propped against one of the walls.

"Are you okay?"

"Just winded. Need a moment. You?"

Edie touched her hand to her face and assessed the rest of her body. She'd be bruised, but the cut on the inside of her cheek where she'd bitten down had already stopped bleeding.

"Bruises. I'm fine." Edie leaned into Skye, taking and giving some strength. She tried to peer into the darkness, though she knew it was useless. "Faina? You okay?"

Edie thought she could hear sounds of scraping and shuffling.

"I think...not."

Alarm snaked up Edie's chest at admission from her friend, the faintness of her voice. Skye moved beside her, and a second later, the light from a cell phone lit up the gloom.

"They never look for more than one phone," Skye said as she flashed the light up the wall above their heads. "No window. Good." She moved the beam down the truck. It was empty except for Faina's inert body right near the centre.

Faina lay on her side, rolling and shaking with the movement of the truck. Edie and Skye crawled toward her, then gently turned her onto her back. Her neck and shoulder were covered in a dark, wet stain. Skye angled the phone and the blood showed up red and awful, splattering Faina's face.

"The shot through the Jeep. Jesus," Edie breathed out. She leaned over Faina and pulled back her shirt. All she could see was blood. "Where were you shot? I can't see it."

"Shoulder, I think. Hurts. It was so hot." Faina mumbled.

Edie wondered how much blood she'd lost. She pulled more forcefully on the neck of Faina's shirt, making her whimper. But she needed to find the wound. There, on the outside of her bicep. Edie bunched up the sleeve of her own shirt and pressed it to the wound. She looked up at Skye, lit from below with the glow of the cell phone. "She needs a hospital."

"We're being tracked. JC isn't too far behind. We just have to hold on until the cavalry arrives." Skye's voice was sure, and Edie felt her skyrocketing pulse re-enter the atmosphere at her certainty. "Faina, you just need to hold on for a little while longer. It's almost over. I promise."

"He's here. My brother. I saw him."

Edie and Skye exchanged a silent look over Faina. Skye looked back down.

"Don't worry about that right now. Just try to conserve your energy. I'm going to call JC, which means I need the light."

"It's okay," Edie said. Faina's blood soaked through the sleeve of her shirt. She needed more material, a better angle. She needed the truck to stop moving.

"JC. Have you got us? Edie and I are fine, but Faina's got a GSW to her upper arm. She's lost a lot of blood already."

"Tell her about Alex," Faina mumbled.

Skye began awkwardly pulling off her long-sleeved shirt. "Faina identified her brother as one of the assailants. Tell Donaldson to send the whole fucking army." She pulled the shirt over her head and passed it to Edie. "You've got us in your sights? And backup? Okay, good. We'll sit tight. They've got my weapon as well as their own. Roger that, fire buddy."

Skye tilted the phone screen back to Faina so Edie could see the wound. It wasn't bleeding very much anymore, but Edie folded Skye's shirt into a semblance of a bandage and wrapped the sleeves around Faina's bicep, pulling tightly until Faina moaned.

"I'm sorry, Faina," Edie whispered.

The sound of the engine changed, downshifting and reducing speed, and Edie nearly fell over Faina.

"Let's move her against the wall," Skye said. "I want us halfway between both doors when they stop."

It was difficult with the constant swaying of the truck and the unexpected changes in speed, but Skye and Edie managed to half drag Faina up against the wall. They sat on either side of her, propping her up. Faina rested her head against Edie's shoulder. She was so pale.

The truck slowed again, bouncing over an uneven road. Then they stopped, the engine idled, and there were voices outside and the sound of scraping metal.

"A gate." Skye tapped into her phone.

The truck slowly lurched forward again, then came to a complete stop before the engine died. The floor shook as people clambered around the vehicle, calling out to each other in Russian. Then Edie heard multiple sirens, their wails taking turns as they climbed to a crescendo before dropping down and making the ascent again, pausing just long enough to give a rapid-fire warning blare. Edie felt relief and hope until she looked across Faina's still form at Skye.

"You both need to listen to me very carefully," Skye said. "We're in a standoff. Rada has brought us here for a reason. He's not only drawn the three of us to this location, he has intentionally drawn the police here, too. He wants something, and we're going to have to figure out what that is."

The relief was gone, hope replaced with a sense of powerlessness. Edie hated that feeling. She dug underneath it, refusing to allow it to take root.

"Tell me how to play it," Edie said, aiming for calm. It was hard with the sirens wailing.

"Ask questions. Get Rada to talk. Do what you do best."

"Okay," Edie said. "An interview. Faina said we should play to his ego. Let him think he's entirely in control."

"Yes," Skye said. "Which is why I'm going to sit back. I'm a threat. He'll feel more confident now that I'm unarmed."

"He doesn't know you," Edie whispered. Skye's face was stone in the edge of light cast from the phone. "You don't need a weapon to be a threat to him."

"Yes," Skye said, soft and dangerous.

Edie jumped at a bang on the far side of the truck. Skye turned off her phone, plunging the interior of the truck into darkness for a second before the side door opened and the back door of the truck was rolled up. Armed men climbed into the truck from both doorways. Artificial light streamed into the truck, and the occasional flash of yellow and white made Edie think the line of police was not far off. She counted the men as they entered the truck. Six in total. The size of their guns momentarily confused Edie. Ottawa, not Kandahar. Canada, not Afghanistan. Home country. Safe and secure. She glanced at Skye, trying to resettle her thoughts. Protected. She was protected.

One man squatted down in front of the three women. Edie guessed it was Rada, and she tried to find traces of Faina in his face. Maybe in the eyes, the spark of intelligence. The love of a puzzle. Edie felt a surge of confidence. She knew men like this. She had interviewed men like this.

"I am Alex Rada," he said in accented English. He spoke directly to Edie. "I want to spend as little time as possible in this truck. I want to let you go. First we exchange information, and then you go. You understand this, Edie Black?"

"Yes, I understand," Edie said. "I need to get Faina to a hospital. Tell me what you want."

Rada glanced once at the slouched form of his sister who leaned against Edie with her eyes only half-open. His eyes flashed with scorn and loathing, before focusing back on Edie.

"You tell me what you know. What you have told the police."

She had no reason to hold back. The only thing she had to sell was her uncertainty that it was all out.

"I know you put things in my head. Faina told us that. Then they used some kind of hypnotherapy. I gave them lines from a poem while I was under."

"How many lines?"

"Four, I think," Edie said, trying to sound uncertain. "Yes, four lines from a poem. They wanted more. They kept asking, but I couldn't remember more."

Rada kept his gaze pinned on Edie, obviously searching for lies amongst the truth. Edie let him search. It was all truth.

When Rada said nothing more, Edie took a gamble. "Is there more? I want it out. I don't care what it is, I don't care that the department of firearms—"

Rada stood suddenly. Edie worried she had made a mistake, had offered up too much too soon. He paced in short bursts, muttering in Russian to his men. Faina shifted and leaned her head back, moaning. Edie squeezed her hand then leaned in when Faina squeezed back with surprising strength and Edie heard her whisper. She leaned closer to catch the words.

"He is saying you know some but not all. He is relieved. Bargaining chip."

Rada returned and knelt in front of Edie again. His eyes were alight, like a predator closing in on his prey. "What did the police do with the words?"

"I don't know exactly," Edie said. When Rada growled, she held up a hand. "I really don't. They think it's a code. They thought I had the key to unlock it, but I kept telling them I didn't know. They talked about cryptographers and bringing in data analysts. If they figured it out, they never told me."

Rada seemed satisfied with this response. He suddenly shifted his gaze to Skye. "You. Can you negotiate with the police?"

"I have no power to make a deal," Skye said. "I'm here to protect Ms. Black."

Rada sneered. "Then you are no good at your job. A bodyguard should not fuck those they protect. Or you will end up in back of truck with men with guns."

Rada laughed and his men followed suit. Skye just glared. Rada stood and reached into his pocket, pulling out a phone and tossing it to Skye. She caught it deftly.

"Call your police contact. The one who has been at your house. Put it on speakerphone."

Skye did exactly as directed.

"Caldwell."

"It's Kenny. Rada wants to negotiate."

"I'm listening, Rada."

"I have information for you regarding multiple drop points and buyers," Rada said, raising his voice. "I assume you are one of the many uniforms outside these gates. Approach the truck alone, unarmed, no listening devices. You break any of these conditions, and I will shoot one of these women. I have not yet decided who."

"Understood," JC said through the speaker. "Two minutes, back of the truck."

The line went dead. Edie couldn't look at the guns, but she imagined the muzzle being aimed at her, at Faina, at Skye. A tremor started in her hands. She wasn't sure how much bravery she had left.

A commotion at the back of the truck signaled JC's arrival. Edie watched as JC easily climbed into the back of the truck. Two men approached and patted her down. JC scanned the interior as she held up her arms, giving no indication she was bothered by the roughness of their search. She glanced at Skye, Edie, and Faina, then she turned her attention to Rada.

"This will be brief," Rada said. "I have no interest in long talks. I can give you dates and times of drops, list of product and suppliers, and names of buyers. I am small piece. You want bigger piece. I give you information, I give you the three girls and my men and I walk away."

JC said nothing, but she nodded throughout his speech, as if they were talking calmly. As if everything he was saying was completely reasonable.

"I'm not going to lie. My superiors have been riding my ass for that information."

Rada smiled the predatory smile. "Good. Then we have a deal?"

JC smiled as well. "Here's the thing. You're about an hour too late. We already have some of that information. It's basically no good anymore."

"What?" The word exploded from Rada, and he turned an accusing glare on Edie.

"Ms. Black didn't know," JC said. "Though I'm thinking Kenny here did."

"What do you think you know?" Rada yelled, looking between JC and Skye. Edie was having a hard time keeping up. Did they really know something? Was this a bluff?

"I take it you got a message from Gordon?" Skye said.

Gordon, thought Edie. *Gordon bouncing on the trampoline in the Twelve.* Skye had given him the code and asked him to crack it. Without permission.

"I sure did," JC said, grinning. Their conversation was obviously unnerving Rada. And as their leader became more rattled, so did the other men. Edie caught the uneasy glances behind Rada's back. JC and Skye were effectively undermining Rada's authority and trust along with whatever plan he had promised his men he could execute.

"I do not believe you," Rada spat. He suddenly seemed aware of the shifting uneasiness of the men around him. He barked at them in Russian over his shoulder. They settled but kept glancing at each other.

Beside her, Faina rolled her head over to rest against Skye. Rada spared her a glance, but when she didn't move again, he looked back to JC.

"Prove it," Rada said.

"Sure," JC said easily. She walked a little farther into the truck. Closer to Rada but also closer to where Skye, Faina, and Edie still sat. Rada stood his ground, but his men shifted back. Edie noticed several of them glancing at the side door. "The first drop is May 31, seven a.m., at the Petit Dejeuner truck stop. My source said you mixed multiple languages in each line of code. Clever. It tricked all of our analysts."

Rada said nothing, but the tension in the truck had increased exponentially. The men at the back of the truck muttered to each other now. Faina shifted again and whispered something in Skye's ear. Skye shook her head emphatically. Faina squeezed Edie's hand, then disengaged and slowly pulled herself to standing. She called out in Russian, and when she had Rada's attention, switched to English.

"You always called me an embarrassment," Faina said, leaning against the wall of the truck. Skye and Edie stood as well, trying to support Faina, who pushed them away.

"You are an embarrassment, sister," Rada sneered. "You and your whore of a mother."

Faina swayed slightly as she slowly approached her brother, one arm held protectively across her body. "I made mistakes. Trusting you and Yana was a mistake. But I am not the one who is an embarrassment to their birth country. Who is sinking quickly. And taking everyone down with him."

"You know nothing," Rada said. "I am restoring the good name of Rada after our father lost it, marrying that Syrian whore and producing you." Rada used his gun to accentuate his point. Edie flinched. Faina continued her slow advance as Rada's shouting increased in volume. "This technology is a gift to the Russian military. It will clear our name."

"A plan gone wrong, Alex. Yana disappeared. Your code is cracked. This locked vault you promised is a sham." Faina stopped in front of her half brother. She poked him in the chest. "You have failed."

Alex's eyes bulged at the insult, utterly enraged. He swung his arm back and screamed in Russian.

"No!"

Edie screamed as JC and Skye launched themselves in tandem at Rada. Skye tackled Faina just as the butt of Rada's gun made contact with Faina's cheek. Faina's cry of pain was lost in the sudden cacophony of noise. Police shouted commands to drop their weapons, JC and two tactical officers took Rada down, and a single bullet was discharged. Edie was tackled from behind and dropped to the floor of the truck. The weight on her back was heavy. Edie started to panic.

"Off." Edie tried to shout above the awful noise in the truck. Screaming and shaking and boots pounding against the walls of the truck, and Edie felt every vibration with her body pressed against the metal floor. She wanted to yell but didn't have enough air in her lungs. Edie angled her head, her vision filled with Skye leaning over Faina, who was blood-covered and still. Skye turned and looked at Edie and she was angry, shouting, gesturing wildly, then suddenly the weight was gone from Edie's back. The shouting was dying down, and fewer jarring thuds rocked the truck. Edie rolled onto her back to see an officer holding out her hand.

"Sorry, Ms. Black. Just trying to keep you out of the line of fire."

Edie took the hand, and the officer helped her up from the floor.

Her legs were shaky, the dump of adrenaline nearly too much for her body to process. She scanned the truck interior, a sea of officers in tactical gear, two to each unarmed Russian who was being pulled out of the back of the truck. JC talking to Rada, her face impassive, reciting something as if from memory. *They are arresting the man who wanted me dead.*

Edie suddenly sank to her knees. It was too much to keep standing, too much to process.

"Edie, just breathe."

That request was harder than it should have been.

"Take a breath. Good. Another one."

Edie breathed, and as the oxygen settled back into her lungs, she connected the voice to the words. Skye was still kneeling beside Faina, though two paramedics had joined her. The truck was lit up now. Dawn had arrived. Faina was shot. Edie had played her part. JC and Skye had kept them safe.

"Faina, is she…"

"She passed out," Skye said firmly. "Look, she's coming around."

Faina opened her eyes and she was struggling to move. Edie shuffled forward on her knees and joined Skye next to Faina's head. She didn't look at the paramedics, but Edie could not ignore the angry red welt and blossoming bruise on one side of Faina's cheek, the imprint of Rada's gun clearly pressed into her flesh. Edie shuddered and carefully touched her hand to Faina's unmarked cheek.

"You're okay," Edie whispered. Faina focused her eyes on Edie for just a moment.

"You? Everyone?" Faina said.

"No one else was hurt," Skye said, her voice was very gentle. "Edie and I are unhurt. JC is fine. They're going to take you to the hospital in a moment, so just rest."

Faina almost immediately closed her eyes again. Skye put her arm around Edie's shoulder and drew her sideways against her body. She was strength and reassurance, and Edie soaked up both wordlessly.

"How long until transport?" JC had walked over, still in full command mode, both hands wrapped around the straps of her bulletproof vest.

"Five minutes, tops," one of the paramedics said. "She's stable, just getting her ready to move."

JC nodded curtly and looked at Skye and Edie.

"We're all going. Everyone gets checked out. No arguments."

Edie did not have the strength to argue. She had a sudden image in her head of Skye being kicked repeatedly. Edie shuddered and tried to ease away, but Skye held her securely.

"It's done," JC said, more softly. "We'll need to get initial statements at the hospital from both of you. But you did it."

"Listen to her," Skye said in her ear. "Just sit with Faina. It's done."

CHAPTER SIXTEEN

Okay, Ms. Black. Here are your discharge papers, signs and symptoms of a worsening concussion. And yes, I know you could write a manual on the subject. Spare me the drama, take the papers, and for God's sake, follow up with your doctor in the next forty-eight hours."

Edie took the papers from Nurse Brian, who had been competently directing traffic in his ER since they had all arrived. Edie had been completely and thoroughly checked over, a CT scan ordered, the cut on the inside of her mouth assessed, bruises counted and discarded as anything more serious than burst blood vessels beneath her skin.

It was Edie's head and heart that hurt.

Her thoughts were a dull ache of confusion at the last few hours, and she felt a mild sense of panic at being separated from Skye and Faina. Skye had been next to her on the ride to the hospital, the triage area, in the chair by her bed as the doctor looked her over, and as an officer came to take her statement. But she'd been constantly on the phone with someone, getting updates on Faina, which she'd passed along to Edie in a neutral tone, answering questions from JC and Donaldson, from her own boss at the security agency.

Edie watched her work, felt the force of her uncertainty. She tried to take comfort from her physical proximity even as she understood Skye was with her yet not. Here and away. Edie could barely think, and it was both a relief and an ache when Skye was called down to x-ray to take a look at her ribs.

But that had been two hours ago, and as Nurse Brian handed Edie the papers and pulled back the curtain, Edie was disappointed to not see Skye there waiting. She spotted Sasha just a few feet away, his eyes wide and cheeks pink. Brian approached him, wrote something on Sasha's inner arm, then walked briskly away. It made Edie's heart hurt a little less, knowing Skye had sent Sasha for her and seeing this sweet, simple exchange between the two men. These were moments, too. Happiness and lightness, ease and anticipation. Edie could find them and let them in, let them erase the recent horrors.

Sasha was still staring down at his arm when Edie approached.

"Hey, Sasha."

Sasha looked up and hastily pulled down his sleeve. Edie raised an eyebrow and smiled.

"Edie. Hi. Sorry. You okay?" He was adorable when flustered.

"I'm good. You?"

Sasha blushed and Edie laughed gently. The sensation felt new somehow.

"Don't tell the boss," Sasha said.

"I won't."

"Speaking of the boss, Skye has been released and is down at the police station. I can take you home or to Skye's place. She says you're welcome to stay at the loft, if you'd rather."

Maybe Skye was not here, but she was looking out for Edie. An extension of soldier Skye's protection, even now that the danger no longer existed? Or was it an invitation, an olive branch, the tentative offer of hope?

"I'd like to see Faina first."

"Fourth floor," Sasha said. "I'll take you."

They walked out of the emergency department and through the confusing maze of hospital hallways.

"How is Faina?"

"She's waiting for surgery to clean up the gunshot wound, though CT cleared her from needing a surgical correction of the crack in her orbital floor from the pistol whip." Sasha stopped as Edie winced at his words. "Sorry."

"It's okay, keep going."

"The docs think the crack will heal fine on its own. The surgery is just to make sure the gunshot wound is clean of debris, but they are confident it hit nothing major. JC is back at headquarters now, debriefing with the team and trying to keep the boss out of hot water. I imagine she'll be back when she can get away."

Edie looked up at Sasha and parsed out his last words. Then she remembered.

"Because Skye sent the information to Gordon."

"Yes. Even after she was expressly forbidden to do so by Donaldson. And JC, actually."

"Is she in a lot of trouble?" Edie said. It hadn't occurred to her that this could end badly for Skye.

Sasha shrugged his easygoing shrug.

"She's run out of favours with all the governmental agencies, but it's hard for Donaldson to be pissed when she handed him exactly what he was looking for. And took away Rada's only real bargaining chip."

They got off the elevator on the fourth floor. It was busy, with nurses in brightly coloured scrubs talking to patients and calling out to each other. Monitors beeped and blared, and nobody seemed too concerned. The efficiency calmed Edie. Faina was in good hands. Sasha pointed to a door and indicated he would wait outside.

Four beds were in this room, each with a curtain that enclosed the patients. Faina was in the bed closest to the window, and she lay very still beneath the white sheets. The midafternoon sun, half shielded by the blinds, brought the violence of Faina's injuries into dramatic light. Edie could see the layers of bruises, old and new and still forming. Faina was a canvas of hurt.

Edie walked to the bed and gently touched Faina's hand. Faina opened her glassy eyes and fixed them on Edie. She tried to smile.

"Hey, no need to wake up," Edie said. "I just wanted to see you."

Faina blinked and gave Edie's hand a light, shaky squeeze. She was heavily sedated, and Edie didn't want to keep her surfaced if it was a struggle. She had a hazy memory of what that felt like.

"Sleep, my friend. I'll be here after your surgery."

Faina closed her eyes again, and her hand went limp. Edie felt tears well up, but she forced them back down. She leaned over the railing of the bed and gave Faina a light kiss on her temple.

When she left the room, Sasha pushed away from the wall and looked at her expectantly. What Edie needed above all right now was comfort and rest.

"I'd like you to take me to Skye's," she said.

The journey seemed endless. Edie watched with dull interest as the world continued to spin around her in its normal, everyday progression. Every person she saw was completely unaware of the events of the early morning. Maybe they'd cursed the snarled traffic as the police had shut down Elgin Street under the Pretoria Bridge for a crash investigation. It was news, an annoyance, a frustration for the morning instead of the nightmare it had been for Edie. And for Faina.

Finally Sasha pulled up outside of Skye's loft, angling into a no parking zone before walking Edie up to the blue steel door. He punched a code into his phone, and the lock disengaged. Sasha escorted her up the stairs and unlocked the inside door, allowing Edie to pass in front of him.

"Skye will likely be a few hours," Sasha said, standing in the doorway. "Is there anything else you need?"

Edie looked at him gratefully. "No, thank you. You've been wonderful. I think I just need to sleep."

"Okay. See you around, Edie."

When Sasha closed the door, Edie listened to the lock engage, Sasha's tread on the stairway, then the clang of the outside door. Now there was just her and silence and the comfort of Skye's loft. Edie didn't know what to do. It had been a long time since she'd been truly alone. Skye had been a constant presence, whether she was making coffee, sitting quietly with her laptop, or even finding a way to release her boundless energy without going very far. Her absence made Edie feel hollow.

Edie considered making herself something to eat, but the effort seemed too much. She slipped off her shoes instead, sinking down into the couch. She closed her eyes and leaned her head back, letting thoughts and sensations and worries and dull pain drift away. And then she curled over onto her side, cheek pressed into the soft grey fabric of the back cushion, and stopped trying to think at all.

It felt like hours later when Edie drifted out of her half sleep to the sound of the door. Her body felt heavy, her thoughts weighed down, far too tired to even worry who was walking into the loft. But Edie knew. She could feel Skye's force. Edie kept her eyes closed, still so close to sleep, and listened to Skye's soft footsteps as she approached. Skye hesitated at the edge of the living room. Edie's heart pounded just a little harder. This moment was suddenly so critical.

The couch dipped slightly as Skye sat down very close to Edie, her bicep inches from where Edie rested her head. They both breathed and the moment settled, and Edie's heart beat a familiar happy rhythm at Skye's nearness. The pull was a gentle gravitational force.

Skye was a full round moon that bathed everything in its light. And that was exactly what Edie wanted. She reached out her hand and rested it against Skye's stomach, feeling her light shudder of breath, the faint contraction of muscles. Heat. After a moment, Skye shifted a little closer, lifting her arm and settling it gently around Edie's shoulder. Edie tucked her head into the crook of Skye's shoulder and neck, held her close, and breathed her in.

When Skye rested her cheek on the top of Edie's head and gave a small sigh, Edie felt tears. She wasn't sad, just swamped by emotions. Edie anchored herself in Skye's strength, confirming her own strength had been there all along.

After a moment, Skye reached across with her free hand and cupped Edie's face. She lightly traced Edie's cheekbone and jaw with her fingers, touching the soft flesh of Edie's ear. The sensation was both sweet and intense, tentative and insistent.

"I owe you an apology."

Edie leaned back until she could look into Skye's eyes. "For what?"

"I shouldn't have left you the other night."

Edie slid her hand over Skye's stomach and held her around her waist. She needed Skye to know she wasn't going anywhere.

"Can you tell me why you did?"

Skye looked away briefly, and Edie felt the tension in her body. But it was only for a moment, then she locked eyes with Edie again.

"I kept thinking I was losing you. That whole day, threat after threat. I had convinced myself I couldn't possibly be enough for you. But that night with you, I kind of lost my mind. I thought I was too much. I've always been too much or not enough. I didn't want to disappoint you. I...I'm very sorry, Edie."

Edie sifted through Skye's words, the tone of her voice. She wasn't apologizing for wanting Edie.

"I forgive you."

Edie was sure Skye needed to hear those words. Skye briefly closed her eyes, then opened them again and gently tilted Edie's face up so she could kiss her. Edie felt like her forgiveness had cleansed them both. Skye's kiss was gentle, a sweet exploration of Edie's lips, an echo of her apology, and a hint of promise.

Skye pulled away slowly but kept Edie's face cradled in her hand. Skye was smiling, and Edie's whole body filled with relief and happiness and hope. This awful part of her life was coming to a close, and she had Skye. Now she needed Faina to pull through this ordeal as unscathed as possible.

"Have you heard from the hospital?" Edie said, leaning back into Skye's embrace.

"They were going to have her in surgery by midnight. When we left headquarters, JC was heading home to tuck her kids into bed and then her plan was to spend the night at the hospital. I said we'd take the morning shift. I hope that's okay."

Edie kissed the corner of Skye's mouth, tasting her sweetness. "Yes, it's perfect. Thank you."

Skye smiled and ducked her head briefly. She obviously wasn't used to this. Edie grinned. That was okay. They had time now. Edie looked forward to the lessons she could teach Skye on how to be loved.

"What time is it?" Edie said, looking around the loft. It was dark outside, but she thought she could still hear the sounds of the city and its movement.

"Just after eight."

"Eight," Edie mused. "That's a good time to start a date."

Skye's eyes widened. "You want a date? Tonight?"

"Yes," Edie said. "I want a date. I'm pretty sure you owe me dinner."

"Uh…" Skye said, looking suddenly concerned.

"Okay, you can make me dinner another night."

"What would you like tonight?"

Edie didn't answer at first. She ran her palm over Skye's hip, fingers dancing over Skye's rib cage, tracing the muscles of Skye's stomach before pressing up between her breasts and over her chest and resting against Skye's neck. Edie felt the wild pounding of Skye's heartbeat against her fingertips. She had never loved a feeling more.

"Tonight I want a shower. With you. And I want you to take me to bed and make love to me." She heard Skye's breath hitch, but she pushed on. This was her date, and she was going to direct it how she wanted. "And then I want you to order your favourite take-out. Lots of it. And when we're done with that, I want to sleep with you." Edie's voice gentled, and she whispered the final words. "I want to fall asleep with you."

"Yes," Skye said before lowering her head and taking Edie's lips in a fierce kiss. Edie tried to push back but Skye was stronger, pressing her into the couch, the stroke of Skye's tongue against her own making her weak. Making her want more. She gripped Skye's hips and guided her body against her as they fell back onto the couch, tangling their legs together, the push and pull of their bodies together rocketing Edie suddenly so close.

Skye broke the kiss and eased back just a little, her hips still rocking against Edie's in a slow rhythm that threatened to undo Edie entirely.

"Shower," Skye said against Edie's lips. "You said shower first."

Edie sucked Skye's bottom lip into her mouth. God, she loved the taste of her.

"Yes. Now."

Skye pulled Edie up in one swift movement, steadying her with an arm around her waist. They walked to the bathroom at the back of the loft, Skye turning on the lights then standing and facing Edie with her hands on her hips.

"What is it?" Edie said.

"I have bruises. On my left shoulder, left hip, and left thigh. One on my back. They're tender, but they don't hurt. I wanted you to know before you saw them."

Skye was on the ground in the dim underpass. She was curled on her side and they were kicking her. Edie couldn't get close enough. She tasted blood in her mouth, the sickness of helplessness.

Skye stepped in closer to Edie and rested her hands on Edie's hips. "You're right here with me," Skye said. "We're safe. Faina and JC are safe."

Edie stared into Skye's eyes, grounded by her hands on her hips. She grasped Skye's upper arms, feeling the muscles under her palms.

"Just take a minute and find your way back here," Skye said.

Edie complied. She walked through their long, hellish day, forced herself to think through decisions that led to terror, the painful fear of their ordeal. And the outcome. Rada in handcuffs. Faina being treated. Skye's touch.

"I'm okay."

Skye welcomed her back with a smile. "I know."

Edie ran her hands lightly up Skye's body, skimming her shoulder. "Can you show me?"

Skye took a step back and pulled her T-shirt over her head. Her black sports bra followed. A red contusion covered the front of Skye's shoulder, and Edie covered it lightly. It was smaller than her hand. Skye undid the button and zipper on her pants, Skye stripping herself bare and standing naked in front of Edie. More bruises, exactly where Skye said they would be. All the same size, the toe of a boot making contact with flesh.

"Edie, it's okay."

"I'm angry," Edie said, unable to look away from the bruises.

"Yes," Skye said.

"They hurt you."

Skye looked down at her bruises as if assessing them for the first time. "They're a little sore. Sasha has given me worse when we spar." Skye reached out for Edie's hand and guided it to her hip, covering one of the bruises. "I'll heal. I'm not worried."

The bruise felt slightly warmer than the surrounding skin. But it was all Skye. And Edie's instinct told her this was all part of loving Skye. Her selflessness. Her physicality. The force of her will and her strength, and her absolute confidence that her body would do what it needed to do. Edie needed to love her for that. Edie *did* love her for that.

Edie dropped her hands and pulled her own shirt over her head. She wanted to be out of these clothes, wash away the grit of the day, the feel of the metal floor beneath her cheek, the smell of guns. Skye leaned into the glassed-in shower stall to turn on the tap, and the sound of water soothed the angry thoughts in Edie's head once steam began to wrap around her bare skin.

Skye tugged at Edie's hand and pulled her into the shower. Edie groaned at the dual sensation of hot water over her own body and the slickness of Skye's skin. Skye kissed her, lips gentle and warm, until Edie's whole body felt liquid and languid. Edie could kiss Skye for days with no need to surface or breathe. And when Skye pulled her closer, fusing their bodies along every point, Edie forgot how her body felt separate from Skye. And she felt the absolute certainty that she would never again need to know.

Water and steam streamed around them as they kissed and touched, separating to find soap, sliding their palms over each other's skin to both clean and claim. Skye watched as Edie washed her hair. Her gaze made Edie feel loved. She could feel it even when she closed her eyes and leaned her head back into the shower to rinse.

Edie felt Skye's teeth on her neck, and the groan that escaped Skye reverberated through her chest. Skye claimed her breasts, covering them both with her palms before sliding her fingers over her nipples. Edie felt weak with the onslaught of desire, but Skye pinned her against the tile wall with her hips. The shock of cold was a contrast to the heat in her body as Skye kissed her neck, her fingers torturing her nipples until Edie had to break the never-ending kiss, gasping for air, trying to calm the rioting in her body as she rocketed so quickly to the edge.

"More," Skye said as she lifted Edie's hips and settled her thigh between her legs. The pressure was intense. Edie cried out and clung to Skye's shoulders, even as she rocked against her, her body completely overtaken with sensation. Skye matched her rhythm, one hand on Edie's hip, the other sweeping up her body, fisting her fingers in Edie's wet hair and taking her mouth again. The heat of Skye's mouth, the friction of Skye's wet flesh against her clit, and the steadily increasing thrust of Skye's hips sent Edie spinning higher with every gasped breath. When Skye broke the kiss, groaning, and bit down on the juncture of Edie's shoulder and neck, Edie thought her head would explode with pleasure. Skye stiffened, and the bite to her neck turned to a kiss as Skye groaned again and eased the pressure of her thigh. Skye shook her head slowly, the lightest sweep of her lips over Edie's flesh sending shivers up her spine. "Gentle," Skye said. "I want to be gentle this time."

Edie tugged at Skye's hair until she leaned back. Skye's eyes were hazy, tortured, intense.

"I know you can be gentle," Edie said. "But you don't have to be." Edie kissed her slowly, drawing Skye's tongue into her mouth and sucking before biting down and releasing her. She leaned back again, sliding one hand into Skye's slick, short hair and cupping her face with the other. "You are enough for me, Skye Kenny. And I promise you will never, ever be too much."

When Skye leaned in to kiss Edie again, Edie felt her full force, maybe for the very first time. Her gravitational pull had been unleashed and Edie had no time to marvel at her strength, but only be overwhelmed. Edie drew Skye against her, insinuating a hand between them, needing to feel the centre of Skye's desire.

Skye groaned but made room between them, dropping her head to Edie's shoulder as Edie dipped her finger down over her stomach and touched the dark curls between Skye's thighs. Skye thrust against Edie's fingers, and Edie felt light-headed with the power she had over Skye. She didn't want to torture her by drawing it out or teasing; she just wanted Skye to feel everything. The rhythm of Skye's thrusts increased as Edie drew wet heat around and over Skye's hard clit, taking her closer and closer.

Suddenly Skye moved away and dropped to her knees, her mouth on Edie's stomach. Edie wasn't sure she could take this. Her whole body trembled, she was so close to coming, needing to feel her own release, already so closely tied to Skye's. So close. When Skye kissed her inner thigh, she sagged. Skye spread her legs and pinned her to the wall with her upper body and held her hips. She traced Edie with her tongue, sucking her slick flesh until Edie could not hold back the rising tide. There was only release, there was only Skye and her own shuddering body, there was only their combined force that burned away everything but the continuous waves that rocked them, released them, fused them.

Edie slowly came back to awareness, sensing the sound of the shower, her own hand cradling Skye's head against her abdomen, their synchronized breath. And the sense that something was newly created. When Skye turned her head and looked up at Edie, she felt a certainty and a connection she had never had in her entire life. This woman, this life, was all she needed.

Skye's smile was as warm and easy as she stood, embracing Edie lightly and kissing her gently. Edie knew she felt it, too. They'd have time to put words to it, but they weren't necessary right now. Everything they had in this moment was enough. And with Skye's arms around her, Edie knew it would always be.

EPILOGUE

Edie piled cookies onto a tin-stamped platter she found in the community church kitchen and listened to Dr. Wallace greet the group's newest participant. Edie made a mental note to sit with the young woman tonight. She was finally starting to find her rhythm in this group, walking the line between participant and mentor. These Thursday nights weren't always easy, but she finally trusted the momentum of her own recovery. Always moving forward, despite some slow days. In six weeks, she'd be back teaching at the university. It was only one course for the fall semester, but it was a start.

Edie stole a cookie from the platter, and then she began the task of making coffee. The newly repaired downstairs kitchen had no temperamental coffee percolators, so Edie shoved in a coffee filter and began counting the scoops of coffee grinds.

Hands on her hips and a soft kiss to the back of her neck startled Edie out of her task.

"Hey," she complained, catching one of Skye's hands and drawing it around her waist. "You made me lose count."

"Nine," Skye said. "And sorry."

Edie continued filling the filter with coffee, smiling at Skye's whispered count in her ear. Edie elbowed her lightly in the ribs and Skye laughed and backed off.

"I can make coffee on my own, Major Kenny," Edie said.

She plugged in the coffee perc and hit the switch. Then she looked at Skye, who had hopped up on the opposite counter. The tan on her face, neck, and arms were evidence of their time spent at Basher's cottage over the summer. There had been a constant parade of guests:

Adelah, JC and her kids, Edie's niece and nephew, and even Faina once she'd been released from the hospital. It had been joyful and busy and exactly what they'd needed.

But they'd also had some days and nights completely on their own. They'd had time together to swim and run and cook. They talked for hours, sharing a beer on the deck. They had long moments of silence, Edie curled into Skye's lap in front of the fire on the wet sand beach. Edie smiled at the memory of Skye's fierce determination to both fit in the hammock. Edie had laughed so hard her stomach muscles had ached. They made love in the early morning, Skye's energy enough for both of them. They'd slept, Skye's protective presence enough to ease any of Edie's early nightmares. One cold spring night under the stars, Edie had told Skye she loved her. She thought she'd never seen Skye look so happy as she accepted the words for the gift and the truth that they were. Then she'd returned the words and kissed Edie with a promise Edie knew she would never break.

"Where did you go, Edie Black?" Skye said gently, calling her back.

Edie shook her head lightly and smiled. She crossed the kitchen and hopped on the counter beside Skye.

"I'm mentally already at the cottage," Edie said, leaning into Skye.

"Tomorrow," Skye said. "The Jeep's all packed. I've got a meeting in the morning, but then we'll head out before traffic gets too bad."

Edie could not possibly describe the happiness these easy moments brought.

"And I'm taking Faina to a doctor's appointment and then we're going out for coffee."

Skye stiffened slightly, then took Edie's hand.

"What is it?" Edie said.

"I have some news. JC called me as I was walking here tonight. Do you want to hear it from me or wait until you see Faina tomorrow?"

"Now, please."

"The three-month extension was approved on medical grounds, but then Faina is being deported back to the UK on November 17."

Even fully anticipating this result, knowing the Canadian government had no other choice but to deport a person residing unlawfully in this country, did not make the news any easier. Edie let out a long, shaky breath.

Skye sat silently and rubbed her thumb over Edie's hand in a calming, repetitive motion. Edie met Skye's concerned look.

"Okay?" Skye said.

"Yeah. I know Faina's immigration liaison is setting her up with contacts and services in the UK. I know she's strong. I know there's part of her that's excited about starting this new life. But she's on her own. I hate that."

Skye leaned in and kissed Edie's temple. "I know. But there's technology. You two can see each other every day if you want. We'll make sure of that."

Edie leaned her head against Skye's shoulder and drew from her unlimited strength. They sat quietly and listened to the coffee percolator burble in the background.

Moments later, Dr. Wallace entered the kitchen.

"My favourite couple," she announced, smiling broadly. She picked up the tray of cookies. "I believe we may be facing a mutiny unless we get the cookies out there. So I'm going to take these out and trust you love birds to bring the coffee when it's ready."

Edie laughed as Dr. Wallace swept out of the kitchen. Skye hopped off the counter and pulled Edie down with her.

"I should get set up upstairs, as well," Skye said. "We'll head home together after group?"

Edie stretched up and stole a quick kiss before Skye could escape. The yellow-green of Skye's eyes danced. Edie knew she could not love this woman more.

"Yes," Edie said. "We'll head home together."

About the Author

Jessica L. Webb spends her professional days working with educators to find the why behind the challenging behaviors of the students they support. Limitless curiosity about the motivations and intentions of human behavior is also a huge part of what drives her to write stories and understand the complexities of her characters and their actions. When she's not working or writing, Jessica is spending time with her wife and daughter, usually planning where they will travel next. Jessica can be found most often on her favorite spot on the couch with a book and a cup of tea.

Books Available From Bold Strokes Books

Canvas for Love by Charlotte Greene. When ghosts from Amelia's past threaten to undermine their relationship, Chloé must navigate the greatest romance of her life without losing sight of who she is. (978-1-62639-944-0)

Heart Stop by Radclyffe. Two women, one with a damaged body, the other a damaged spirit, challenge each other to dare to live again. (978-1-62639-899-3)

Repercussions by Jessica L. Webb. Someone planted information in Edie Black's brain and now they want it back, but with the protection of shy former soldier Skye Kenny, Edie has a chance at life and love. (978-1-62639-925-9)

Spark by Catherine Friend. Jamie's life is turned upside down when her consciousness travels back to 1560 and lands in the body of one of Queen Elizabeth I's ladies-in-waiting…or has she totally lost her grip on reality? (978-1-62639-930-3)

Taking Sides by Kathleen Knowles. When passion and politics collide, can love survive? (978-1-62639-876-4)

Thorns of the Past by Gun Brooke. Former cop Darcy Flynn's heart broke when her career on the force ended in disgrace, but perhaps saving Sabrina Hawk's life will mend it in more ways than one. (978-1-62639-857-3)

You Make Me Tremble by Karis Walsh. Seismologist Casey Radnor comes to the San Juan Islands to study an earthquake but finds her heart shaken by passion when she meets animal rescuer Iris Mallery. (978-1-62639-901-3)

Complications by MJ Williamz. Two women battle for the heart of one. (978-1-62639-769-9)

Crossing the Wide Forever by Missouri Vaun. As Cody Walsh and Lillie Ellis face the perils of the untamed West, they discover that love's uncharted frontier isn't for the weak in spirit or the faint of heart. (978-1-62639-851-1)